Trail of Bodies

Kreig W. Vens

PublishAmerica
Baltimore

© 2007 by Kreig W. Vens.
All rights reserved. No part of this book may be reproduced, stored in a retrieval system or transmitted in any form or by any means without the prior written permission of the publishers, except by a reviewer who may quote brief passages in a review to be printed in a newspaper, magazine or journal.

First printing

All characters appearing in this work are fictitious. Any resemblance to real persons, living or dead, is purely coincidental.

At the specific preference of the author, PublishAmerica allowed this work to remain exactly as the author intended, verbatim, without editorial input.

ISBN: 1-4241-6480-X
PUBLISHED BY PUBLISHAMERICA, LLLP
www.publishamerica.com
Baltimore

Printed in the United States of America

Other titles by Kreig W. Vens

Prosecuted Innocence

To Jan
Read Fast, The Movie
Is Coming

Kreig W. Vens

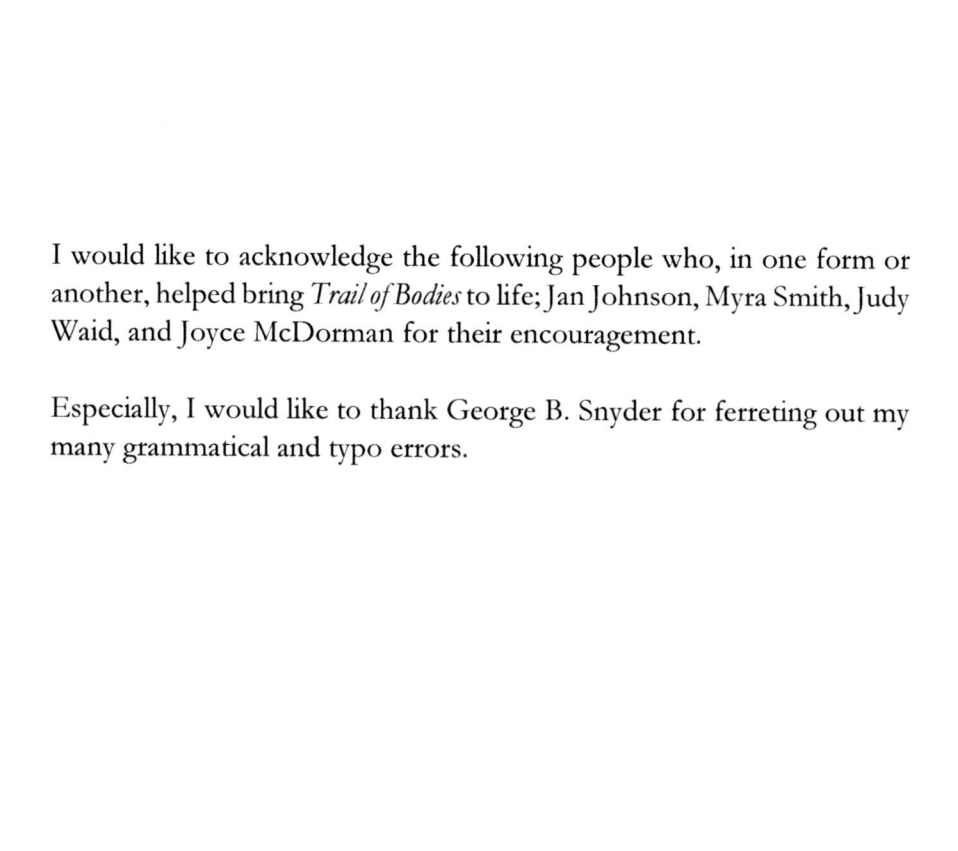

I would like to acknowledge the following people who, in one form or another, helped bring *Trail of Bodies* to life; Jan Johnson, Myra Smith, Judy Waid, and Joyce McDorman for their encouragement.

Especially, I would like to thank George B. Snyder for ferreting out my many grammatical and typo errors.

Prologue

Bullets packed with the right combination of magnesium perchlorate and strontium salts create bright trails when fired—tracer rounds.

Tracer rounds whined overhead like an angry swarm of fireflies searching for an easy, or careless, mark. The squad's unlucky number, thirteen, came about as a result of United States Marine Corps, private first class Dalton Brook's careless head peek over the embankment of the washed-out rut they were hunkered down in. A sniper's bright yellow firefly entered Brook's right eye, and, in a bright red mist, evacuated most of his brain matter through a softball-size hole at the back of his head.

Under fire, Captain Robert Benjamin Daniels was as cool as a penguin on an ice flow, and about as vicious as a mother polar bear protecting her cubs. Nearing the end of his third tour of duty in the jungles of Vietnam, Captain Daniels, for the past several weeks, had been giving serious thought to volunteering for a fourth stint. While he loved his job, and his job was to kill as many of the enemy as possible, it was his love of being in charge that explained why as a commissioned officer he'd chosen to accompany the recon-squad into the jungle for the scouting mission.

As the battle intensified, Daniels sat calmly with his back pressed against the eroded embankment of tangled roots and mud, casually cleaning "gook dirt" from beneath his fingernails with a sharpened twig. He extended his hands out at eye level and inspected his manicure. Satisfied, he snatched the sawed-off Ithaca model 37 Featherweight 12 gauge shotgun (its seven shot magazine loaded with 00 buckshot) from his lap, and shouted overtop the small arms fire raining down on them from the front flank.

"Bricker!"

It had not been Corporal Michael Dakota Bricker's intent to spend his nineteenth birthday pinned down in a muddy ditch halfway around the world, fighting an enemy he could not see. Hunkered down below the line of fire, and only because he couldn't reach the military-issued shovel stuffed into his backpack to dig any deeper, he crawled over the legs of his fellow soldiers toward Captain Daniels.

"Sir?"

"Crawl your Limey-ass over here!" Daniels yelled above the racket of chattering AK-47s and Chicom machine gun fire.

* * *

The Bricker children, Dakota, and sisters Virginia "Ginny" and Maryland "Mary" had each been named after one of the states in the Union. It was their father's subtle reminder that while they all had been born abroad, they were still citizens of the United States of America, and according to Colonel Thaxton Bricker, that knowledge was imperative.

Before retiring, Colonel Bricker spent the better part of his United States Air Force career traveling the globe with wife "Trish", who peddled her secretarial wares to the various embassies where they were stationed. The Colonel ran his household with the same military precision as the bases he oversaw. The Bricker children had learned early on not to complain about their globetrotting lifestyle. When the Colonel gave the order that they were "bugging out", the family packed up their essentials, said goodbye to temporary friends, and then moved on with their lives. By the time Dakota was eight years old he, and his siblings, had lived on every continent with the exception of Australia.

After Trish's untimely death in Southeast Asia (the result of a snakebite) Colonel Bricker settled in as commander of the US Air Force base in Lakenheath, England, where Dakota spent his formative years, and developed his telltale English brogue. He graduated from the base high school and, much to the Colonel's chagrin, applied to culinary arts school rather than follow in his father's substantial footsteps. While at Corus Hotels Institute at Bracknell, Dakota met Emaline "Emy" McCartney, and promptly fell head over heels in love. Both graduated with honors before making a hasty departure to the United States. Dakota's plan was to take the newly budding Las Vegas Strip by storm, billing himself as a European trained Master Chef while Emy rode on his coattails as Director of Housekeeping; his plan was quickly derailed by a quirky U.S. law that required all males over the age of eighteen to register for the draft. After the "Uncle Sam wants you!" Selective Service lottery was drawn, Bricker found himself in second position. At the time he'd given serious consideration to an immediate departure for Heathrow Airport, but decided that if his father found out he was a draft dodger, the Colonel would no doubt load him onto a military transport and personally escort him back to the good old U.S. of A. Dakota Bricker accomplished two things during his brief stay in Las Vegas: he changed Emy's last name to Bricker, and he enlisted in the United States Marine Corps' food service, not jungle patrol.

* * *

Bricker kept his head below the line of fire as he slithered through mud and roots to where Captain Daniels sat, seemingly oblivious to the increasing swarm of rounds chopping a hole in the vegetation on their rear flank. He scooted next to the captain, his British accent barely audible over the gunfire, and said, "Sir, you called for me?"

Captain Daniels reached into the shirt pocket of his battle dress uniform and pulled out a pair of foam earplugs, handed them to Bricker, and shouted, "Stick these in your ears, boy. It's about to get real noisy around here. I called in for a little air support."

Bricker had barely worked the soft earplugs into place when a Cobra gunship screamed up from the misty valley below, its pulsating blades thumping a hurricane downdraft and bending tree branches into painful arches. The Air Calvary paused overhead for a moment, verified the "friendly's position", and then unleashed their payload; four Sidewinder rockets and three two-minute bursts from twin .50 caliber machine guns mounted on each side of the hull. Hot shell casings rained down on the Marines as the munitions found their mark a half-click ahead. The thick jungle erupted into blinding flashes of orange-red flame, followed by clouds of billowing black smoke that swirled through the air in the helicopter's downdraft. A millisecond later the ground shook with seismic proportion. The co-stick flashed a thumbs-up to the grunts below and then banked the helicopter left, disappearing back down into the steamy valley.

Several thousand pounds of ordinance was all it took to end the torment of the enemy's gunfire. Those that had not been blown to bits by the rockets red glare, or shredded into unrecognizable corpses by the heavy machine gun fire, retreated into the labyrinth of subterranean tunnels and caves that the Viet Cong used to conceal their movements. Except for a roaring brushfire the jungle was mortuary quiet.

Captain Daniels climbed to his feet, brushed the dirt from his clothes, and said, "Let's move out!"

Bricker chanced a cautious forward peek. "Sir? Aren't we going to check for wounded?"

Daniels stopped dead in his tracks, his head snapping around to face his squad, most of them still huddled below the line of fire.

"Tell you what, Brick, old Chap," Daniels drawled with a mocking accent. "Why don't you crawl your Limey-ass up the hill and explain to the poor wounded slope lying on an armed grenade that you're there to help him. As for me," Daniels thumbed over his shoulder, "I'm headed for EVAC two clicks the other direction." Daniels ran piercing, unforgiving eyes over the squad, spat on the ground, worked the saliva into the dirt with his boot heel, and said, "That's all I plan leaving of me in this Godforsaken shithole." He slung the shotgun over his shoulder, pushed through his troops, and stopped, momentarily, to look at the only casualty of the mission thus far.

Twenty-four uninterrupted months in Viet Nam and Daniels had witnessed more close up death than most people would see if they lived four lifetimes. A *gallows' humor* grin spread across his face as he looked over his shoulder with a smirk. "Would one of you ladies be kind enough to pick up Brookie? I'm thinking he's a little bit lighter now."

After his honorable discharge, Bricker returned to Las Vegas where he found Emy working in housekeeping, not as Director, but as a maid at the Sand's Casino. He also quickly learned, as did most returning Nam vets, that being a veteran and twenty cents *might* get him a cup of coffee.

Bricker stood behind a Blackjack table dressed in a starched white shirt, black vest and bowtie, while lethargically dealing cards to alcohol-plied guests who spent more money than they could afford to loose trying to beat the odds stacked heavily in the casino's favor. He barely noticed the players' faces as he tossed cards across the felt, pausing long enough to help inebriated players tally their cards, rake in the loosing bets, and then start the process all over again, hundreds of times a shift. Not until the table's maximum bet, five hundred dollars, was placed in the bettor's circle did he lift vacant eyes from the felt and focus on the face.

It had been three years since they'd served together in Viet Nam. Captain Daniels stood on the patron's side of the table holding a glass of Captain Morgan's Spiced Rum over shaved ice.

"Figured you'd own one of these places by now, Brick," Daniels said, smiling and sipping his drink.

Bricker beamed back a grin and nodded to the man who'd twice saved his life in the jungles. "Figured you, of all people, Sir, would know better than to waste your hard earned cash in a casino," he said.

Captain Daniels took a seat at the table.

Bricker, like millions of other *Life Magazine* subscribers, had flipped through the August 25th 1967 issue, its propaganda cover photo a U.S. Marine walking alongside a Vietnamese boy on crutches. Bricker's interest had settled on the small article at the back of the magazine. The feature profiled a certain Captain R.B. Daniels's rocketed ascent (pardon the pun) up the financial ladder, a result of his newly designed computer chip and software program pioneering LASER guided military weaponry.

Bricker dealt the cards and flipped the dealer's second card face up— Ace of spades. Beginning to his left, Bricker pointed to each player and offered "insurance" against the dealer's potential Blackjack. All but one player declined. He worked his way around the table pausing in front of each player and waiting until they motioned for another card, or waved that they would "stand pat". Seats two through five motioned for cards and as each hand "busted", Bricker raked in the five and ten-dollar loosing bets.

Bricker was every bit as good at card counting as any professional gambler, and with nearly two-thirds of the deck played out, also taking into consideration the Captain's top card was a heart-six, he knew the odds were unlikely Daniels could build a winning hand.

The Captain leaned back in his chair and gulped down his drink, snapped his fingers at a passing cocktail hostess, ordered a refill, and then rested his elbows on the padded rail holding up the game until she returned with his beverage. He set his glass in the cup holder with a derisive smirk, stacked five additional black chips beside his original bet, and then leaned back in his chair.

Bricker shook his head; surprised Daniels would "double down" with such a weak hand. Daniels, however, stared into Bricker's eyes long enough he drew the attention of the Pit Boss, who stepped behind Bricker and let his eyes land on the hefty bet in front of seat number six. "Is there a problem, sir?" he said.

Daniels grinned arrogantly at the balding pudgy face hovering over Bricker's shoulder. "Not unless my winning is a problem for you, sonny."

"We encourage our guests to win." And for benefit of the others at the table, added, "Good luck to you, sir." He stepped back and nodded for Bricker to deal the cards.

Daniels saluted the man with his drink, and then with his pinkie finger sporting a diamond clustered gold band, flipped over his hole card—King of hearts.

Bricker dealt Daniels's double up card face down and then flipped the dealer's hole card—nine of diamonds. He bounced his fist on the table in front of seat number one and announced a "push", or tie.

With a confident smirk the Pit Boss stepped closer to the table. "Dealer has twenty. Pay twenty-one."

Bricker noticed the same display of confidence he'd seen exhibited on Daniels's face in the jungles. The table waited while the Captain took a long, slow draw on his cocktail, pausing with his glass near his smiling mouth. He finally reached down and flipped his hole card.

The Pit Boss craned his neck over Bricker's shoulder—five of clubs. "Congratulations, sir, twenty-one. Dealer, pay the lucky bettor," he said, with forced geniality.

The Pit Boss stepped from the table and brought the security phone to his ear, asking for a review of the last dozen plays on Blackjack table number seven, particular attention being paid to seat number six.

Bricker plucked a thousand dollars worth of chips from the dealer's chip tray and stacked them next to Daniels's original bet.

The Captain picked up his winnings, tossed a hundred dollar token across the table, and said, "I'm looking for a ranch hand-cum-butler. It pays five hundred...let's make that seven-fifty a week. Just in case you know anyone looking for a job."

Bricker rolled the *tip chip* over the back of his fingers with nimble precision, watching as Captain R. B. Daniels disappeared into the crowd.

The anonymous face seated in number three position, anxious to part with more money, said, "Hey, buddy, you dealing cards, or what?"

Bricker dropped Daniels's tip into the communal tip bin attached to the backside of the table, clapped and showed both sides of his hands for benefit of the overhead security cameras, and stepped away from the table. "I don't think so, *buddy*," he said peeling off his bow tie. "I quit."

That incident took place over thirty years ago and it was the last time Dakota Bricker set foot in a casino. The following day he and his beloved Emy moved their belongings to the servant's quarters at Daniels's secluded ranch, where they became lifelong employees of Daniels Industries, Inc., effectively quadrupling their income.

Chapter 1

The Dalton Brook having his head blown off dream snapped Dakota Bricker bolt upright in bed, frantically swiping ghostly images of brain matter from the front of his uniform. The decades that had passed since he'd worn a camouflage battle dress uniform, and nearly as long since he had fought in the jungles of Viet Nam, didn't change the vividness of that recurring dream.

The electric charge that jolted him from a deep sleep tingled across his clammy skin. He crawled from bed and stripped out of his sweat-soaked pajamas, moved to the open window and bathed in the cool desert breeze that gently lifted the drapes away from the window.

What Bricker wanted most was to put an end to the nightmares and go back to sleep. But somehow nightmares and sleep, placed side by side, never seem to commingle well. Most of the nightmares came from his battle experiences, while others came from having witnessed the things Captain Daniels did to young Vietnamese girls and boys to frail to resist. He knew the Captain's drunken tumble down the main staircase and breaking his neck, almost twenty years ago, his blood alcohol three times the legal limit to operate a vehicle, was no accident. The abuses that Captain Daniels bestowed upon the Oriental race had been avenged.

Bricker, still employed by heir to the Daniels dynasty, from the shadows of his room, let his eyes drift across the stamped concrete deck surrounding the swimming pool, skim across its placid waters, and come to rest on *Mr. Daniels's* den window. An iridescent blue light glowed from the second story window, which meant Mr. Daniels was again up late, working on his computer.

Chapter 2

A casual stroll carried him across the parking lot. In the waning sunlight he barely drew the attention of the young mother of infant twins, preoccupied with wrestling a bag of groceries from the hatch of her minivan while keeping the quarreling two year olds from going to the pavement in a full-blown hair pulling, arm biting brawl. The killer, a master chameleon, was so non-descript he could stand at a busy intersection beneath a streetlamp and still go totally unnoticed by both vehicular and pedestrian traffic. For a moment, and only for a moment, he considered stopping to lend the young mother a hand, but to do so could prove counterproductive to his purpose for being at the apartment complex in the first place, not to mention jeopardize his anonymity, and Shadow Man knew anonymity was a serial killer's best friend.

He climbed the open-air staircase running along the outside of the building and stopped on the fourth floor landing long enough to peer through the small window in the fire door. Finding the hallway empty, he entered the floor walking directly to the apartment of interest, pausing in front of the only door with double deadbolt locks, evidence the selected target was at least cautious, if not paranoid. After a furtive glance in each direction, he slid a thin flexible lock pick into the keyhole and, with nimble fingers, worked the shank back and forth and up and down until he breached both locks. Twenty eight seconds later he was standing inside a predator's world ready to go about his work.

Most of the images downloaded across today's Internet would shock the conscience of all but a jaded law enforcement official, hardcore pedophile, or devoted vigilante. The Internet had changed, changed dramatically from its original purpose as an information-sharing medium. It is now a worldwide, searchable database of perversion. The proliferation of child pornography streaming across the Internet is of magnanimous proportion; point of fact, any ne'er-do-well with a modem and mediocre surfing ability can whet his salacious appetite. Adorning the Net in distressing numbers appear photographs of prepubescent girls performing fellatio on men old enough to be their fathers, and some are; their innocent vaginas stretched taut by the manhood of a degenerate letch. Instead of playing with dolls and dreaming of being happily married to a doctor, or lawyer, some fifteen years to the future, they grimace pained smiles for the benefit of the reprobates who direct the action from behind the anonymity of a camera lens. And neither is pedophilia restricted by gender. During his Internet *hunts*, Shadow Man had seen hundreds of pictures of teenage boys sodomizing each other and handing out oral sex like so many smooches at a carnival's kissing booth.

Try as they might, law enforcement is about as successful at eradicating child pornography as they are stemming the blizzard of white poison invading the country from South America. That's not to say there is not a concerted effort within the law enforcement community to squash kiddy porn, but like the drug problem, it's larger than life. The energetic efforts of the Federal Bureau of Investigation, on down to the local constables, occasionally reels in a malignant fish. Those rare "catches" are trumpeted through the media, both electronic and print, lest the public realize the cold fact: child pornography is like an iceberg; it's the unseen portion that offers the most danger. Regurgitated figures released by the Attorney General's Office fools only the naïve. For each statistical catch hundreds, and in all probability, thousands more continue producing and distributing videos of kids being abused by adults, and of children abusing children. No one was more aware of the psychological damage that kind of abuse can cause than was Shadow Man.

The disheveled tiny apartment he had entered was a hodgepodge of mismatched secondhand furniture. Bolted against one wall in the living room was an elaborate entertainment system, frugally housed on shelves of scrap lumber and cinderblock, on another wall was an enormous glass terrarium. Wood crates served as record album and compact disk holders while secondhand store end tables graced each side of a brown and yellow flower-print couch that clashed hideously with a lime-green chair covered with a knitted, rose-colored throw.

The first thing Shadow Man did was slip into a pair of generic, white cotton gardener-style gloves, not meant for dexterity, rather, so any trace fibers left behind would identify only the brand of glove and not a specific location of purchase. The killer had no need of precision to handle videotapes and computer disks belonging to his pedophile target.

The first order of business was to locate the target's computer, which he did by tracing along the telephone cord plugged into a wall jack in the living room to its final destination in the kitchen. Tucked into a corner of the breakfast nook a scratch and dent sale computer stand and USB cables connected a high-tech Hewlett Packard Pavilion 7955 to a printer/scanner/copier/fax machine. A second cable snaked to the top shelf where the predator's DVD recorder (for transferring standard camcorder and digital camera images into high grade DVD/ROM format) was housed. Shadow Man walked across the kitchen and powered up the system. While waiting for it to hum to life, he mused that any footage found on the hard drive would, in all likelihood, not be images of the last family reunion.

He turned a curious ear toward the living room and the sound of children's laughter. He crossed the room on light steps, leaving shadowy footprints in the carpet's thick brown pile, and parted earth tone Venetian blinds ever so slightly. Peeking beyond the narrow balcony, where a lone green and white frayed lawn chair and camp-size propane grill atop a cinderblock sat, he looked four floors below. A half a dozen squealing youngsters frolicked in the shallow end of a swimming pool while PABA-free coconut scented, sun block smeared mothers chatted idly, casting intermittent glances toward the pool and doing a quick headcount. When Shadow Man turned from the window his shoulder bumped against a powerful set of six-power binoculars hanging from a hook, no doubt used to ogle children around the pool.

He returned to the kitchen and guided the mouse pointer across Windows' desktop, stopping on the Windows Explorer icon. He spent several minutes perusing the computer's brain until he found a folder, cleverly hidden inside a subdirectory of Microsoft Office. The folder was divided into subcategories of boy, girl, and miscellaneous. Within the miscellaneous folder were dozens of G-rated pictures of children, most taken of the kids playing in and around the pool. The boy-girl folders were a horse of a different color.

Inside those folders he found hundreds of illicit pictures, many captured from, and, traded across the Internet, while still others appeared to be more of the "homemade" variety. Regardless, it was the bull's-eye he'd hoped for. The evidence on the computer's hard drive proved with certainty that he had correctly matched the screen persona to a real person. He shut down the PC and began searching the rest of the apartment. If past experience proved correct he knew tangible, hard copy evidence existed somewhere inside the apartment.

Over the years the death toll of Shadow Man's *calling* stood at fourteen. For close to two decades he had surreptitiously invaded homes, condominiums, and apartments, gathering necessary evidence to justify his labors; with a personal pledge that insisted on hard copy evidence—sordid images on computer hard drives, floppy disks, DVDs, or actual photographs—before he moved forward with a liquidation. Over the years the serial killer had grudgingly spared several prospective targets due to an inability to locate incriminating proof; but those foolish souls who maintained a tangible copy of their perversion—hidden in the strangest of places; inside empty toilet tanks; between furniture cushions; inside toolboxes; between rafters and under floorboards; taped to the underside of desk drawers; one had buried his stash in a kitty litter box—paid the Piper, and it was a heavy and fatal price they paid.

Shadow Man conducted a thorough search of the target's kitchen cabinets, checked inside the dishwasher, opened lids on the pots and pans in the oven's drawer, moved boxed and canned food in the pantry, and rummaged around the inside of the refrigerator before he was satisfied no secret hiding place in the kitchen had been overlooked. He scoured the living room with the same diligence, and then moved deeper into the apartment, exploring the bathroom medicine cabinet and vanity drawers.

Shadow Man stood in the doorway of the lone bedroom for a moment, surveying its surroundings. While searching the bedroom he was careful not to disturb the order of clothes as he rummaged through the rickety chest of drawers. Inside the closet he slid hanging clothes to one side and then the other, groping through the disheveled pile of shirts and sweatshirts on the top shelf and dropping to his knees to check shoeboxes stacked in a corner on the floor. A frustrated sigh escaped after a fruitless sweep of his hand between the Queen-size box spring and mattress. He smoothed the plain green comforter and then bent down for a look underneath the bed.

In the corner nearest the headboard a darting tongue air-tasted his scent, a pair of unblinking black beads stared back at him. Shadow Man nearly screamed as he fell backwards and crab-crawled across the room, putting as much distance as he possibly could between him and the four-foot boa constrictor. *That explains the empty terrarium in the living room*, he mused, cautiously backing out of the room.

He stood in the narrow hallway between the bedroom and living room, his clenched fist pressed against his chin. It appeared as if this target would escape a date with destiny. Why additional "fruits of the crime" had not been found perplexed him. He was positive they existed. The target had been so cavalier with his postings on the newsgroups discussion boards, bragging about how he had "unlimited access to fresh and original pixs".

One of the many internal voices Shadow Man conversed with spoke: "They're here, somewhere. You know it, you feel it." And then a different voice cautioned him that for every second he remained inside the apartment he risked discovery. "Maybe one more quick look around," the first voice said. "No! Leave now!" the second warned.

He shrugged with an acquiescent smile and started toward the door, covering less than five strides before freezing in mid-step, his head slowly turning over his right shoulder. He backpedaled into the hallway and stopped in front of the linen closet door next to the bathroom. He was slipping. How had he missed the tiny closet?

Shadow Man groped through towels rolled up like miniature bedrolls. He slid aside arrays of bottled colognes and lotions, gave the 4-pack of toilet paper a vigorous shake, but still nothing. His brow furrowed with disappointment as he closed the door. For no explainable reason he looked down to the floor and noticed an arch in the carpet's nap. Squatting to his haunches, gloved fingers worked loose four wing nuts holding a plumbing access door in place. He swung the plywood cover aside and found concealed inside the wall all the evidence he needed, and then some.

On the floor inside the cubbyhole was a shoebox filled with 3.5 floppy disks, along with dozens upon dozens of compact disks. Next to the treasure chest was a foot-high stack of magazines. *Go figure*, the internal voice said with a smirk, *a NAMBLA subscriber.* Shadow Man wagged his head in disgust. This was the first target he had selected that was a bona fide, card-carrying member of the North American Man/Boy Love Association.

Photobug and Don Mathers were the same person; the pedophile he'd been tracking across the Internet for nearly six months. A mental note was entered to return to the apartment after cleansing the gene pool of *Photobug*-Mathers's DNA, and make sure the hidden stash was easily found—posthumously of course—by the cops who would search Mathers's apartment. They would find his alcove of perversion and make the connection why he had to be eliminated, liquidated, erased, murdered.

He gave the apartment a quick once over and satisfied he had left behind no telltale sign of his presence, other than footprints in the carpet, Shadow Man pulled out a handkerchief, wiped his fingerprints from both sides of the door handle (the only place touched without gloves), tucked the gloves into the waistband under his shirt, and stepped into the hallway glancing at his wristwatch.

Twenty-six minutes was a little longer than he had expected being inside the apartment, but when panning for the gold of the computer's hard drive, one does not pass up the twenty-four karat nugget of magazines and boxful of disks. Soon, very soon, the Internet would be free of another predator, and another notch would be added to the moniker: Shadow Man.

Chapter 3

The previous Friday morning Don Mathers had stood in the church parking lot like a prima donna, sipping coffee from a Styrofoam cup, watching eleven boys ages ten through fifteen said goodbye to their parents. Camcorders rolled and still cameras flashed as the boys tossed bedrolls and sleeping bags through the emergency exit door at the rear of the church bus. After motherly hugs, fatherly handshakes, and backslapping jokes about how three days in the wilderness would turn the boys into men, they loaded onto the bus. Class-A campsites with electric and water hookup, a bathhouse with hot and cold running water, and State Park Rangers patrolling the Valley of Fire State Park in east central Nevada could hardly be called a wilderness. About as close as the boys would come to experiencing true pioneer hardship would be when they used the latrines.

Mathers watched the parting display with keen interest; he was in the information-gathering mode. Which group of boys showed indifference to spending a weekend away from their families? More importantly, which displayed apprehensiveness? While the former *may* be manipulated, it was the other group Mr. Mathers set his sights upon. Strong leadership would show the latter group that befriending the camp counselor could bring with it certain *fringe benefits*.

It was late Sunday afternoon when Mathers returned to his apartment, tossed the military surplus duffel bag to the floor, wriggled the camcorder case from his shoulder and set it on the coffee table next to a cardboard pet carrier he had bought at "White's Pets-N-More" on his way home. He turned to the five hundred gallon terrarium against the wall next to the entertainment center. The lid was closed, but the tank was empty. He rushed across the room in three panic-stricken strides and peered, eyes wide, into the empty tank. Whoever broke into his apartment and stole Oscar was in deep trouble? He would kill for Oscar!

Mathers dropped to his knees and frantically scanned under the living room furniture while calling out in a shrill voice. "Oscar!"

As if he recognized his name, Oscar slithered around the corner, his tongue darting, and coiled into a ball in front of Mathers. Mathers breathed a sigh of relief, scooped the dwarf boa constrictor up off the ground, draped four feet of oozing reptile over his shoulders, and kissed the snake's scaly head as he climbed to his feet.

"You were a bad boy while Daddy was gone," Mathers sniggered. "I see Daddy needs to put a new latch on your pen so you can't get out." He kissed the snake a second time and returned it to the five hundred-gallon, self-contained glass ecosystem.

If only Oscar could speak he would have prattled on until his forked tongue fell off, conveying to his owner how frightening the stranger dressed in all black inside the apartment yesterday was. The constrictor slithered across the cedar chips lining the bottom of the terrarium and took up a lazy position in a corner of the terrarium.

Mathers returned to the cardboard pet carrier on the table and scooped out one of three white rats scurrying around inside. Holding it by the tail at eye level, he said, "Guess who were having for dinner?"

He stood over Oscar's pen dangling the rat over the opening for a moment, and then dropped it inside, slid the cover closed, bent over at the waist, and in anticipation of the show brought his face close to the glass.

Instinctively, Oscar coiled into a tight motionless ball, tasting the rat's scent on the air. The confused rodent stood still for a few moments before cautiously edging forward to explore his new surroundings. He made hesitant dashes along the edge of the glass, stopping every few steps and rearing up on his hind legs, sniffing the air with his wiggling pink nose. It paused and scratched the glass at Mathers's sneering face on the outside of the tank. Because he blinked, Mathers missed the strike but not the effect. A high-pitch, tortured squeal escaped as Oscar knotted his body around dinner and did what Boa constrictors do, that being squeeze the life out of its prey.

Mathers's remained fixated on the show until the rat's legs stopped thrashing. He turned from the display with a maniacal laugh. "Daddy has to unpack, baby. Don't forget to wipe your mouth when you're finished," he said as Oscar slowly devoured his prey.

Mathers picked up his camcorder, carried it into the kitchen, and set it on the battered computer stand. He had nearly thirty minutes of digital footage needing transferred to *.mpg* format and posted to the Net. He would screen capture the better images later, (video of the younger boys being forced by the teen group leader to strip and jump into "Mouse's Tank", a watershed catch basin deep within the belly of a remote canyon inside the state park) footage taken surreptitiously, and trade them with select newsgroup *friends*; those who better knew Mathers as *Photobug*. Provided the pictures were of good quality there was a better than average chance he would acquire some new pictures from his newsgroup contacts. But all of that would wait until he had more time; little did Donald Mathers know that his time was running out.

He booted up his computer, made a cup of microwave coffee, sifted through Friday and Saturday's junk mail, and breezed through the August issue of *PHOTOgraphic Magazine,* its cover photo a snapshot of a blazing orange sunset over the Atlantic Ocean. When the microwave's timer chimed he tossed the magazine aside, carried his coffee to the table, and checked his email account. Finding nothing of interest he returned to the living room and picked up his duffle bag before walking to the bedroom to unpack.

Fifteen minutes after leaving his apartment Mathers pulled his lime-green and black Kawasaki Ninja ZXR into the parking lot of the "Iron Works", pushed the kickstand down with his heel, and dropped his feet to the pavement.

The Iron Works was not your typical Las Vegas yuppie-puppy health club. It did not have any of the new-fangled, state-of-the-art, dial-up resistance machines with cables and pistons, and neither did the patrons of the Iron Works believe in treadmills or stair climbers. Those who exercised at the facility used good old-fashion iron plates, and if one wanted the benefits of aerobic exercise one donned jogging shoes and took to the track or stadium bleachers across the street at Eldorado High School. And neither was the sweaty cinderblock interior painted in those sissy shades of mauve and taupe found in the more stylish clubs. No fancy gold-framed deco art adorned the walls. The Iron Works' décor was adorned with faded and taped posters of world-class body builders the likes of Frank Zane, Lou Ferrigno, Arnold Schwartzenegger, and Lee Haney—to mention but a few. Inside the clammy steroid and testosterone charged gym the uniform of the day was a sweat-stained tee shirt with the sleeves ripped off and faded sweat pants with more holes in them than a screen door.

Fellow bodybuilders shouted encouragements that bordered on insults, while serious weight lifters huffed and grunted unbelievable poundage toward the ceiling. The chipped concrete floor was a testament to muscles pushed beyond the brink of exhaustion. The hand-printed sign taped to the locker room door said it all: "Girly-Men Go Home!"

Mathers unpacked his gym bag and changed into his workout clothes, a black sleeveless sweatshirt and yellow sweat pants cut off at the knee. He was seated on a gnarled wooden bench tying his shoes when The Iron Works' owner, Bojan "Bo" Vjekoslav—an aging former Mr. Nevada contender whose desk displayed a yellowing autographed picture of him on Venice Beach spotting Frank Zane's three hundred forty seven pound bench press—walked into the locker room.

"Where you been, Donny? No see you all weekend," Bo said with a heavy Croatian accent.

Without looking up from his laces, Mathers said, "Took the kids from the church bible school camping this weekend. We went to the Valley of Fire Park and did a little hiking and rock climbing."

"Good 'dat you take time wit' 'dos boys."

The 'dos boys' Vjekoslav was referring to were a group of underprivileged kids the Youth Ministry sponsored for summer bible study, and camping and hiking expeditions. Mathers volunteered to chaperone the outings whenever it did not conflict with his work schedule as a security guard at the Tropicana Casino.

"Kids nowadays?" Vjekoslav slapped the air with a dismissing wave of his hand. "Too soft! Pampered by computers and the telly-vison. My grandson? The closest he come to sports is to play the football with his thumbs." Bo danced his thick digits over an imaginary videogame controller. "He play game for hours, but you think I can get him into backyard to throw da' football with his Poppa Bojan?

"Look at equipment." Vjekoslav pointed beyond the locker room door. "He never come in here. Bojan remembers Sibenik."

Before old Vjekoslav could drone on about how tough life had been growing up on the cobblestone streets of the ancient Adriatic Seaport, Mathers cut him off. "He's still young, Bo. He'll come around."

Vjekoslav's face twisted into a lemon-sour pucker. "Not da' way his mama makes excuse for him. I'm surprised he's out of the diaper."

Vjekoslav gave Mathers's shoulder a mighty swat, folded still substantial arms across an equally well-developed chest, and said, "It's a good thing you do to take interest in 'dos boys. Not let them become the panty waist."

Mathers's interest in the boys, Bobby Sheer in particular, had nothing to do with altruism; his purpose ran much deeper, and much darker. And not unlike his veiled agenda with Bobby Sheer, Mathers's interest in bodybuilding had little to do with creating the chiseled exterior he sported. It had everything to do with concealing a fragile interior. He slipped into a pair of fingerless black leather weightlifter's gloves and stepped into the gym to pump up his façade.

Chapter 4

Special Agent MacKenzie Stevens and his partner stepped from the Federal Bureau of Investigation's private jet, and down to the tarmac at the North Las Vegas Air Terminal. "Well, that was totally unproductive," he said.

"I don't know about that," his partner replied sporting a wide grin. "It was pretty lucrative for me."

Stevens's partner John Dowe (pronounced Doe)—a surname that nearly kept him out of J. Edgar Hoover's FBI—was fifteen hundred dollars to the plus side thanks to a lucky four king draw on a five-dollar video poker machine, followed up by a straight flush, queen high. A half-dozen well played double downs added an additional three hundred dollars to his wallet; while Stevens strolled around Reno's Atlantis Casino Resort sipping coffee and reflecting on how this was the first time the elusive Shadow Man serial killer had dared to venture so far from home base, Las Vegas. Eight of the suspected thirteen previous homicides occurred within a hundred mile radius of Las Vegas, and now number fourteen showed up on the chart—Or was it the work of a copycat?—in Washoe County in the extreme northwest corner of the state. The latest murder threw off all predictions the Behavioral Science Division in Washington had managed to come up with.

A Teletype across the police National Crime Information Center computer system is what had alerted the Bureau's Las Vegas field office to the murder, hence Stevens and Dowe's trip to Reno. The Nevada Highway

Patrol's Investigative Division did the initial investigation, and quite admirably. The crime scene photos Stevens viewed at the NVHP Reno Headquarters showed the crime scene was staged, as were most of the prior scenes Stevens had inspected. Neatly arranged around the Washoe victim were photographs of him having sex with children, prompting a search warrant of the "victim's" residence. Inside the single story log cabin nestled deep in Squaw Valley Resort near Lake Tahoe they had found computer disks, pictures, as well as other proof that the *victim* had a number of victims of his own. All evidentiary fingers pointed to the unidentified suspect of the Bureau's "Operation Candy Cane"—Shadow Man.

Stevens found himself wandering around a mortuary slab eating a ham and cheese on rye, peering over the county coroner's shoulder, watching victim fourteen be forensically dissected. The autopsy verified the victim was killed elsewhere before being strung by the neck from the rafters of a remote roadside rest stop along Interstate 80. He had been dangling there for two days, maybe more. A pair of softball-size discolorations on his chest—the one on the lower left rib cage broke two ribs and punctured the superior lobe of the left lung, the other directly over a cracked and displaced sternum—indicated "blows of tremendous force", or so said autopsy vernacular. The victim bled to death internally the result of a torn aorta. "Homicide caused by blunt force trauma to the thorax" was the official ruling.

Back in Las Vegas Stevens drove the unmarked agency car toward the Bureau's office on E. Charleston Boulevard, nestled amongst commercial office buildings three blocks off the Las Vegas "Strip". Stevens loathed Las Vegas in general and the boulevard in particular. He despised its constant flow of tourists, taxis, and limousines. He stuck to the back roads and watched out of the corner of his eye as Dowe peeled hundred dollar bills from his pocket, counting his earnings for the umpteenth time.

Inside the Bureau's office Agent Stevens sat at his desk deep in thought, chin supported on cupped hands, the cup of coffee on his desk having chilled to room temperature.

Dowe strolled into their shared cubicle with a coffee in one hand and a rolled up *Las Vegas Sun* in the other. He dropped to the chair behind his desk, set his coffee on top of a disheveled pile of reports, and snapped the newspaper open to the sports page.

"Daydreaming, Mack?" Dowe said with a smirk. "Louis wouldn't appreciate you wasting the taxpayer's dollars sitting around daydreaming."

Agent Stevens chose decorum by not referring to the Director of the Federal Bureau of Investigation by his first name. "I'm sure Director Freeh will walk through the door any second now, John."

"In the old days Hoover might have," Dowe said, and then buried his head behind the newspaper's thoroughbred horses posting.

Stevens raised his head from his hands and his eyes to his partner. "In case you haven't noticed, John, this isn't the old days."

Mackenzie Stevens was fifteen years into an ambitious career he hoped would carry him to the upper echelons of the FBI. He resented Dowe's twenty-nine year and eight months—three months from retirement—complacency. If crime fighting no longer held his interest why didn't Dowe pull the plug and walk out? Three months wouldn't benefit his pension package by more than a few dollars a month.

Stevens rose from his desk and leaned balled fists on the thick "Operation Candy Cane" folder. "How do you suppose our boy moves around the state in total anonymity?" he said. "That's assuming the murder up north was done by Shadow Man and not a copycat."

Dowe glanced overtop the newspaper with an innocuous grin. It was time to have a little fun at Stevens's expense. He carefully folded the newspaper closed and set it on his desk. "Maybe he doesn't move around in 'total anonymity', Mack. I'll wager a paycheck that he never leaves his house."

Stevens's pencil thin eyebrows creased together at the bridge of his nose. "What're you talking about?"

Dowe leaned forward, clapped his hands together, and brought them to rest on his desk. "Maybe he offs his victims remotely without ever leaving the comfort of his La-Z-Boy. Yeah, that's it! He kills them remotely."

Stevens rolled disgusted eyes toward the ceiling and pushed away from his desk. He knew the direction his partner was heading.

Dowe closed his eyes and brought fingertips to his temples, intoning his mantra: "I am Shadow Man-Shadow Man-Shadow Man," he echoed. "I will you dead, Mr. Pee-Pee toucher killer. Hummm."

Stevens sighed and shook his head with disgust, sorry he had ever confided in Dowe his interest in the military and C.I.A.'s clandestine research into remote viewing: the purported clairvoyant ability to view distant or future events using paranormal thought processes; extrasensory perception, a.k.a. ESP.

Late on a Friday night Stevens had been sitting in his easy chair sipping a glass of wine, listening to the "Coast to Coast with Art Bell" AM radio program, mortified when Dowe's voice leapt from the speakers. Dowe actually had had the gall to phone the nationally syndicated talk show claiming, anonymously of course, to be a retired CIA expert on "Star Gate"—the CIA's code name for their remote viewing experimentation. Dowe duped the host out of nearly five minutes of airtime before Mr. Bell queued in on the caller's sniggering and hung up on him, explaining to his audience that an occasional "crackpot" gets past the call screener.

"You know, John, you really are to be pitied," Stevens said, his feathers sufficiently ruffled. "I don't know why I even bothered trying to have intelligent conversations with you." He picked up his cup and snatched the "Candy Cane" folder from his desk, the contents spilling to the floor at his feet.

Dowe pounced on the calamity and took full credit for the mishap.

"Don't mess with me again, Mack. I swear…" He married his fingertips to his temples, and with a triumphant giggle, said, "Next time I'll drop your pants to the floor right here in front of everyone." He leaned back in his chair, snatched up the newspaper, and penciled in his picks for the afternoon races.

Stevens glared at him for a moment and then, amidst grumbling curses, knelt down and gathered together the file, stuffing loose pages into the folder until it looked like a tangle of Medusa's hair. "If you're such a believer in RV, John…Why is it you never seem to pick the right horse?"

TRAIL OF BODIES

Dowe snapped the paper taut in front of his face. "Not my fault the horses don't believe," he said.

Special Agent Silifax poked his head around the doorjamb. "Mack. There's a Sheriff Austin on the phone for you. Says he has some Intel on Candy Cane."

Stevens turned and said, "What's he got?"

"No idea." Silifax shrugged and held up three fingers. "Line three."

Reese Daniels sat on the floor at the center of his tiyuguan (Chinese for gymnasium) crossed legged, motionless. The back of each hand rested on the insides of his knees, thumb and forefinger in light contact; palms faced the ceiling, sweat dripping from his face. After an exhilarating workout he was focused on lowering his respirations to deep, rhythmic inhalation and exhalations, two per minute. Internally centered, eyes closed, he not only saw the flickering flame on the altar two meters away; he felt its heat. Conscious effort directed his chi, his life force, through the meridians of the body, barely taking notice of swollen hands that registered no pain. Reese Daniels did not feel pain in a traditional physical sense. He had learned long ago how to turn off the brain's neuron receptors that told him he was in pain. In a shadowy corner of the studio, one-inch thick slabs of block lay crumbled on the floor, rendered useless from bone-crushing blows learned in his youth. Tian Xian Huo, Grand Master of traditional Chinese Wu Shu, had he still been alive, would have smiled a crooked, yellow-toothed smile, proud of his xuésheng (student, pupil, disciple).

Chapter 5

Cody Austin turned west off Interstate 93 and followed the two-lane asphalt ribbon officially designated as Nevada State Route 375 for several miles, finally edging his two-tone brown and tan Ford Bronco to the side of the road near Coyote Summit. He brought the vehicle to a smooth stop on the narrow shoulder, slipped the gearshift into park, closed his eyes and let his head to drop back against the headrest, and stretched his long arm across the top of the passenger seat. A funnel of cool air from the air conditioning vent crawled up his sleeve and cooled his sweaty armpit.

Austin was a big man, and it had always been so. It wasn't long (sixth grade as he remembered) before he shot up like a sprout and passed most of his classmates; big enough in boot camp he became the favorite target of the drill sergeant. Big, however, did not imply oafishness, quite the contrary. Cody Austin stood six feet six inches tall and tipped the scale at two hundred sixty five pounds of muscular agility.

He reached down and picked up the clipboard resting on the console between the bucket seats, opened his eyes, and carefully reread every word on the sheet of paper. It all matched what he had been speculating for some time, but the question was how to go about proving a mystery the FBI's vast resources had to date failed to unravel. And more importantly, did he want to be right? He tossed the clipboard to the passenger seat, let out a heavy breath, dropped the gearshift into drive, snapped forward in his seat, and drove down a sand and gravel trail that resembled an abandoned gas well road more than a driveway. Dust billowed from beneath the Ford's chassis as he jostled and shimmied deeper into the foothills of the Timpahute Mountain Range on the west side of Lincoln County. More than a mile from the paved highway Austin stood hard on the brakes at the crest of a steep hill, gravity pulling him forward against the safety belt's shoulder strap. He could not help but smile at the thought of Sitting Bull looking down on Little Bighorn. The desert floor looked as if God had taken a moment out of his busy creation schedule and ladled out a scoop, leaving behind a barren sinkhole in the midst of the foothills. If not for the sprawling estate in the middle of the divot the landscape resembled an ocean gone dry, or the lunar surface as viewed through a telescope.

Austin eased his foot off the brake pedal and let the Bronco coast down to the oasis on the valley's floor, guiding his vehicle around the apex of a circular crushed limestone driveway with Joshua trees rising from the mounded island. He stopped his vehicle and shoved the gearshift up into park.

The house's exterior—if one can call a thirteen thousand square foot structure a house—was beige stucco capped with red clay Spanish roof tiles, and contrasted gracefully with the barren desert landscape. An interlocking jigsaw puzzle flagstone sidewalk lined with indigenous Multiflora Rose Shrubs and squatty Yucca plants led to the front porch. Standing defiant against the sun on each side of the shaded veranda's arched stone entrance stood two eight-foot tall centurion-like Saguaro cacti.

Austin extricated himself from behind the steering wheel, plopped a sweat-stained faded Stetson on top of his graying crew cut while reflecting how, on his income, he might marginally afford the servant's quarters at the rear of the sprawling two-story mansion. Vast wealth brings with it opulence for which most would be willing to trade a few body parts. His dusty brown cowboy boots clicked against the flagstone squares as he quickened his pace for the shaded porch.

Ringing the doorbell was but a formality at the Daniels ranch. Austin had been to the place enough times as a child, and as Lincoln County's sheriff, to know that a state-of-the-art security system, complete with pressure plates, motion sensors, and video surveillance had already alerted the occupants of his arrival. The hacienda's original owner, R.B. Daniels, had even prepared for a power failure. At the slightest drop in voltage a 27kw Perkins generator, with automatic transfer switch, fired up to supply enough power to run a moderate-sized office building. From behind the heavy double oak doors muted chimes sang his arrival and, all things considered, Austin was pleasantly surprised the door opened as quickly as it did.

The homeowner greeted him in Chinese. "Hao chen, jingcha Austin."

"Good afternoon to you, too, Reese," Austin said, taken aback the homeowner answered the door. Usually it was the ranch manager-maintenance man-butler who responded to the doorbell, not Reese Daniels.

Glistening with sweat, Reese stepped out of the doorway and waved Sheriff Austin inside. "Please, won't you come in?"

Austin peeled off his mirrored aviator sunglasses and tucked the stem into his shirt pocket. "Thought you'd never ask," he said with a grin.

"Warm enough for you?"

"If the marquee in Pioche is right, 112 degrees," Austin said, grateful to be out of the sun.

"Bring your swim trunks?"

Austin came to test the waters all right, but not those of Daniels's swimming pool. He scanned his host's face for a hint of surprise, or concern, or anything. "Having a slow day so I thought I'd drop by and say howdy."

Coming from someone whose physical attributes leaned heavily toward the Oriental side of his Chinese-American heritage, Reese's, "Well, howdy back." seemed clumsy at best.

Austin stepped into the palatial, air-conditioned foyer and removed his Stetson, mopped his brow with a red paisley handkerchief, and then returned it to his back pocket.

Sunlight blazing in through floor-to-ceiling windows reflected across the foyer's imported white Spanish Onyx Crema Marfil marble floor. Rooted in mammoth terracotta pots strategically placed throughout the foyer a half dozen scabrous palm trees stretched their branches toward the twenty-foot vaulted ceiling. Expensive abstract paintings showcased with soft illumination lined the walls. No matter how many times he had been inside the house Cody Austin always marveled at the elegance of Daniels's estate.

Reese sealed out the afternoon heat with a push of the door. "I'm glad you dropped by, Sheriff. Would you care for a lemonade?"

"Sure," Sheriff Austin said.

"I just finished up with my work out." Daniels wiped his face on the towel draped across his shoulders. "You know your way to the kitchen, Sheriff. Make yourself at home. I'll grab a quick shower and join you in a few minutes."

Reese turned toward the sweeping spiral mahogany staircase; the same staircase Daniels Industries founder, the late Captain R.B. Daniels, tumbled down nearly two decades ago breaking his neck.

Austin's hand brushed against the pearl handle .45-caliber auto pistol strapped to his right hip and with nervous eyes darting about the atrium, he said, "Where's Kitty?"

Reese paused with his foot resting on the first step and his hand on the banister. He turned to the sheriff with a smile.

Kitty was Reese's idea of a pet, if one could call a flat-out mean feral coyote a pet. His naming a male coyote "Kitty" was but just one example of Reese's inimitable sense of humor, which so happened to match one of the traits listed on the FBI's serial killer profile lying on the passenger seat of the Bronco.

Several years ago Reese found Kitty suckling his dead mother's teat near the north property line of the fifteen thousand acre ranch. Kitty's mother died a thirty-caliber death, and let there be no doubt, if Reese ever found out who had shot the lone coyote and stomped three of her four offspring to death on his property, he would most happily introduce their rifle barrel to their colon. Kitty respected Reese, tolerated Dakota the ranch hand, and distrusted most others. The rare intrusion that the perimeter alarm missed Kitty didn't. In Reese's company the coyote was as well behaved as Lassie, without him close by, meaner than Cujo.

"He's outside someplace. No doubt sleeping in the shade," Reese said, and then bounded up the staircase taking four steps at a time.

In less than ten minutes Reese strolled into the kitchen wearing a pair of lightweight green hospital scrubs and bright yellow sleeveless cotton shirt. "How's business?" he said with his head buried in the refrigerator.

"Slow. As usual." Sheriff Austin sipped the lemonade he had poured himself.

Lincoln County, Nevada, situated north of Clark County (home of Las Vegas) and east of Nye County (home of the government's mysterious Area 51 and nuclear test sights) is ten thousand plus square miles of barren, mountainous desert with a population hovering around four thousand souls. Made up predominately of expansive ranches it's about as stereotypically desolate as a Clint Eastwood spaghetti western, and nowhere near as filled with desperadoes.

"Slow isn't bad, is it?" Reese said, pushing the stainless steel refrigerator door closed with his foot.

"Hell's Bells no!" Austin almost shouted. "Slow is a good thing. It means me and my deputies are doing what we get paid to do, and that's keep the peace."

"Good point." Reese padded across the tile floor to the island countertop at the center of the kitchen.

Sheriff Austin watched with a cop's intuitive gaze as his host set a Tupperware container filled with lemon slices on the counter and pried the cap off a bottle of Corona. Next he pulled a white linen napkin from the drawer and cleaned the bottle's neck, pushed a lemon wedge inside with his thumb, and then wiped the neck a second time before depositing the towel into a wicker hamper in the pantry. Reese turned to the sink, squeezed a quarter-size glob of Purell hand sanitizer into his palm, and worked it over his hands. He covered the opening with his thumb, tipped the bottle upside down, and watched with childlike interest as the lemon floated to the upturned bottom.

Reese took a sip of his beer, set the bottle on the counter, and turned to the sheriff. "I see the *Lincoln Record* endorsed your reelection."

"Kinda' silly considering I'm running unopposed," Austin said, with a grin and listless shrug of his shoulders. He took another swig of lemonade. "Like anyone wants this job."

"Someone has to do it," Reese said.

"Not many takers," Austin countered. "Most people can't handle the sudden poverty."

Reese leaned his arms on the countertop and grinned. "I'd be willing to support a tax if it all went to your office," he said.

Easy to say when you have enough money that Trump probably drops what he's doing whenever you call. "I'll recommend you to chair the committee," he said, sardonically.

Reese paused his drink in front of his lips. "So what brings you all the way out here today, Sheriff?"

"Nothing in particular. Happened to be in the neighborhood, hadn't stopped by in a while, so here I am."

Considering Daniels's estate was secluded in a remote valley in the northwest corner of the county, and hidden more than a mile into the desert off a desolate stretch of SR 375, no one just "happened to be in the neighborhood", and Reese knew that.

He walked to the refrigerator and brought out the pitcher of lemonade, topped off the sheriff's glass, and said, "Well I'm glad you dropped in. Would you care to join me out on the patio?"

Sheriff Austin followed Reese through the set of French doors overlooking the pool deck. Reese set his beer on a glass top patio table, walked across the sprawling concrete deck to the wall nearest the family room doors where he flipped a switch to activate a rollout awning. Sheriff Austin took a seat in the shade, mentally preparing himself to pick the brain of a serial killer.

Cody Austin was a teenager the stormy night Reese Daniels was born. Thirty some years later and he could still vividly recall his father's late night summons to Daniels's ranch, but more importantly he remembered the next morning's breakfast conversation.

For nearly three decades before hanging up his scalpel to manage Cody's bid for sheriff, Dr. Travis Austin served as Lincoln County's Coroner. Immediately after the election, Dr. Austin retired to the thick pine forests of Kodiak Island, Alaska, where he spends the majority of his time salmon fishing the icy creeks within walking distance of his secluded log cabin.

It was no secret around Lincoln County back then that old Captain R.B. Daniels had more money than most third world countries, and that his wealth earned him certain latitudes with many local politicians, Dr. Travis Austin nearly at the top of the list. Money certainly can buy a lot of things, but in the words of Lennon and McCartney, "Money can't buy me love", because R.B. Daniels's daughter Libby spent the better part of her teen years running away and hanging out on the streets of San Francisco. The night Reese was born Dr. Austin "…responded to the Daniels ranch to find sixteen year old Elizabeth Daniels in the latter throes of childbirth…" or so said his report. Unfortunately, Libby passed away minutes after birthing a baby boy; "massive hemorrhaging" entered on the cause of death line.

It was his father's comment the following morning at the breakfast table that brought then teenage Cody's eyes overtop the sports page.

"…and a damn good thing she died. The boy's a half-breed."

"Negro?" mother Austin asked while flipping over sausage patties.

Dr. Austin paused with a fork-load of hotcakes in front of his mouth. "Worse," he'd said.

"Worse?" mother Austin's brow wrinkled. "What could possibly be worse?"

"The boy's a half-breed chink; we all know what Mr. Daniels thinks of Orientals."

Reese shook the sheriff's hand with a genial smile. "Stop by anytime, Sheriff. You know you're always welcome here."

The hour-long conversation had revealed nothing noteworthy, much to Austin's chagrin. He zigzagged his way back toward civilization more certain than ever that Reese Daniels was emotionally vacant enough to be the mysterious serial killer—Shadow Man.

Reese stood in the driveway scratching his short-cropped black hair, contemplating the real reason behind the sheriff's visit. He watched Austin's Bronco disappear overtop the ridge on the west side of the valley and then, with a shrug, walked back into the house.

Chapter 6

The Federal Bureau of Investigation rarely concerns itself with a local murder investigation unless the resident police force asks for assistance, which in the case of the "Operation Candy Cane" murders had not happened. Nearly all the victims came from the more populated Clark County, whose sheriff's office, auspice the Las Vegas casinos, was well funded. Nye County to the northwest semi-claimed two "possible" victims, and now Washoe County to the north had entered the chart, provided Shadow Man's legend had not produced a fan club of imitators. The Bureau's five-year involvement in the case came as a result of victim number nine's relationship with a certain high-ranking Washington D.C. politico.

The serial killer had tracked Lee Whaler, son of U.S. Senator Jack Whaler, across the Internet for two short months before connecting the screen persona with a real person. It proved to be one of Shadow Man's quickest hunts. Once he made the connection he visited his target within a week, finding the senator's son and his lover writhing like perverse snakes on the living room floor of Whaler's exclusive condominium. Like a cool breeze, Shadow Man entered through an unlocked sliding door and snapped Whaler's neck like a dried chicken bone, gone before his lover could get a glimpse of the killer. At the police station Whaler's boy-toy (who turned out was only seventeen) confessed to a two-year affair with the senator's much older son, and when the cops asked the sobbing teen for a description of the murderer, he blubbered: "I have no idea what he looked like, officer.

All of the sudden he was there. And all the sudden he was gone. Like a shadow man."

At the conclusion of yesterday's meeting with Daniels Sheriff Austin made the call from his vehicle before he reached the highway. Normally punctual for his appointments, Austin was running late. Like a tardy student sneaking into the classroom he quietly opened the door with the blue and gold FBI logo painted on frosted glass, walked to the receptionist's window wearing a sheepish grin, announced his arrival, and then took a seat near the door expecting he would be kept waiting long enough to chastise his tardiness. The whole situation reminded him that he was the Chihuahua seeking audience with the Great Dane of law enforcement. Surprisingly, it was only a few minutes before the receptionist buzzed him through the security door and escorted him to a medium-size conference room at the end of a narrow carpeted hall.

"Make yourself comfortable, Sheriff," she said with an indulgent smile. "Agent Stevens will be with you in a moment. He's on a conference call with the DD." In case the sheriff didn't understand federal jargon, she added, "The Deputy Director that is."

Austin gave a silent nod and waited until she left the room before sliding a chair from beneath the table at the center of the room and taking a seat. He poured himself a glass of ice water from a plastic decanter on the table and used the heel of his hand to mop up droplets that splashed over the edge of the glass. The dark walnut paneled room was absent distractions, save a framed portrait of J. Edgar Hoover, whose suspicious eyes seemed welded to Sheriff Austin's every move. It was as plain and businesslike as the receptionist's countenance.

The door swung open and Special Agent MacKenzie Stevens stepped into the room, crisp white cuffs poking beyond the sleeves of his charcoal-gray suit jacket, a plain black tie pulled tight to his neck. He stepped forward with his hand extended. Sheriff Austin felt underdressed in his chocolate brown uniform slacks and khaki shirt with dark epaulets and pocket flaps. He stood and wiped his hand on his pant leg in case the diaper wipes he kept in the console had missed any of the grime from an impromptu tire change for a lost tourist on US 15.

"Sheriff Austin, my pleasure. I'm MacKenzie Stevens," the agents said amiably.

Sheriff Austin reached forward and clasped the agent's hand firmly enough to convey to the "suit cop" that he was a frontline, hands-on, no nonsense sheriff, and for his efforts, Sheriff Austin found an equal pressure returned.

"Thank you for taking the time to see me, Agent Stevens."

"From the sound of yesterday's phone call, it's I who should be thanking you. And it's MacKenzie, Sheriff, most people just call me Mack."

"Cody." He released Stevens's hand. "And most call me Cody."

Stevens grinned and waved him to a chair. "Please, Cody, have a seat."

The two lawmen sat on opposite sides of the table and adjusted their chairs until facing each other.

"I know you federal boys are real busy so I'm going to jump right in here. I've read the FBI's profile on the serial killer you folks call Shadow Man," Austin said without mincing his words. "I'm pretty sure I know who he is."

Jumping right to the point was an understatement, Stevens mused, leaning back in his chair. "How so, Cody?" he said.

"Ever heard of Daniels Industries, Mack?"

"The same Daniels Industries that pioneered the guidance system for our smart bombs?"

"One in the same."

"I don't know much about it except what I've read over the years in the *Wall Street Journal* and some old news periodicals. If I recall correctly, the founder made a boatload of money off the Department of Defense for all the good it did him. I was finishing up at the National Academy when I read, someplace, that he fell down a flight of steps and died of a broken neck."

Sheriff Austin pursed his lips, bobbed his head, and reached for his glass, taking a couple of healthy gulps. He wiped his mouth on the back of his hand and leaned forward. "Maybe, and then again, maybe not. I think R.B. Daniels, that's the founder of Daniels Industries, was Shadow Man's first kill. And maybe Shadow Boy is the more accurate term."

Stevens's head drooped toward his right shoulder and his brow creased. "Explain."

Austin sagged forward until his elbows came to rest on his knees. "Mack, my father was Lincoln County's Coroner for a whole bunch of years before I took over as sheriff. After I got elected, and mostly out of curiosity, I looked at a couple of old files. Both involved what some of my older deputies called 'questionable deaths'. Both, coincidentally, involved the Daniels family."

The expression on Stevens's face let Austin know he had piqued the agent's interest.

"Let me start off with some ancient Lincoln County history.

"Back when I was about fourteen or fifteen I remember sitting at the breakfast table listening to my old man tell Mom about Daniels's daughter giving birth in the middle of the night. And, I might add, that was no big surprise.

"Libby and I—Libby was old man Daniels's daughter—were friends all through grade school, right up until ninth grade. That's when she started hanging around some of the..." Austin paused to find the right phrase. "...less desirables, if you know what I mean. We sort of went in separate directions.

"Although I never saw her do it, rumor back then had it that she started smoking marijuana and got the reputation of being a little loose. You know how teenage boys like to brag about that kind of thing. According to the way the guys on the football team talked...let's just say it was a well-deserved reputation. She developed this habit of disappearing for months at a time, running away to hang out with a bunch of hippies over in San Francisco. I suppose that kinda' stuck hard in old Daniels's craw, him being a decorated veteran and all.

"Libby supposedly died during childbirth. 'Massive hemorrhaging' according to Pop's report."

The building's air conditioning was playing havoc with Austin's sinuses. He pinched his nostrils together, popped his ears, and snorted loudly.

"But there's a slight problem with Pop's official report," he continued. "I went down to the courthouse and looked at Libby's death certificate.

According to it she died two weeks *after* the baby was born."

"A typo-error?" Stevens offered, anxiously waiting for Austin to get to the Shadow Man part of this story.

"Or a Freudian pen-slip," Austin countered. "Then again, maybe my old man intentionally left a hidden trail for someone to pick up on. Goodness knows my predecessor was tighter with Daniels than my old man was, so I can only imagine how thorough the investigation into Libby's death was. Hell's Bells, Mack, not one deputy on my department remembers anyone going out there that night other than the former sheriff himself.

"And there's another weird twist to this. The date on Libby's death certificate was handwritten, not typed in. It's my Pop's handwriting. That kind of struck me as odd. I pulled up a whole bunch of death certificates just for grins and giggles. On all of them except Libby's death certificate the date and time of death is typed in, not handwritten."

"Did you ever ask your father about the discrepancy?" Stevens asked.

A cynical smile turned up the corners of Austin's mouth. Idly, he swept imaginary debris from the table. "I sure did."

"And?"

"When I called Pop and confronted him about the discrepancy I heard him choking on the other end of the line like he'd swallowed a scorpion. I don't think when he left the trail—if that's what it is—he anticipated me becoming the sheriff. He recovered quickly enough, said he must have filled in the wrong date by mistake."

Stevens folded his hands on top of each other, laid them on the table, and said, "Sounds plausible to me, Sheriff."

"Sounds like BS to me, Stevens." Sheriff Austin leaned back in his chair, folded his arms across his chest, and let his head dip to one side. "Look, Stevens…Mack, I may not be the sharpest knife in the drawer but I know when I'm being spoon-fed. And I'm pretty sure what Pop was feeding me was pure, unadulterated, one hundred percent longhorn cowpat."

"Why would your father falsify this girl's death certificate?" Stevens said.

Sheriff Austin stared directly into the agent's eyes, his voice compelling. "Because I think the drunken *Captain* murdered his daughter, that's why."

Stevens's sat up a little straighter in his seat. "Motive, Sheriff?"

"Daniels's grandson is a half-breed Chinese." Austin leaned back in his chair as if the statement alone was self-explanatory.

Stevens deflated in his seat with a chortle. "Hardly a motive for murder in this day and age, Austin."

"It wasn't in 'this day and age' Stevens. It happened nearly twenty years ago." Sheriff Austin lowered his voice and slid to the edge of his seat. "There's a reason everybody around Lincoln County called him the Captain," Austin's voice was almost a whisper. "Granted, he liked his Captain Morgan's rum and all, but that ain't the reason."

"He owned a yacht?" Stevens mocked.

"A couple of them as a matter of fact," the sheriff retorted. "And more politicians than will ever be known. I 'spect my father and the former sheriff ran neck and neck for top of the list honors.

"That old nasty man wouldn't hesitate for a second buying anyone he thought could help his cause, whatever that may have been at the moment." Austin relaxed his big hands in his lap. "The good Captain was a highly decorated Nam veteran. Hell's Bells, he had three Purple Hearts and a Silver Star pinned to his chest when they planted him in the ground. You don't get no chest full of medals for fraternizing with the enemy, Stevens. You get 'em for killing...And kill he did.

"Rumor has it he was personally responsible for over two hundred Vietnamese kills during his overseas tours. *Tours* is plural. Rumor also has it not all of them were enemy combatants."

Austin sat back and gave Stevens a moment to chew on the new information, and then continued. "Agent Stevens, you didn't know old man Daniels. The Captain had an obsessive hatred for anything Oriental. I'll assume it came with his war experiences, the stuff he saw over there. Then his daughter goes and gets knocked up and delivers a half-breed chink?" Austin's brows rose to stamp an exclamation point on his theory. "There's your motive."

Stevens's hand stroked his clean-shaven chin and after an appropriate pause, Austin resumed the story.

"Now for part two. Rumor also has it, and rumors are aplenty around my county, that as the child grows up he's spoiled rotten by the Captain's wealth. Not out of love mind you, no siree-bob. Daniels despised his Chinese grandson with the same passion you folks down here set aside for panhandlers in the lobby of Caesar's Palace. He absolutely hated that kid, Stevens."

"Then why not whack the kid too and be done with it?" Stevens said. "According to your theory, Sheriff, mom's already dead so there's really no one to stop him."

Austin raised a hold-that-thought-for-a-moment finger toward the ceiling. "I'll get to Dakota Bricker in a minute.

"The whole time Reese—that's old man Daniels's grandson—is growing up he's not allowed off the ranch. Very few people ever saw the kid, and even fewer even knew he existed. It was like Daniels wanted to keep his Oriental bastard offspring hidden from the public's prying eyes.

"Can you imagine growing up in total isolation? A prisoner in your own home with no other kids to play with, no friends." Sheriff Austin shook his head in sympathy. "That would have to twist anyone's bubble.

"Captain Daniels had highly paid tutors brought to the ranch rather than send Reese to public school.

"I was at home on leave once when my old man told me the story of how Daniels flew a Martial Arts expert in from China when the kid got interested in karate. No one knows how many years the little guy spent out there at the ranch teaching young Reese karate, but gossip has it he didn't speak a lick of English. So what did Daniels do? In step with the Daniels way, he spent more money and hired an interpreter to teach Reese Chinese.

"He set the little Chinaman up with his own trailer in Rachel, paid for everything. According to Pops, Bricker picked the guy up every morning and hauled him back to Rachel in the afternoon after Reese's lessons. No one knows for sure how much Daniels paid Kung Fu Joe, but I'll bet that Chinaman is one of the richest peasants in his village if he's still alive.

"Jeepers, Mack, Reese speaks Chinese like he grew up over there. I've been to the ranch; he not only listens to Internet broadcast Chinese radio stations, he talks back to the radio like he's in the studio. I asked him why he listens to that crap and do you know what he told me?"

Stevens shook his head.

"He said it's so he can stay in touch with his 'roots'.

"I'm a lot older than Reese, but I'd occasionally see him when Pop dragged me along with him out to Daniels's ranch. After I got out of the service and decided to make a run for sheriff my old man took me out there so Daniels and I could have a *chat*.

"Reese would have been about twelve or thirteen at the time. When we got to the ranch, Reese's arm was in a cast. God only knows how that happened, and Pops wouldn't say. I felt kinda' sorry for the kid, him being isolated out there in the middle of nowhere. I tried getting his grandpa to let me take him campaigning with me. I figured since him and my old man was so tight he wouldn't mind.

"I'm here to tell ya' Stevens, that spiteful old man had a huge problem letting that kid out of his sight."

Austin tipped his head down and looked at Stevens through bushy eyebrows. "But he didn't have no problem offering me ten-thousand dollars in nice crisp fifties and hundreds, tucked inside a plain white envelope. 'For unexpected campaign costs' he'd said.

"I told him no thanks and handed it back; told him I intended to run an honest campaign, and an honest office.

"Daniels blew a gasket. He screamed and cursed at me, said I'd never be sheriff as long as he was alive." Austin shrugged his shoulders with a snigger. "Maybe that was the first time anyone had had the stones to tell him no.

"Needless to say, Pops was hot under the collar for me telling Daniels to shove his money. By the time we were ready to leave Daniels calmed down enough to at least shake my hand. Pops went to the car and purposely left me standing on the front porch alone with Daniels.

"I have to give the old buzzard credit for having some big balls...sorry," Austin blushed slightly, "fortitude. When I turned to leave he said, and these are his exact words, 'Cody, you'd better rethink my offer if you want to be sheriff. Without my support you'll never make it past the primary.' "

"You'll never guess what he did next." Austin didn't wait for a response. "He slapped that cash-filled envelope against my chest with one of his crap eating smiles."

"Did you take the money?" Stevens asked.

"Ten thousand dollars? You bet I took it—"

Until his confession to public corruption Austin had earned Stevens's respect.

"—and then I dumped it out at his feet. Old man Daniels was about my size. I stepped up nose-to-nose with him and told him if he ever offered me money again, whether or not I was the sheriff, I would break his G.I. Joe neck. I was a lot younger back then and a whole bunch more vocal," Austin said with an embarrassed smile.

"Hope my promise to Daniels," Austin said as an afterthought, "doesn't make me a suspect in his death."

Stevens grinned.

"That was the last time I saw the old man alive," Austin said. "Three months before I was elected to office Daniels took his famous nosedive down the steps, or so goes the story."

Stevens adjusted himself in his chair, flicked a piece of lint from his dark trousers, and said, "Cody, what does any of this have to do with the Shadow Man investigation? And who is this Bricker character you mentioned?"

"Hold onto your federal paycheck, Mack," Austin said, tongue-in-cheek. "I'll get to Dakota Bricker in a minute.

"Unless I'm mistaken, and I don't think I am, you federal boys didn't get too interested in the Shadow Man case until a certain Senator's kid, pardon the pun, got caught with his pants down. Then y'all got the secret handshake, or whatever you call it, to stick your nose into the investigation."

Stevens leaned forward, rested his cheeks on his hands, and remained taciturn.

"I'll take your lack of an answer as a yes." Austin squinted his eyes. "Mack, it don't take no rocket scientist to figure out the reason the FBI's in the case is because victim number nine's father just so happens to be a U.S. Senator, and Mom's brother a deputy U.S. Attorney."

The agent remained aloof and Austin snapped forward in his seat. "Look here mister high and mighty FBI..." and then softened his tone, "Mack, we're on the same team. I'm trying to stop a serial killer. And I ain't talking about a guy who goes around knifing boxes of Coco Puffs in the supermarket."

"So what's your theory, Sheriff?"

"My theory?" Austin scoffed. "My theory is that Reese Daniels is the elusive Shadow Man."

"Elaborate."

Austin let a sigh of frustration escape. "Reese's teenage momma gives birth to a half-breed Oriental son; grandpa Daniels is so pissed off that in a fit of rage kills his own daughter, most probably witnessed by ranch hand Dakota Bricker.

"Let's say, just for sake of conversation, that Bricker comes on the scene seconds after Daniels strips a gear on Libby. He's too late to help her but keeps the old drunk from murdering his grandson, too. The next day, when Daniels sobers up and realizes what he's done, he offers Bricker more money to keep his mouth shut than a ranch hand could possibly make in three lifetimes.

"By the way," Austin interrupted his account, "guess under whose command Dakota Bricker served in Viet Nam?"

Austin saw the bombshell had landed on target.

"That's right, Stevens. Bricker served two tours under Daniels's command, Special Forces!

"Now let's again say," Austin said, returning to his original train of thought, "for conversation that is, that Daniels swears an oath—Semper Fi! and all that crap—the kid will never want for anything, at least not materialistically. Libby's dead and nothing's going to bring her back, so Bricker strokes the Golden Goose and goes along with the old man's scheme. Let's also say that years later Reese finds out grandpa killed his mommy. But he's not a little kid anymore; he's a teenager with years of that Kung Fu crap under his black belt.

"He catches grandpa all juiced up one night and sees his chance to get even; to avenge his momma. He uses one of them karate chops," Austin sliced the air with his hand, "and busts the old fool's neck, and then makes it look like an accident by tossing grandpa's body down the steps. No one is the wiser."

Austin slid his chair back, folded his hands behind his head, and stretched his long legs out under the table, crossing them at the ankle.

"Here's the part I'm not so sure about, Mack. Does Bricker know Reese whacked grandpa, or did he actually believe Daniels took a drunken swan dive into the hereafter?"

Stevens's skepticism was thawing.

"Okay, Sheriff, for now let's go with your premise. But why hunt pedophiles on the Internet and systematically kill them?"

"Ah, there's the rub. Maybe, just maybe there's more going on out there at the Daniels homestead than anyone knows about, or suspects," Austin said with a wry grin. "Maybe that's exactly why Libby kept running away. We know rapists don't rape for sex, they rape to exert a perverse sense of power and control over their victim. What better way for the Captain to exert power over a race he hated so much than to rape an Oriental; the half-breed grandson he detests."

Stevens smacked his lips audibly while considering the sheriff's reasoning. "I have to tell you, Sheriff Austin, you're taking some huge leaps in logic."

"I don't think so, Agent Stevens. Unless I'm mistaken, all of Reese's—" The sheriff paused and corrected himself. "—Shadow Man's victims have died of blunt force trauma; crushed tracheas, ruptured aortas, broken necks. Correct me if I'm wrong, but to the best of my knowledge there has never been a weapon used." Austin's shoulders shrugged. "Am I correct."

Stevens was reluctant to share details of the "Operation Candy Cane" file with the locals so he remained silent.

Sheriff Austin drove nearly three hours out of his way to share information that could possibly solve a fifteen year old mystery and— characteristic of the FBI's participatory view of law enforcement, local cops participate by funneling information to the federal level—he was being stonewalled. He exhaled a heavy sigh and trudged on.

"Obviously the Shadow Man character is someone highly trained in the art of killing. I don't think I need to remind you of the years Reese spent learning with the Chinaman, do I?

"Mack, Reese Daniels is a walking weapon! And he comes complete with the financial freedom to move about totally undetected." Sheriff Austin intertwined his fingers and dropped them to his lap. "While I'm at it, let's take another leap in logic.

"What if Daniels and Bricker are a team? Let's say Daniels hunts pedophiles on the Internet, Bricker supplies the transportation by taking Reese out to do his thing, and afterward returns the monster to the castle in the desert?"

A team? That was a point Stevens hadn't even considered. He eased from his chair and paced the room deep in thought. Was it possible that a rural sheriff who spent more time chasing tumbleweeds than he did bad guys used his gray matter to outthink a mystery the mainframe computer in Washington couldn't unravel? The context with which the sheriff delivered his theory not only made sense, it was completely plausible. Stevens paused and fixed his eyes for a moment on the framed portrait of the legendary J. Edgar Hoover, and then returned to his seat.

"Sheriff, I've got to tell you that this is one hell of a conspiracy theory you've come up with. I'm not sure I'll can make the hard sell to the Deputy Director to justify additional assets."

But he knew he would do his best; all while leading the DD to believe it was his theory. The arrest of the elusive Shadow Man could be his one-way ticket out of Las Vegas, provide him the means to a more cushy position in the Bureau, not to mention a transfer to a more reasonable climate.

Sheriff Austin looked at the agent with an amused smirk. "Tell me something Stevens, what have your resources accomplished up to this point? As best as I can tell, and I certainly ain't got all the information you federal boys got, there are somewhere around a dozen murders attributed to Shadow Man. So exactly what have you got to lose?"

Good point, Stevens internalized. He looked hard into the sheriff's eyes. "What's in this for you, Austin?"

Austin almost laughed in his face. "To stop a serial killer you pompous jackass!"

Chapter 7

The morning sun shone in brightly through the kitchen's east windows. Spider plant tentacles of new growth dangled two feet below handcrafted Shoshone Indian ceramic pots, and hung from macramé holders attached to ceiling hooks. Beams of sunlight danced across the jade-colored granite countertop and spilled onto the polished mahogany hardwood floor, creating deep, red, glowing pools. White ash cabinets stylishly divided the dark floor from the dark countertop. The spotless kitchen was as elegant as the rest of the mansion and could easily have adorned the centerfold of *Better Homes and Gardens*.

"Good morning," Dakota Bricker said in his heavy English accent.

Reese strolled to the kitchen table wearing a pair of orange and black Harley Davidson sweatpants and a white tee shirt. He slid a chair from beneath the table and took a seat. "Morning, Dakota," he yawned.

Prior to his untimely death the late Robert Benjamin Daniels arranged for Bricker's well-being with simple clause in his Last Will and Testament: "…as for my loyal servant, Michael Dakota Bricker; should my heir, or heirs decide Dakota's services are no longer necessary, he shall receive in severance pay the amount of $250,000.00. Along with an annual stipend of $75,000.00 for his sole use, free and clear of any claims by my aforementioned heirs, so long as he shall live." The sole heir to the Daniels fortune never gave a moment's thought to dismissing Dakota.

After he turned eighteen, Reese found himself in the enviable position of being the sole heir to the Daniels Industries empire…net worth, at the time, an estimated one hundred and seventy eight million dollars, making him one of the richest men/boys west of the Mississippi. Before the birthday candles melted, several corporate attorneys descended upon the ranch jockeying for Reese's favor, encouraging him to "...split the stocks and go public...initiate a hostile takeover of our competitor's assets...drive them out before they organize against us..." Reese had had the good sense to follow the advice of his grandfather's trusted counsel, Nelson Grover, along with some strong influence from Bricker. In a private one-on-one meeting at the ranch Grover cautioned against a hostile takeover that could ultimately bring about a monopoly complaint from the U.S. Attorney General. No one wanted to see Daniels Industries follow the Microsoft Corporation into a quagmire of legal posturing against the U.S. Government. Grover's closing comment had said it all: "I think those at the top of the Daniels Industries ladder have more than enough assets to survive quite comfortably for the rest of their lives." Reese decided to leave well enough alone.

The microwave chimed and Bricker pulled out a steaming bowl and set it on the table in front of Reese next to a tumbler of orange juice. A holdover from his years in Great Britain, Bricker said, "I've made porridge this morning for breakfast."

Reese chuckled. "Dakota, how long have you been living in the United States?"

"Long enough to know that porridge and oatmeal are the same dish so it matters little how I refer to them." He returned to the island countertop. "I noticed you were up rather late last evening."

Reese's smile faded to a nervous grin. "And I noticed you weren't around all day yesterday," he countered.

"I had errands to attend to in Pioche," Dakota said.

Reese buttered two slices of wheat toast without looking up at his housekeeper. "I had work to do last night," he said.

"From the light emanating through the den window, shall I assume you were on the computer?"

Reese's butter knife clanged against the china plate. He looked at Dakota with a darkening mien. "Are you finished Sherlock Bricker?"

"No," Dakota said. "I'm concerned about you. You seem preoccupied as of late. Maybe you're not getting enough rest."

After the death of his grandfather Dakota, along with Grover as court appointed attorney ad litem, stepped into the role of guardian and father figure and raised Reese. Their relationship was a peculiar one, indeed. During Reese's early years Bricker served as an adult role model, but as his ward matured, grew into a man, Dakota became like a best friend or big brother; and now that Reese was in his thirties Dakota's position had come full circle, regressing more in line with his original appointment.

"I'm getting plenty of rest, Father Goose," Reese said genially enough to temper the conversation.

Dakota rinsed his breakfast dishes and placed them inside the dishwasher, segueing into his role as butler/housekeeper. "Will you be teleconferencing with the Board of Directors this morning, Sir?"

"Dakota, knock off the 'Sir' crap; and in answer to your question, no. I spoke with Nelson yesterday afternoon. He has my instructions, he'll fax me the minutes this afternoon."

"Very well then, Mr. Daniels." Dakota wiped his hands on a dishtowel and deposited it in the pantry's hamper. "If you have nothing of importance needing my attention, I promised young Timothy I would take him riding this morning."

Reese sniggered at Dakota's stiff British-butler vernacular. And he also knew full well that Dakota was trying to get under his skin. He saluted the attempt with a spoonful of oatmeal. "By all means, take Timmy riding. I intend to work out a little this morning, and then lounge around the pool and go over some stock quotes." Reese blew across the spoonful of steaming porridge and sank the spoon in his mouth continuing to talk, knowing his vulgar table manners would get under Dakota's proper English epidermis.

"Why don't you invite Timmy's mother along? You never know..." He gave his eyebrows a twitch.

"Honestly, Reese! Will you please not talk with your mouth full of food? I find it completely disgusting when you do that. Besides, it's the

Big Brothers program not the Lonely Hearts Club. Mrs. Robbins is more akin to your age."

Both Nancy's age and her presence at the ranch had not gone unnoticed by Reese.

"Mother Bricker would disapprove," Dakota said. "Mrs. Robbins is far too young for an old geezer like me." He set the timer on the dishwasher.

Although Bricker's dear Emaline had been gone for nearly twenty-five years he still missed her as if she had died only yesterday. When not busy occupying himself with ranch hand duties, he retired to his quarters and lamented his loss. But there's only so much reading, watching television, and contemplating life one could do to fill the void of a lost soul mate. Having never fathered offspring (thanks to the side affects of the defoliant, Agent Orange) he had initially hesitated becoming involved with the responsibility of molding a young life. After all, if God intended him to father children it would have happened naturally. That was the excuse he used the day Reese handed him an advertisement clipped from the *Pioche Record*: "Seeking mature, family oriented male to invest a few hours a week in America's future." Dakota's mentoring of Timothy Robbins through the Big Brothers/Big Sisters of America program was in its second year.

Reese creased open the morning newspaper (the paper delivery lady being well-paid for her long trek from the highway each morning before sunrise) to the page with the NASDAQ quotes.

"Dakota," Reese said, "I seriously doubt Emy expected you to remain a widower for the rest of your life. If you'd like, Timmy can stay with me by the pool while you and Nancy go riding."

"I told you, Mother Bricker would disapprove," he said over his shoulder hurrying toward the rapid-fire door chimes.

"Have fun," Reese said, his eyes dropping back to the newspaper. "Tell Timmy I said, *hey*."

Dakota waved over his shoulder and quickened his pace. Twelve year olds have no patience.

Reese traced down the columns with his finger until he found the stock ticker he sought. The drop in value brought a twinkle to his eye; one man's misery is another's good fortune. He hoped the decline by another fifty-two cents would make the offer he had instructed Grover to make seem more palatable.

Timmy Robbins's voice lilted down the hall and into the kitchen, "Hi, Reese, bye, Reese," quickly followed by the clatter of cowboy boots dashing across the atrium toward the family room. Three shrill chirps from the security system signaled a breach of the sliding doors as Timmy's feet carried him on a cloud of dust toward the barn.

By the time Dakota reached the barn Timmy was standing on the bottom rail of the stall brushing black bangs from the chestnut mare's eyes. "High, Mollie, old girl," he said. "You going to be a good horsy today?" Mollie wrapped her lips around the apple held out in his flattened palm. "Sure you are."

Dakota grinned with fatherly pride from the doorway while Timmy talked to Mollie ("...so she recognizes who you are...") and gently worked the bridle into her mouth before leading her out of the stall. He tied the reigns to a hitching ring nailed to the wall, carried her blanket and saddle from the tack room, and with one hundred percent effort and seventy percent ability, saddled his mount. Dakota walked into the barn and checked the cinch belt, making sure it was neither too tight, nor too loose.

"If I didn't know better, Mr. Robbins," he said, "I'd swear Mollie knew you were coming." Dakota tipped his head back and sniffed the air. "Maybe she smelled you."

"Very funny, Dakota. Hardy, har-har."

Dakota tossed Timmy's shoulder-length blonde hair as he walked past with a square blade shovel. He stepped into Mollie's stall to fulfill one of Dakota's many rules when it came to the horses: 'The stall shall be cleaned before any riding takes place.'

He scooped up horse dumplings, carried them to the manure pile behind the barn, stopping at the wellhead and rinsing the shovel on his way back inside. After returning the shovel to the tack room he laid a fresh bed of straw in Mollie's stall, climbed the ladder nailed to the wall, wrestled a bale of straw to the edge of the loft, and kicked it to the floor with a dusty thud.

They started off at a slow trot to give the horses a chance to work out the kinks from being cooped up overnight. Dakota glanced down at his watch. It would take a little over an hour to ride to the remote northwest corner of Daniels's estate.

Reese stood on the concrete deck, forearms resting atop the stonewall surrounding the pool, until Dakota and Timmy rode out of sight. He carried his coffee cup back into the kitchen, cleaned up his breakfast dishes, and then went upstairs and changed into a black satin Kung Fu uniform.

He paused in the doorway of his tiyuguan and offered the oil portrait of Tian Xian Huo hanging over the alter the traditional Kung Fu standing salute; left fist surrounding right hand, held in front of the face so as not to obstruct the vision. Only then did Reese step into the room. Kitty flopped down outside the door with a groan and brought his head to rest on his paws.

Reese lit two sticks of jasmine incense and then moved to the center of the room and took a seat on the floor, where he spent nearly a half hour stretching his limbs beyond the point most would find painful. Sufficiently limbered up he stood, closed his eyes, relaxed his chi, and flowed through Tai Chi Chuan's Yang-style long form. At the conclusion of "Close Tai Chi" Reese sprang into the dynamic Northern Praying Mantis form (characterized by low stances and snapping kicks) following it up with the Tiger Crane form's swift and powerful, yet soft and graceful movements. He concluded his two-hour workout with the Zhen Shan Gwun 16 technique staff routine.

He returned the six-foot bamboo staff to the weapons rack bolted against the wall. Neatly arranged were bamboo staffs, broad swords, Tiger forks, a Monk's spade, and an assortment of spears: all of them deadly in the hands of an expert, and Reese was highly skilled with each of them. He bowed to Mr. Huo's portrait, stepped from the studio, bent down and patted Kitty on the head, and then went upstairs and showered.

He strolled out onto the pool deck wearing an aqua-green Speedo and carrying a lightweight pair of white cotton trousers draped over his shoulder. He tossed the pants to the lounge chair on his way to the pool. Not yet ten o'clock and the temperature was already pushing the ninety-degree mark. After finishing a few lazy lengths of the pool, Reese plopped down on the lounge chair. With Dakota and Timmy gone for the next couple of hours he had the house to himself. He slipped into a pair of Gargoyle's and settled back in the chair for a little crisping under the pre-noon sun, along with some serious consideration regarding some *pending business* that needed his attention.

Dakota and Timmy reached the northwest point of the ranch, accessible by four-wheel drive, ATV, or horseback, in a little over an hour. A florescent orange fiberglass pole with a frayed yellow windsock attached to the top marked the end of Daniels's ranch, and the beginning of the Marzdeck property.

Dakota unsaddled Gus and Mollie in the shade of a curious rock formation rising inexplicably from the desert floor. Left behind by retreating glaciers, etched by millenniums of wind and sand it resembled a gigantic clamshell whose fan curled overhead and created a shallow cave where temperatures were twenty degrees cooler than standing in the blazing sun.

Inside "Seashell Rock" Timmy sat on "Nature's Bench"—names bestowed upon the formation during his first visit there over a year ago—peeling off boots and socks and rolling his jeans up above the knee. He ran across the hot sand to the marker pin, unclipped a five gallon plastic bucket attached to the pole with a short cable, and waded out into the half-acre artesian well pond in front of Seashell Rock. He rinsed sand from the bucket and returned to Seashell Rock, offering Mollie and Gus a drink of cool spring water.

He sat cross-legged on the bench picking sand from between his toes while Dakota unpacked the saddlebags. The first item set out was a twenty-quart plastic garbage bag. Timmy mused that it was somewhere around Dakota rule #52: '…absolutely, positively nothing shall be left behind to soil the landscape…' Only once had Dakota left anything behind at Seashell Rock, Emaline Bricker's ashes.

Dakota set two cans of Del Monte peaches and a can of baked beans; along with four PB&J sandwiches in zip lock bags and a can opener between them. While Timmy attacked the baked beans with the can opener, Dakota popped the lids off the peach cans and deposited them in the garbage bag. Cold baked beans and peaches were a perfect compliment to peanut butter and jelly sandwiches and ice-cold water straight from the canteen. Dakota was in the process of passing the baked beans back to his young ward when Timmy's question landed with all the subtlety of a C-130 on a crowded beach.

"Dakota, do you think Reese is gay?"

The big man's chewing slowed as if his jaw was suddenly rusting shut.

"What I mean is…I've been coming 'round for about what, a year or so?"

"Or there about," Dakota acknowledged, sliding his sandwich into the plastic bag and setting it down on the stone bench. "Timothy, what would cause you to ask so outrageous a question?"

Timmy paused the fork load of baked beans near his mouth. "Well, I've never seen him go out on a date, or have a girlfriend over, or nothing like that. I know he sneaks away every once in a while because a couple of times when I've stayed over I heard the garage door go up and saw the Lincoln leave." Timmy crammed the plastic fork into his mouth.

Dakota rolled his eyes at the absurdity of the conversation. He handed Timmy a paper towel, a silent request to wipe the bean juice dripping from his chin.

"I, likewise, *never have a girlfriend over, or nothing like that*," Dakota said.

"Yeah, but you're old. No one expects you to date."

Dakota rolled his eyes, the audaciousness of youth, he mused. "Tell me something, Timothy. Exactly how many *boyfriends* have you seen Mister Daniels with?"

Timmy gave the question a moment's thought. "Well…none, actually."

Dakota sipped from his canteen and then methodically replaced the lid, dabbing the corners of his mouth with a paper napkin. "If one is to assume Reese is gay based on a lack of female companionship, would it not be an equally fair assumption that based on a lack of male companionship that he's heterosexual?"

"He's not out picking up hookers, is he?"

Dakota arched an eyebrow. "Why is it you ask such outlandish questions lacking foundation or thought?"

Timmy cocked his head to one side. "How's comes when I ask you a question you always answer it with another question?"

When Dakota first began mentoring Timmy Robbins he thought he had made the acquaintance of a pint-sized truck driver. Such foul language he had not heard since his military days, and coming from an eleven year-old only served to make it that much worse. It was during their second outing Dakota insisted Timmy stop using the F-word with reckless abandon or he would terminate the relationship. Timmy's "So who gives a fuck?" bought three weeks of severance before he telephoned Dakota and apologized.

"The 'how's comes', young Master Robbins," Dakota reached out and poked Timmy's forehead with his finger, "is to stimulate your brain."

"Well thank you very much, Mr. Bricker." Timmy wiped his mouth and dropped the napkin into the garbage bag. "I forgot we was in desert Psychology-101."

Bricker's forced western drawl, mixed with his British accent, sounded like Wyatt Earp meets James Bond. "Gist 'cause yous in the desert, Robbins, don't means yous gotta' forget your fetchin' up."

Timmy chuckled and swept his shoulder-length hair behind his ears. "When we get back can I give Mollie a bath?"

Dakota corrected him again. "You certainly *may*."

After the refuse was packed and stowed it in the saddlebags they rode southeast toward an out-of-the-way canyon where Dakota had found a pair of bald eagles nesting in the cliffs.

Chapter 8

Mack Stevens sat in the maroon leather Stratolounger in his living room staring listlessly at the television screen, vaguely aware the Eastern Kentucky Colonels were trouncing his favored Tennessee State Tigers. His thoughts were fixed on his meeting with Sheriff Austin, and more particularly how a Podunk desert sheriff could have solved a fifteen-year old crime the old fashion way, with brainpower. Austin's common sense filled theory made it all the more convincing.

Theories, Stevens pondered, are like statistics; the presenter cleverly manipulates the facts in support his point of view, but make no bones about it, the Daniels character Austin referenced was indeed filthy rich, as verified by his income tax return. And as the sheriff had said, "that could afford him a certain degree of anonymity and travel resources." Daniels's estate, or farm, or ranch, or whatever the heck it was called on the western side of the country, was definitely out of reach of prying eyes. Stevens entered a mental note to check the Bureau's computerized database of aerial photographs commissioned from military satellites. He could zero in on any address in the world, and if the pictures didn't show enough detail of Daniels's ranch he could always make a clandestine visit.

Austin's hypothesis about Daniels being an abused child certainly gave credence to motive. Anyone with a badge knows that a majority of abusive parents were themselves victims of abuse. Because Daniels had been held prisoner in his own home for his entire childhood, and now that he was an adult he may be leading a double life, possibly possessed with multiple personalities. It was feasible that Reese-*the mega-millionaire-*

Daniels may have no idea of what Reese-*the mega-monster*-Shadow Man does for a hobby; seeking vengeance upon people like the person who had abused him was clearly understandable.

Stevens gave the side of his head a sharp slap. His job was to catch the bad guys, not conjure up an insanity defense. He needed to stay focused on the evidence and let it lead him where it may.

Stevens switched his attention to the folder spread across his lap and began sifting through the pages. According to the information contained in the file Michael D. Bricker wandered the globe as a military brat until after his mother's death. Bricker's father settled the family down to a more permanent residence on the USAF base in Lakenheath, Great Britain. Colonel Bricker even declined a promotion to Brigadier General to avoid moving his family again. He rode out his remaining years of service to his country in Lakenheath. Bricker's youngest sister Ginny still lives in Liverpool, the proprietor of a ceramic doll import shop on the east end docks; the older sibling, Mary, died in a freak automobile accident in Paris more than a decade ago. Colonel Bricker was resting peacefully in Arlington National Cemetery next to his wife. Stevens flipped through more yellowing pages of Michael Bricker's military career. Austin was right again. Bricker served two tours of duty in Vietnam, Third Battalion, 5th Marine Division, Lima Company, under command of Captain Robert Benjamin Daniels. Not many butlers commanded the wage R.B. Daniels paid Bricker for his multi-faceted services, and as R.B. Daniels's wealth soared, so had Bricker's income. Nothing really stood out in Bricker's file other than he was a highly paid non-entity that, from all appearances, was hired to kiss R.B. Daniels's rich behind.

There was virtually no information available on Daniels. Except for some corporate papers and income tax returns, the enigma Reese Daniels seemed nonexistent. His personal affairs appeared buried in the corporate business of Daniels Industries, far out of reach without a search warrant.

Stevens plunked the footrest down with a bang, gathered the file together, and then walked to his office at the back of the house. He sat in front of his computer, entered the password linking him to the field office's computer, and ultimately to the mainframe in Washington. He updated the "Operation Candy Cane" file with the first credible information of substance as to the "*possible*" identity of Shadow Man.

Chapter 9

Nancy Robbins's early arrival at the ranch to pick up Timmy was not a mere coincidence. Wearing a pair of frayed blue denim cutoffs, a pink halter-top beneath a sleeveless white cotton blouse and sandaled feet, she stood on the shaded front porch ringing the doorbell. In all the times she had been to the ranch to either drop Timmy off, or pick him up, not once had Reese answered the door. So it was no surprise that after several more rings the door remained unanswered. She walked around the side of the house thinking the boys may be in the barn tending to the horses, or better yet, out by the pool. Reese was unquestionably a puzzle she had yet to figure out. At times he was childishly entertaining, while at other times foreboding, preoccupied, borderline morose.

She neared the backside of the mansion and heard the whining gibberish of Chinese blaring from quadraphonic speakers cleverly disguised as stones and carefully hidden in the landscaping. She stopped to listen to the rising and falling tones of a language she knew she would never understand.

Nancy hopped onto a sandstone-landscaping boulder the size of a beach ball and peeked over the wall. She saw Reese stretched out on a lounge chair next to the pool, dark shades covering his eyes, arms folded behind his head, skin glistening with perspiration and tanning oil, apparently dozing. She leaned against the wall, rested her chin on her arms, and watched Reese sunbathe, a tiny smile tugging the corners of her mouth.

As if he had built-in RADAR, Reese suddenly snapped upright and homed in to where she ogled him overtop the wall, the abrupt movement startling her enough so that she lost her balance, fell to the ground, and landed on her backside with a dull thud. She found herself squinting up at Reese's face, silhouetted against the cloudless blue sky.

He shot a helping hand over the wall, and said, "Are you okay?"

"I'm sorry." She took hold of his hand and pulled herself to her feet. "I rang the doorbell," she said, almost defensively while brushing Cypress chips from her shorts, "but no one answered. I thought everyone was in the barn."

Reese's smile was noncommittal, he pointed to the wrought iron gate. "C'mon around and I'll let you in." He jumped down and crossed the deck, speaking to her over the wall. "You sure you're, okay?"

Nancy stepped onto the deck with a sheepish smile. "The only thing bruised on me is my ego."

"Last time I checked," he plucked a Cyprus chip from her hair, "egos heal pretty quickly."

She followed Reese around the pool and watched him slip on the white cotton pants draped over his chair, pull the drawstring tight, and walk to the outdoor wet bar and turn off the Chinese broadcast he was listening to. Then he washed his hands.

Nancy sat at a glass top patio table that was sparsely shaded by a palm tree. "You understand that nonsense?" she said, opening a faux bamboo umbrella to further shelter the table.

"It's not nonsense, it's Chinese," he said curtly, and then changed the subject. "Dakota and Timmy should be back any time now. Would you care for something cold to drink?"

"What do you have?"

He tipped his head down and looked at her over the top of his sunglasses. "A little bit of everything I suppose. Sodas, beer, wine, liquor, you name it, and we probably have it."

Nancy slid her chair deeper into the shade. "A beer will be fine."

Reese drew out a bottle of Corona from the refrigerator under the bar and held it up. "Lemon or lime?"

Nancy rested her elbows on the table and propped her chin in her hands. "Surprise me."

A precursor to Dakota and Timmy's return Kitty (who had gone searching for Dakota and Timmy after Reese's workout) bounded over the wall and immediately spotted Nancy sitting at the table. He folded his ears flat, rolled his lips back and exposed his fangs, dropped his head behind a low guttural growl, and slinked between where Nancy sat and Reese stood behind the bar.

On his way to the table Reese patted the coyote's flank to calm him. "Yi nan, ta shuren."

He handed across the table a frosted mug with a slice of lime and a slice of lemon floating beneath the foamy head. "Here you go." He set his Jack Daniel's and water on the table and sat opposite Nancy.

She slid her hand through the mug's handle. "What did you just say to Kitty?"

He repeated the phrase. "Yi nan, ta shuren loosely translated, means, 'easy boy, she's a friend'."

Nancy sipped her beer while keeping an eye on Kitty, and he had both of his welded to her. "Timmy brags all the time about how you can speak Chinese."

"Zhongwen-meiguoren." Reese flashed a nervous smile as he said, "Chinese-American."

"Chinese on your father's side I assume?" Nancy said, taking another sip from her mug.

If she noticed that Reese changed the subject anytime time she mentioned something of a personal nature, she didn't let on.

"Are you sure you didn't get hurt?" he said.

Nancy pulled the mug from her lips, set it on the table, and licked away the foamy mustache. "I grew up around five older brothers. Trust me, Reese, I've tumbled down, or been thrown from more life-threatening heights than that."

"I guess it's a good thing I put the cactus garden over there, huh?" He thumbed over his shoulder to where Kitty had taken a place in the shade of the wall, his piercing yellow eyes still glaring at Nancy.

Nancy idly spun her glass on the table with a chuckle. "Now that could have proved painful."

Reese's eye caught the distant movement of Dakota and Timmy cresting one of the small knolls on the north side of the barn. When Timmy spotted his mother sitting near the pool with Reese he kicked Mollie into a gallop, the chinstrap of his black cowboy hat kept it from blowing off. He skidded Mollie to a dusty stop outside of the wall and touched the brim of his hat with two fingers.

"Well howdy there, Miss Nancy."

She batted her eyes and spoke to Reese in the best Southern Bell voice she could muster. "Why, my dear sir, I do believe that handsome young cowboy over yonder is trying to make time with me."

" It 'peers so, Miss."

Reese joined the charade. He tossed his sunglasses to the table and with his arms arched at his sides, faced Timmy. "You best be ready to slap leather mister, ifin' you're fixin' to steal my lady."

Timmy whipped an imaginary six-shooter out of an equally imaginary holster and fired.

Reese clutched his chest and fell back into the chair. "Dang, he got me. Everything's a-growin' dark. Oh, woman! Tell the children I love 'em." He covered his eyes with his forearm and collapsed over the side of his chair to the cement.

The confused coyote raced to Reese's side and licked his master's face.

Timmy blew smoke from his fingertip, dropped the gun into his holster, and slid out of the saddle. "Tinhorn," he said, tying Mollie's reigns to the gate.

Boot heels clicked loudly against the terra cotta concrete on his way to his mother's chair. He wrapped his arms around her neck and rested his sweaty forehead on her shoulder. "Hi, Mom."

Nancy patted his arm. "Did you have a good ride, honey?"

He barely got "Yup!" from his lips before Reese leaped from the ground starling Kitty into a tail tucking crouch, wrapped an arm around Timmy's waist, the other around his chest, and swept him off his feet.

"Hey!" Timmy shrieked. "You're supposed to be dead."

Reese hoisted him overhead. "You only winged me."

"I'm warning you ya' mangy polecat, you'd best put me down," Timmy cackled.

Reese looked at him, and then started for the pool. "Tinhorn? Polecat? Well see about that," he said, stopping where concrete met water.

Timmy glanced at the sparkling water, and then to Reese. "You ain't got the balls."

"Timothy Michael! You watch that mouth of yours," Nancy said.

Reese dangled Timmy out over the pool. "What is it I don't have, sport?"

Nancy's halfhearted "Reese, don't!" was unconvincing.

With Timmy held high overhead Reese turned and faced her. "Ah, come on, please?"

She wagged her head back and forth and picked up her mug.

Reese lowered Timmy to half-mast, and said, "You're lucky the little lady came to your rescue, punk."

Timmy stuck out his tongue. "I told you that you didn't have the *stuff*."

Reese looked into Timmy's mischievous blue eyes and grinned. "Right, sport," he said, and then fell backward into the pool, letting go of Timmy as they hit the water.

Timmy was first to surface, the waterlogged brim of his hat hanging limply in front of his eyes. He slapped the water with both hands and spun to Reese. "You idiot! No you didn't just throw me into the pool with my clothes on."

He launched at Reese, who pushed him away, paddled to the opposite side of the pool, and climbed out. Timmy crawled out of the water and sloshed to the table, picked up Reese's glass, walked to the wall, and poured Reese's drink over the cactus bed.

"Go get changed," Nancy managed to say, between fits of laughter.

Timmy drew his fingers into menacing cheetah claws, pawed the air while snarling revenge. "Paybacks are a b-word, mister." He dripped across the patio while stripping down to his boxers, bundled the sopping clothes into a ball, and disappeared inside.

Once he was out of earshot, Nancy said, "Now that was truly funny."

Reese gave his eyebrows a playful bounce, picked up his glass, and pointed to Nancy's. "Another?"

"Sure." She gulped down the last of her beer and handed him the mug.

Reese poured Nancy another mug of beer, remixed himself a Jack and water in a clean glass, and set both on the table. "I'll be right back," he said. "Dakota could probably use some help getting Mollie and Gus put up out of the sun."

He sprinted to the pool, dove in, surfaced on the opposite side, and climbed out. "C'mon, old girl," he said, taking hold of Mollie's reigns and starting toward the barn. "It's too hot out here for you."

Reese pushed a hand-painted blue and ivory ceramic bowl across the table. "More potato salad, sport?" he said.

Timmy leaned back in his chair and patted his belly. "Not for me, thanks. I'm stuffed."

Nancy kicked his leg under the table. "Is that thing hollow? Three hamburgers, two helpings of potato salad, and dessert; no wonder you're stuffed."

Timmy let loose a huge belch. "Excuse me," he said bringing his hand to his mouth.

Dakota worked his way around the table gathering up the dishes from their impromptu cookout. It was evident to him that Reese was fond of Nancy and enjoyed Timmy's presence at the ranch. The spoiled rich kid had found a playmate to share his toys with; swimming pool, horses, pool table, big screen television…and considering Reese's social life was somewhere between zero and nil, neither had it gone unnoticed by Bricker how he seemed to always find a way to get Nancy to spend more time at the ranch than she had planned. Reese's behavior was unacceptable. This temptation of Timmy's materialism brought about more than a few discussions between the butler and his employer.

Dakota leaned the serving tray on the edge of the table. "Since Reese has once again cleverly managed to delay your departure, Mrs. Robbins," he shot Reese a circumspect glance, "perhaps, you and Timothy would enjoy indulging in a movie. I procured the newest Steven Seagal release while in Pioche yesterday."

Timmy bounced up and down on the edge of his seat. "Can we, Mom? Can we stay a little bit longer?"

"Talk about me always pulling off a fast one, Dakota," Reese said. "Now look who's doing the tempting."

Nancy rolled her eyes. "Go watch your movie."

Reese pushed away from the table and stood. "Dakota, I'll clean up out here. You and Timmy go watch the movie."

"It shall take but a moment for me to finish," Dakota insisted.

They played tug-o-war over possession of the tray until Reese finally won.

Timmy's vote was cast with Reese. He sprang from his chair with a whoop. "Come on, Dakota. I've been waiting all week to see Seagal kick some bad guy's—" He glanced at his mother's raised brow. "—butt."

"It appears I've been outvoted," Dakota ceded with a chuckle.

Timmy bounded toward the house, shot through the family room doors, and disappeared down the hallway leading to the media room's Sony seventy-inch rear projection screen television, with Dolby Digital Surround.

Nancy climbed out of her chair and helped Reese carry dirty dishes to the kitchen. While Reese scraped the leftover hamburgers into Kitty's bowl, Nancy covered the remnants of the potato salad with plastic cling wrap and shelved the bowl inside the refrigerator. Reese rinsed the dishes, loaded the dishwasher, sanitized his hands, and then walked out onto the patio through the kitchen's French doors. Nancy sat at the breakfast bar sipping French almond coffee, watching as Reese walked to the wall and rested his arms on the top row of stone. She wondered what was going through his mind as he stared at the sun dropping behind the mountains.

Reese Daniels certainly is a strange breed, Nancy mused aloud, *a breed unto himself.*

Chapter 10

Reese always maintained a healthy respect for, if not a downright fear of, horses. Ever since Blaze—his grandfather's stubborn black Arabian Stallion, immediately sold after Reese assumed control of the ranch—bucked him into a wrist cast, compliments of a house call by Dr. Austin, at the age of twelve. And the Captain, never one to overlook an opportunity to serve up a little psycho-trauma on his grandson, ordered him back onto Blaze for a trot around the corral, wet cast and all. Reese had held onto the stallion's reigns for dear life while the Captain, from his perch on the corral's top rail, shouted intimidating encouragement. "You have to get back into the saddle you little chink bastard! Otherwise you'll be afraid of horses for the rest of your worthless, pathetic life!" As if life could not continue unless a terrified twelve-year old with a freshly broken wrist showed a headstrong stallion who the boss was. When Blaze started his nervous prancing, usually a telltale sign he was ready to make a mad dash for the barn, Reese jumped from the saddle and raced to the house, chased by his grandfather's malevolent laughter.

Timmy twisted around in the saddle with an impish grin, and seeing how Dakota was busy caressing Gus's muzzle, out of earshot, he turned his attention to the amusing scene unfolding inside the barn. While Reese may be a fearless martial arts expert, he absolutely sucked when it came to the elementary task of mounting a horse.

Reese had a death grip on the saddle horn and one foot tentatively hoisted to the stirrup. Each time Trixie moved, he danced around her nervously.

"Come on chicken shit. Get on the damn horse," Timmy goaded, making another quick peek out the door.

Reese shot an angry glower over his shoulder, his embarrassment of trying to mount Trixie paled miserably to his embarrassment of being challenged by a twelve year old.

"I'm not a chicken shit, sewer lips. The stupid horse won't hold still," he said, hopping on one foot in time with Trixie's impatient sidesteps.

Timmy tipped his cowboy hat back until it came to rest even with his hairline, saddle leather creaking as he leaned forward and peered down at Reese. "Stupid horse, Reese? Trixie has feelings too, dontcha' know. If I was old Trix I'd buck your chicken ass to the dirt." He cut loose with a mocking laugh eerily reminiscent of the Captain's, and then trotted Mollie out of the barn, ducking his head as he passed through the double doors.

Reese pulled his foot from the stirrup and walked around to the front of the horse, brought his lips close to Trixie's ear, and whispered in Chinese, "Here's the deal you glue bag on hooves. You promise to be a good horse and in exchange, I promise not to beat you to death with my bare hands."

Reese stepped back to Trixie's side and eased himself into the saddle of a horse about as aggressive as a cat napping in a sunbeam.

When Reese and Trixie finally plodded out of the barn the temptation was too much for Timmy. He pounced on the rare moment of being able to "one up" Reese. He spurred Mollie to a gallop like he was chasing a calf straying from the herd. Reese tensed visibly in the saddle when Timmy skidded his mare to a dusty stop. Trixie turned her graying muzzle to the side and whinnied her disapproval at this intrusion into a sedate lifestyle, which caused Reese further anxiety.

Timmy stood in the stirrups and sniggered. "Relax, man. You look like you have a damn board pounded up your ass."

Reese carefully relaxed back into the saddle, and said, "If I wasn't up here on this horse you little punk…"

Timmy yanked back hard on Mollie's reigns, hard enough she reared up on her back legs and pawed at the air. "You'd have to catch me first," he scoffed before dashing off to join Dakota, who watched the show with great amusement.

With a gentle tap to the ribs Trixie trudged wearily ahead. The ride to Seashell Rock would take twice the usual amount of time, because Reese insisted on holding his *raging steed* to a fast walk, which was entirely acceptable to Trixie.

They finally reached Seashell Rock and after unsaddling, watering, and tying the horses in the shade, Timmy stripped down to his swim trunks, hotfooted across the sand, and dove into the artesian pool. He was floundering in the cool water on a lazy backstroke when something suddenly grabbed his ankles and yanked him under water. He broke the surface screaming for Dakota.

Reese treaded water out of his reach. "Who's the chicken shit now?" he said with a sneering grin.

Timmy raked cupped hands across the pool and sent a violent wave in Reese's direction. "You dork! You could have made me drown."

Reese turned and swam toward the shore, Timmy climbing onto his back and trying to dunk him under water as he passed. For his efforts Timmy found himself pitched off and forced underwater, held there longer than he thought came even remotely close to funny.

He surfaced, choked out pond water, wiped his face, and sent another wave toward Reese. "You fucktard, bitch!" He swam to shore and stomped into the safety of Seashell Rock.

Dakota tossed him a towel. "You mustn't get so angry, Timothy. When you show your anger you play into Reese's childish game."

"Screw him, he's an asshole. I could have drowned." Timmy dried his face and then tented the towel over his head.

From the middle of the pool Reese pointed at Timmy, laughed, and then rolled onto his back like a crippled submarine, spitting fountains of water into the air.

"Timmy, I think you're being melodramatic," Dakota said. "I hardly believe Reese would let you drown."

On the verge of angry, embarrassed tears Timmy popped his head out from under the towel and growled, "Fine! You go out there and let him hold you upside down underwater. We'll see how much you like it." He retreated under the towel.

TRAIL OF BODIES

Reese crawled from the pool and walked to the edge of Seashell Rock, where he sprawled out on a sun-baked bolder to dry his jeans.

"What's he so pissed about?" Reese said, bouncing water from his ears.

"I believe you startled him holding him under water for an extended period," Dakota said.

"Oh my goodness, Dakota. He knows I'd never hurt him." Reese dried his face with the towel Dakota had tossed him.

"He's only twelve years old, Reese. It doesn't take much to denigrate one's manhood at such a tender age." Dakota waited until Reese's eyes peeked out from beneath the towel before he continued. "Indeed, I would think you of all people should recognize how demoralized he must feel at this very moment." Dakota abruptly turned and walked back into the shade.

Reese considered the gentle reprimand for a moment, and then approached Timmy with his hand extended. "Sorry, sport. I didn't mean to scare you."

Timmy turned his face deeper toward the back of Seashell Rock. "I wasn't scared, jerk off."

"Yeah, right. Neither was I," he said, self-deprecatingly, "back at the barn when I was trying to climb onto Trixie."

Timmy's snorted laugh sprayed mucus and pond water from his nose. The image of Reese dancing around Trixie in the barn, one foot on the ground the other in a stirrup, brought watery blue eyes out from under the towel. He swiped his nose with a corner of the towel, and said, "You did look like you were about to piss your pants."

Reese patted his wet jeans. "I think I did."

Timmy peeled the towel from his head and looked at up at Reese. "You know something, you can be such a jerk sometimes."

"Tell you what, sport." Reese stuck his hand out again. "Why don't we call a truce and hit the pond, together?"

Timmy's response was somewhere between laughing and crying. "Why, so you can finish me off?" he said.

"I promise not to hold you under water any longer than it takes to fill up one lung," Reese raised his right hand, "so help me God!"

Timmy threw the terrycloth towel into Reese's face and dashed from Seashell Rock, yelling over his shoulder, "Bite me!" as he dove into the water.

Chapter 11

For the past half hour Reese had repeatedly checked the monitor in the security closet, the driveway view camera locked onto the screen. Nancy's jalopy rattled into sight and paused at the top of the crest on the west ridge, momentarily swallowed by the pursuing cloud of dust. He waited until the car began its slow descent before he rushed to the master bath and checked his appearance in the full-length mirror attached to the bathroom door. He wore a black silk button down shirt open to mid-chest, white cotton deck pants with black sandals, around his neck a Paiute shell and bead leather necklace. He swished and gargled a capful of mouthwash to freshen his breath, ran his tongue over his teeth, and rushed downstairs to welcome his guests.

By the time Nancy's car rounded the driveway's island planter and rolled to a stop Reese was already pacing the veranda. He was hurrying down the flagstone path on his way toward the driver's door when the passenger door flung open and Timmy hopped out, lining up in front of him and demanding a round of *Push Hands*—an ancient Chinese drill of maintaining light contact with your opponent while seeking the advantage of balance.

Ever since Reese agreed to teach Timmy martial arts, his protégé had become an ardent, and at times, overzealous student. What Timmy lacked in natural athletic ability he bridged with concerted effort and was slowly inching his way toward a semblance of proficiency.

Reese toyed with Timmy for only as long as it took Nancy to crawl from behind the steering wheel and make her way to the back of the car.

Reese watched out of the corner of his eye as she keyed open the trunk and leaned inside. Her yellow shorts crept high up the back of well-defined legs, taut from years of teaching aerobics. Nancy wrestled a large plastic bag from the trunk, and when it seamed she was struggling to lift it over the lip Reese launched Timmy aside. "Beware when the white stork displays its wings," he said, describing in Chinese a Tai Chi Chuan movement before stepping to the car and lending Nancy a hand.

Timmy regained balance, amid loud protests. "You cheated!"

"I did not." Reese lifted the bag of birthday presents out of the trunk and slammed the lid three times before the latch caught.

"Sometimes the lock sticks," she said pocketing her keys.

Timmy continued to gripe as if Reese was listening to him. "You cheated, Reese! You moved your foot."

His unrelenting bellyaching distracted Reese's amorous appraisal of Nancy, and he shot an askance glance at the birthday boy. "What?"

"You moved your foot, that's cheating!"

"I did not move my foot."

"Did so."

Timmy stepped in and blocked his path to the porch, insisting on a rematch.

Reese stepped around Timmy and followed closely behind Nancy. "Maybe later," he said.

"No, cheater! Right now."

"I said maybe later," Reese growled under his breath in Chinese.

Nancy stepped onto the shaded porch and turned to the dispute with a wide grin. "You boys fight nice now, hear?"

Reese trotted onto the porch and reached around her to open the door. "After you, Mrs. Robbins," he said with a chivalrous wave of the hand.

Nancy flashed a coy smile. "Why thank you, Mr. Daniels," she said stepping into the foyer.

Timmy tried to muscle his way through the door ahead of Reese and found himself standing on the porch with the door slammed closed in his face.

Nancy rolled her eyes and opened the door with a heavy sigh. "Honestly, Reese, I'm not sure which of you is the bigger kid."

Reese pointed an accusatory finger at Timmy as he stepped inside with a menacing glower.

"Sorry, sport," he shrugged innocuously, "I thought your were already inside."

Timmy slammed the door and gave Reese a squint-eyed sneer. "Dork!"

Reese hoisted the bag over his shoulder making sure it hit Timmy in the chest and knocked him off balance. "Dakota's in the kitchen finishing up your birthday cake. Why don't you go see if he needs a hand?"

Timmy's mother turned toward the family room and seeing how she wasn't looking, Timmy used the opportunity to flip Reese off before bolting for the kitchen, sweeping a hand under Kitty's jowls as he passed. With a throaty growl and vigorous tail wag, Kitty looked between Timmy racing for the kitchen, and Reese disappearing down the hall chasing Nancy's heels. He decided his protective services were not needed so he scampered after Timmy.

Reese set the bag of gifts down on the pool table and then joined Nancy on the pool deck. He took his place behind the smoking grill.

"So." Nancy leaned against the bar. "Are you going to tell me what you got Timmy for his birthday?"

Reese turned the steaks, gave her a furtive wink through the cloud of smoke billowing up from the grill, and said, "It's a surprise."

"Remember? It's Timmy's birthday, not mine."

"True!" he said. "We'd need a lot more candles."

He waved the smoke away from in front of his face with a spatula. Reese already had a gift idea picked for her birthday, and it had everything to do with replacing her aging Taurus. Nancy would look even more remarkable than she already did seated behind the steering wheel of a gold-mist Cadillac Escalade.

"I have a suggestion where you can put those extra candles," she said, helping herself to a bottle of raspberry flavored spring water from the refrigerator behind the bar.

"Now I see where Timmy gets it from," he chuckled, picking up a set on barbecue tongs and pointing toward the edge of the bar. "Steaks are done. Would you be so kind as to hand me the serving plate, Mrs. Robbins?"

She carried a china plate wrapped in a white linen towel to the grill and handed it to him. Returning to the bar she sat on a chrome stool and watched Reese load enough seared flesh onto the plate to open a buffet. "Expecting a crowd?" she said sarcastically.

Reese looked up, a questioning expression on his face. "Excuse me?"

"With all that food," she nodded toward the plate filled to the point of overflowing, "I'm thinking maybe you invited the entire state of Nevada?"

Reese smiled and carried the covered plate to the table. "Today, Timmy's officially a teenager." He set the plate down and clicked the tongs like castanets. "And teenagers eat like horses."

"Don't I know that," Nancy replied. She glanced to the mound under the towel, and said. "But I think you've made enough to feed him until he's twenty one."

"You know how much Kitty likes leftovers." Reese hung the tongs from a hook on the side of the grill, turned off the flame, and carried his drink to the table.

Timmy stepped onto the deck from the kitchen doors and, cradling his birthday cake on outstretched hands, began crooning, "Happy birthday to me, happy birthday to me…"

As he neared the table the toe of his tennis shoe caught a bump in the cement and pitched him forward. Nancy leaped from the stool frantically trying to catch the cake Timmy juggled to the table. He slammed the pineapple upside down to the patio table hard enough it shifted to a perilous edge of the milk glass serving dish.

Dakota's cheeks puffed a sigh of relief from the doorway.

"Whew! That was close," Timmy said with a sheepish grin. "Dakota would've kicked my ass if I'd have dumped the cake."

Nancy's eyes drew down to angry slits. "And I still might if you don't watch that mouth of yours. I've already warned you twice today about your cussing."

Reese pointed a mocking finger at Timmy. "Yeah trash mouth; what she said."

"Mom!"

Nancy turned to Reese. "Reese, stop it. I have enough trouble keeping him in line without your adding to it."

Timmy hooked his protruding front teeth over his bottom lip and gnawed at Reese with a face only a mother could love.

Reese burst out laughing. "You could eat grapes through a picket fence with those choppers."

Timmy's overbite was a *major* embarrassment to him. "Mom! Tell him to shut the hell up."

Nancy collapsed to a chair at the table. "Not today, please," she said gritting her teeth. "You're both really starting to piss me off."

Reese made a childish face at her.

"Reese!" she scowled.

"Nancy?" he replied with an innocent smirk.

"I mean it," she fumed.

Dakota arrived at the table, slid the cake to the center of the plate, and covered it with a clear plastic lid.

"Would the two of you, *adults*, please try and remember that this is Timothy's birthday party." Dakota's ominous eyes bounced between Reese and Nancy. "Let us try and set a proper example, shall we?"

With the adults properly chastised, Dakota offered a round of beverages. Nancy and Reese held up their respective glasses.

Timmy slid his chair to the smorgasbord, and said, "I'll have a beer, Dakota."

Reese eased his sunglasses to the tip of his nose. "Right, sport."

"Okay then," Timmy shrugged, reaching for the bowl of coleslaw, "a 7-Up will do."

Reese set his Jack and water on the table. "Budding martial artists should drink water. It's much healthier."

Timmy stopped loading his plate; eyes glanced to the stout glass in front of Reese, his face melted to a smirk. "Jack Daniel's and ice. Is that some sort of ancient Chinese health tonic, Reese?"

Dakota guffawed. "I believe Master Robbins evened the score with that one, Mr. Daniels."

Reese's countenance grew childishly defensive. "I'm not a *budding* artist. It just so happens that I know what I'm doing. So there."

"All right," Timmy said. "Jeez, I'll have a water."

"Under the bar in the refrigerator. You may help yourself," Dakota said as he served up plates full of grilled Kobe steak, baked potatoes, grill-roasted corn on the cob, and homemade coleslaw.

Timmy scraped his chair away from the table and helped himself to the last bottle of raspberry-flavored spring water. "I thought it was supposed to be my birthday," he grumbled on his way back to the table. "So much for getting waited on hand and foot."

After a dinner and a huge slice of pineapple upside down cake topped with two scoops of coconut sherbet, Timmy helped Dakota clear the table. He returned to his seat, plopped down, clapped his hands together, and said, "Bring on the presents."

Nancy looked first to Reese, and then to Dakota. "Presents?" she said. "For what?"

Reese looked to where Dakota stood towering behind Timmy's chair. "Beats me," he said. "Do you know anything about presents, Dakota?"

The chef's big hands landed on Timmy shoulders with a heavy thud. "No one mentioned this to me, Mr. Daniels. My instructions were simply to prepare a hearty dinner and make a birthday cake. Presents? This I know nothing of."

Timmy tipped his head back and found himself in the unenviable position of looking into Dakota's hairy nostrils. "Ha-de-ha-ha. You guys are a real comedic scream team. I've got it! Why don't you can call yourselves something original," He snapped his fingers and looked around the table. "How about Goldberg, Williams, and Crystal. That's original."

Reese scooped his glass from the table with a laugh. "Since I'm the minority here, I'll be Whoopi."

"My name's Robbins," Nancy joined in with a tittered. "I'll be Robin." She splayed her fingers. "Shazbut, Dakota. You must be Billy. Nanu-nanu."

Timmy was fast growing bored with these shenanigans. He slammed his chair to the table. "Just bring on the damn presents, will you?"

The twinkle in Nancy's eye faded like the last dying ember of a campfire. She leaned forward and propped her chin on balled up fists. "One more cussword out of you this afternoon, buster, and there won't be any 'damn presents'. You got it?"

Timmy's eyes fell to the table. "That ain't fair. You guys can sit here busting my a balls…teasing me and I ain't allowed to say nothing back."

Dakota came to his rescue.

"I think we've had enough merriment at young Master Robbins's expense. Mrs. Robbins, if you would be so kind as to follow me?" Dakota stepped behind Nancy's chair and brusquely tugged it away from the table, beckoning her to follow.

"Timothy, close your eyes," Dakota said from the family room doorway, and then disappeared inside with Nancy.

Reese slid his chair from the table, carried his empty glass to the bar, and mixed a fresh drink in a fresh glass. "Big thirteenth, huh, Timmy?" he said.

Timmy rolled his upper lip over his teeth and squirmed in his seat. "You know, Reese. I was thinking. Now that I'm a teenager and all…" he turned toward the house and finding himself safe from his mother's ears, continued, "…maybe we should drop the *Timmy* shit. Let's just go with Tim."

Reese returned to his seat with a smile. "It's your name, sport—sorry—Tim."

Nancy emerged from the house first. She carried an armload of brightly wrapped packages to the table, set them in front of Timmy, moved behind his chair, and covered his eyes with her hands. "Close your eyes, honey."

The birthday boy wrapped his hands around his mother's wrists and, as if he had a choice, closed his eyes.

Dakota peeked his head out through the kitchen doors. Once he was certain the coast was clear he wheeled a chrome-plated Mongoose trick bicycle onto the deck, stopped next to the party boy's chair, and steadied the bike with one hand.

At the "Power of the Pedal" bicycle and skateboard shop in Pioche he had questioned the absence of a kickstand until the young goateed salesman—body adorned with copious amounts of tattoos and body piercings—explained that a "fag brace" could cause a "mondo-rad-mega-wipeout." After the salesman's baroque explanation, complete with animated body gestures, Dakota left the shop still not sure he understood the reason for the missing kickstand.

Reese sipped at the drink in his hand, and said, "OK, sport. You can open your peepers."

Nancy pulled her hands away and dropped them to her hips.

Timmy's saucer-size eyes blinked Dakota's gift into focus. He almost knocked his chair over when he leaped up and reached out his hand. "No shit! A freakin' Mongoose!"

Reese saw Nancy's darkening mien. He tapped her leg with his foot and shook his head, a silent beg for her to let Tim's slipup pass by unnoticed. She resigned with an exasperated sigh.

Timmy snatched hold of the handlebars, threw his leg over the center bar, and parked his butt on the seat with a heavily exhale. Dakota backed away as Timmy rocked the bike onto its back wheel like a rearing pony and free-spun the handlebars, the sun glinting off chrome with each revolution. He dropped the front wheel to the ground and grabbed the handlebars with a white-knuckle grip, taking the bike on its maiden voyage around the swimming pool. Timmy alternated popping wheelies and squeezing the front brake to bring the rear wheel off the ground. He executed a one hundred eighty degree turn, balancing for a moment on two wheels, as if suspended in time. He pumped the pedals and skidded sideways next to Dakota, encircling his mentor with an enthusiastic hug.

"Thanks, Dakota," he said.

"You're welcome, young man." Dakota patted his back lightly. "Indeed, you are more than welcome."

Timmy climbed from the bike and gingerly leaned it against the chair, took a step back for a view with a different angle. "How did you know I wanted a Mongoose?" He glanced at Dakota for a moment and then back to his pride and joy. "You even got the right color."

"Your mother mentioned that your bicycle had been stolen and that you had your eye on this particular model." Dakota beamed with pride at having selected the perfect gift.

"You'd better remember to lock this one up in the shed before you come in for the night," Nancy interjected.

Not only would he lock the Mongoose *in* the shed, he would chain it *to* the shed, as well as double padlock the door. If someone wanted to steal this bike they'd better be ready to take the whole building.

Timmy walked around the table, wrapped his arms around his mother's neck, and squeezed tight. "You're the greatest, Mom." A mischievous smile found his face. From behind his mother's back he stuck his tongue out at Reese, and said, "No matter what Reese says about you when you're not around."

"Me?" Reese choked indignantly.

Timmy managed a straight face when he said, "Don't act all, like, innocent and stuff, Reese. You know how you trash talk her when she's not around to defend herself."

Reese grinned and saluted Timmy with his glass. "Well done, very well done *Timmy*. But have you already forgotten who fell into the pool the last time you lipped off?"

Timmy returned to his bike and yanked it to attention, climbed aboard, and, amidst handlebar spins and one wheel stands rode to the opposite side of the pool. Once he was safely out of reach, he said, "Yeah, but now you can't catch me."

Reese set his glass on the table, tightened his grip on the armrest of his chair, and started to rise. "Don't bet on it," he said; then thought better of having to prove Timmy wrong. He settled back into his seat with a snigger; after all, it was his birthday so he let the challenge pass.

Timmy entertained the idly chatting adults with his limited repertoire of tricks: wheel stands, 180-degree turns, bunnyhops, and handlebar spins.

"It looks like you found the ideal gift, Dakota. Thank you." She turned in her chair to Reese. "Thank both of you for everything you do for us. You guys really are something else."

Grinning at the display of youthful exuberance taking place on the other side of the pool, Dakota said, "You're more than welcome, Mrs.

Robbins. And I think I speak for both of us when I tell you it's a pleasure having young Timothy spend his free time here at the ranch."

Reese was far less versed in the social graces so he raised his glass in a simple salute, and said, "Ditto."

He hollered across the pool and motioned Timmy back to the table. "Come back over here, you have some more presents to open."

Timmy took far less time tearing through the brightly colored wrapping paper of his *practical gifts*—clothes and socks and underwear—than it had taken Nancy to wrap them. After giving the new additions to his wardrobe a cursory glance he stuffed the gift-wrap into the bag Dakota provided, and turned to Reese. "So what'd you get me?"

Nancy was incredulous. "Don't you think you're being a little rude?"

Timmy turned in his seat and rolled his eyes at his mother. "You know he got me something." He turned back to Reese. "So you can stop acting like you didn't know was my birthday."

Reese set his drink on the table with a shrug. "Wait here," he said, before he disappeared into the house.

It was several minutes before he returned carrying a medium size box neatly wrapped in heavy-gauge brown shipping paper. He set it on the ground next to Timmy's chair and reclaimed his seat with a triumphant smile.

"Don't you think you should say, thank you?" Nancy said.

"Not until I see what's inside. Maybe I won't like it."

"Timothy Michael!"

He picked up a box that felt empty. After several vigorous clue-shakes and still unable to guess what was inside, Timmy slid his chair away from the table and pinned the box between his feet. He stared at it for a moment and then looked at everyone seated around the table. Apparently they weren't going to give him a hint so he tore through the first layer of paper, finding a Huggies Diapers shipping box sealed with duct tape.

Suspicious eyes rose slowly to Reese. "Is this supposed to be some kind of statement or something, Reese? Or, is it just some more of your weird sense of humor?"

Reese spit the ice cube he had been crunching back into his glass. "No statement," he laughed. "But I wish I'd have thought of it that way. I could have gotten some real mileage out of that one."

"Glad you didn't," Timmy said.

He spent the next few minutes working his way through boxes of descending size, each meticulously wrapped in coarse paper and concealed inside a box the next smaller size. Finally, he reached the last box—he hoped—and unwrapped a shoebox size package. Inside the shoebox sitting on a bed of tissue paper was a round tube wrapped, go figure, in more brown paper and duct tape. He tore the paper off and found a plain cardboard paper towel roll.

Timmy looked at the paper scattered around his feet. "What am I missing here?" he said totally bewildered.

Nancy's face did not belie her puzzlement; Dakota gave a curt shrug; Reese, on the other hand, gazed into the desert sipping his drink and pretending to be paying no attention.

In case he had missed something, Timmy set the tube on the table and rummaged through the paper at his feet. Not until he glanced up at his mother did his eyes lock on the tube and, much to Reese's relief, noticed there was a piece of paper tucked inside the paper towel roll. While Timmy busied himself working the paper out of the tube, Reese excused himself from the table and went into the house. He stood inside the family room doors until Timmy unrolled the advertisement for a high-end Inspiron 700M, Dell's top of the line notebook computer.

Barely able to contain his childlike excitement, Reese carried the real McCoy to the table. He set the monogrammed gray leather travel case in Timmy's lap.

Timmy's eyes were, again, Mongoose-wide. "For me?"

Reese picked up his drink and returned to his seat, voice echoing out of his glass as he spoke. "I think you're the only one having a birthday today, sport."

Timmy spent the next several minutes caressing the case before carefully unzipping it and, with brain surgeon delicate hands lifted the computer out and set it on the table. "Holy-moly! Check it out, Mom. My very own laptop."

"It comes with a year's free online subscription to AOL." Reese said. "That way you can chat with your buddies from school."

Timmy looked across the table with a smile slightly broader than his host's. "Thanks, Reese. This is way, too, cool."

He jumped from his chair and gave Reese (obviously uncomfortable with the outward show of affection) a tight hug before returning to his seat. He pulled his chair close to the table and opened the cover. "Awesome," he said, with another beaming smile in Reese's direction.

Reese smiled back; grateful he had been spared another huggy-touchy-feely episode.

Nancy scooted her chair around the table closer to Timmy's. "A little expensive don't you think, Reese?" she said.

"Before you get started with that Timmy…oops, sorry Tim, I've got one more thing to show you."

He motioned for the group to follow as he strode across the deck, flung open the iron gate, and continued toward the barn on a hurried pace. As he struggled to keep up, Timmy's thoughts ran rampant to what was hidden in the barn. He had his eye on a Barrel Racer saddle at the "Tack Shoppe" in Pioche and hoped like all heck that Dakota happened to mention it to Reese.

Reese stood in front of the barn doors, his hand on the handle, impatiently waiting for Nancy and Dakota to catch up.

"Ready?" he said, tugging open both doors as the same time.

If Timmy's eyes bugged out when he saw the Mongoose and laptop computer, they nearly popped from their sockets at what awaited him inside the barn.

Chapter 12

Timmy fidgeted anxiously during Dakota's fifteen-minute safety lecture and once he had finished, roared from the barn astride his new red and white Yamaha Raptor quad runner, with color-coordinated helmet. No longer would he have to sit behind Dakota or Reese, hanging onto their waists like as girl, when they went four wheeling in the desert. Now he could cruise on his own machine; and cruise he did, right up until sunset. He blasted more than a dozen laps around the barn and corral, charged as many tours around the main house, and jumped the small moguls of the barn more times than could be counted on two hands and a pair of bare feet.

At sunset, with the combined efforts of Reese and Dakota, along with some serious pleading from Timmy, Nancy was convinced to spend the night at the ranch. Freshly showered, Timmy sat at the heavy oak table in the family room wearing a green tank top and white shorts (his ranch wardrobe had a much wider selection than his tiny closet in the trailer in Rachel) going over the laptop's owner's manual with Dakota.

Reese traded his black silk shirt and white pants for a pair of black jeans and a white tank top and no shoes. He strolled out of the kitchen carrying a steaming cup of Chinese green tea and ambled across the pool deck. Silver prisms of light projected by the swimming pool's underwater lights undulated against the sandstone wall, where he found a comfortable place to lean his forearms, his tea cradled in his hands. He was squinting into the sun's ebbing rays, but before he had a chance to sort through his thoughts he *felt*, rather than heard, Nancy's presence sneaking around the darker shallow end of the pool.

"Sunsets are so beautiful," he said softly.

She snapped disappointed fingers and took a place against the wall next to him. She studied the weary lines etched on his face, his deep brown eyes fixed on a spot in the desert that didn't exist, as if looking into the future, or maybe the past.

"I like sunrise better," she said, turning her eyes to the desert to see what he was looking at.

"Why's that?"

She thought about it for a moment and then said, "Because the sunrise…at least to me…signals a new beginning, the promise of a new day, of things to come. Sunsets remind me of the end…the death of the day."

Reese set his cup on the wall and folded his hands behind his neck, arched his shoulders and squeezed his elbows together in front of his chin. "All in perspective I suppose."

Nancy turned back to his profile and watched his dark lashes flutter with each blink. "Excuse me?" she said.

"I said it's all in perspective." He pointed to where Kitty trotted into the lengthening shadows on the east side of the barn. "To the nocturnal world it's the sunset that promises a new beginning."

Nancy pursed her lips and nodded. "True. But it seems more natural that light marks the beginning, darkness the end."

"Cyclical. Life and death. Black and white. Yin and yang," he said, stoically.

While they each saw the same landscape, their views captured vastly different images.

"We enter the world of light," she said, "from the darkness of the womb. When we die we return to the darkness of the grave. So yeah, sort of cyclical. Black and white."

She wasn't sure about delving into the philosophy of yin and yang, particularly with a person whose culture invented the concept.

Under the impending cover of darkness an imperceptible smile came to Reese's face and he chanced a look in Nancy's direction. "The concept of Yin and Yang has no beginning, nor an end."

In the Nevada hinterland conventional sunrise and sunset does not truly exist. Dawn bursts forth over the horizon and shocks a new day into existence, while darkness obliterates the landscape as quickly as a blanket pulled over the head of a frightened child hiding from the monsters under his bed.

"All life has a beginning and an end, Reese. None of us gets out of here alive. We're all born, we live our lives and do the best we can for those we love, and then in the end we die and get buried."

"Not if you enter death's darkness by way of light," he said, wryly.

"Huh?"

"Not if you're cremated."

It was time to change the topic lest Nancy discover things about Reese Daniels he preferred remain concealed. "Timmy seems to have had a good time today."

"A good time?" Nancy laughed. "My goodness, Reese. He got everything a kid his age should want, plus some. Which brings me to another point."

Nancy turned from the wall and caught Reese staring at her. He quickly turned away, piquing her curiosity why he always diverted his eyes, never engaged her with direct eye contact for more than a few seconds.

"You and Dakota spend way too much money on Timmy. You guys are going to spoil him."

"Spoiled isn't so bad. Look at what a well-rounded person I've turned out to be," he said with a sardonic laugh, eyes fixed on the shadows beyond the wall. "Timmy's a good kid, Nancy. What's nothing wrong with him having some of the things he desires."

"Reese, the things *he desires* should be a Gameboy, or a video game, or maybe on the outside a PlayStation, or whatever they're called. Don't you think a four-wheeler, a top-of-the-line laptop computer, and the best trick bike money can buy is a little much?"

Reese gave an innocuous shrug. "Dakota picked out the bike. I told him you would think it was over the top but he wouldn't listen."

Nancy brushed loose strands of wheat colored hair from her eyes. "I'm sorry if I sound ungrateful, I'm not. I just don't want...how should

I put this...I don't want Timmy thinking of you and Dakota as his personal ATM machine."

Reese laughed at the analogy. "It's okay, Nancy. I have more liquid assets than most banks have in their vaults."

"That's my point! He's acting like your wealth is his wealth. I overheard him on the phone the other night bragging to one of his chums about how he can get anything he wants from his 'rich friends'."

"Maybe, Nancy, he was just being truthful."

She might as well be having a conversation with the wall. Her hands snapped to her hips. "Reese!"

He turned to her for a rare moment of eye-to-eye contact. "So I should cancel the Lamborghini I have on order for his sixteenth?" He picked up his cup, turned away from the wall, and the conversation, and padded around the pool toward the family room.

Nancy's cheeks puffed out an exasperated sigh. "Reese, I'm serious."

Reese paused with his hand on the door handle. "So am I," he said, and then disappeared inside.

Nancy sat at the heavy oak table across from Timmy and Dakota, chin propped in her hands, deep in thought, listlessly watching as they set up Timmy's AOL account, only half hearing Dakota's warning about the dangers of the Internet if one ended up in the wrong area of the World Wide Web.

After their poolside conversation Reese went upstairs and changed clothes before retiring to his tiyuguan, where he spent forty-five minutes seated on the floor meditating on what it was about Nancy that confused him so. The answer bubbled out of the subconscious side of the mind and broke the surface of conscious thought.

He was in love.

Reese blinked his eyes open with a broad smile. It was a new and wonderful sensation. He rose from the floor and glided across the room on light steps, cupped his hand behind the candle and blew out the flame. He stood in the semi-dark for a moment watching velvety wisps of smoke climb from the two incense sticks glowing on each side of the altar. He stopped in the doorway and bowed his respects to the portrait of Tian Xian Huo, paused in the family room doorway to say goodnight to his guests, and, before anyone could respond, bounded up the steps to the second floor master bedroom suite. He took a cold shower and crawled into bed contemplating how much to tell Nancy, if anything, about his *business dealings.*

Nancy was still staring at the empty doorway when she spoke to no one in particular. "What is it with him?"

Dakota queued in that something was wrong when Reese entered the house. He closed the lid on Timmy's laptop and leaned back in his chair, thoughtfully.

"Mrs. Robbins, Reese is a very private person; extremely introverted and insecure, secretive. I sensed when he entered the house that he was perturbed. And while indeed it is none of my affair what the conversation between the two of you on the patio entailed, I must inform you that Reese has a tendency to switch to…shall I say…the avoidance mood if someone draws too close."

Timmy shot a disparaging glare across the table. "Smooth move, Mom. What'd you say to piss Reese off?"

Nancy's face wilted as she fell back in her chair and mulled over the poolside conversation, trying to recall what might have been said to offend him, or was of such a personal nature he would sulk to his room like a child, ignoring his guests.

It was nearing midnight when Dakota ordered Timmy off to bed. He wanted to get an early start in the morning. Rather than riding Gus and Mollie to Seashell Rock he had acquiesced to taking the quad-runners. They would also take the side trip to "Desperado's Canyon" (Timmy had romanticized names for every location on the ranch) where the bald eagles nested. Dakota even agreed to take along his digital camera with the zoom lens so Timmy could shoot as many pictures as the camera's memory card would hold. When he got home tomorrow night he could download to his laptop and email them back to Dakota. As much as Timmy loved hanging out at the ranch he couldn't wait to get home, hook his new computer to the phone line in the living room, and send out his first honest-to-goodness email.

Chapter 13

By the time Nancy awoke the following morning and found her way downstairs to the kitchen, Reese had already finished an early morning workout, indulged a light breakfast of Chinese green tea and cinnamon bagels smeared with buckwheat honey, dragged the patio table closer to the pool, and was sitting in the shade of the umbrella with business papers scattered across the table before him.

Nancy stood in the kitchen yawning off the foggy memory of Dakota and Timmy firing up their quad-runners shortly after dawn. She helped herself to a cup of coffee, and then walked out onto the patio.

When Reese glanced up from his notes he would have to have been blind to miss Nancy's unbridled breasts, nipples erect in the chilly morning air and pressing against the oversized tee shirt, muscular legs and red toenails carrying her to the table. Caught staring at her again, Reese quickly dropped his eyes to the table.

She pulled a chair out from under the table and took a seat, curling her legs under and tenting the shirt over her knees. "Morning, Reese."

Without raising his eyes, he said, "Good morning, Nancy."

She sipped her coffee, decided it was too hot, set the cup on the table, and watched Reese fumble without purpose through the stack of papers in front of him.

"What are those?" she said, craning her neck across the table.

He quickly gathered the pages together as if she was cheating his answers from a test. "Nothing really. Just some accountant projections on Daniels Industries business."

"Really? Projections on what?"

She was a little too interested for his liking. "A business enterprise I'm…Daniels Industries is considering getting involved with." Before raising his eyes to hers, he slipped into a pair of sunglasses. "Why do you ask?"

"I don't know." Nancy wrapped her fingers around her cup. "I just wondered what it is that Daniels Industries does, that's all."

Reese leaned back, pretentiously. "Daniels Industries is a rather complex and diversified corporation, Nancy. It's all really quite confusing."

"And I'm not smart enough to understand it?"

"That's not what I meant."

It was her turn to switch gears in mid-conversation. She squirmed in her seat, sampled her coffee again, still too hot, and said, "Look, Reese. I'm sorry if I made you mad last night, if I said something I shouldn't have."

He found it far less complicated looking into her beautiful hazel eyes from behind the safety of dark lenses. "I wasn't mad, Nancy. Tired was more like it."

She flashed a sardonic smile that said 'tired' was a weak excuse at best. "Can I ask you a question?"

"Sure," he replied, knowing that any other response would not keep her from saying what was on her mind; outspokenness, just one of many traits he liked about her.

"Why is it you never leave the ranch? It's like a hermit's lifestyle fits you all too well. Don't you ever get bored with having no external stimulation in your life?"

He squeezed his glass of iced tea tightly, checked his anger, frustration, and relaxed. "Actually, Nancy," he said. "Recluse is a more appropriate term. To call me a hermit implies I'm on some sort of religious sabbatical, which is hardly the case. On the other hand, my being a recluse states I've made a conscious choice to withdraw from society, and that is precisely the case."

Her eyes told the tale; she was not amused with his answer.

"Recluse, hermit; eccentric, weird; semantics," she said stringently.

His index finger rose, and so did a nervous smile. "Ah! Do you know the difference between eccentric and weird?"

Nancy wondered if he was being condescending, trying to be witty, or had again switched to the avoidance mode Dakota spoke of last night. She hoped her stoic expression conveyed that she had no interest in engaging in a verbal joust.

"Anyway," he continued, "an eccentric person has money, usually lots of it; whereas weird people more often than not are poor." He shrugged an idiotic grin. "That makes me an eccentric recluse, not a weird hermit."

She closed her eyes, drew in a deep breath, and came to her point; the same point she had tried to get to last night before he left her standing alone on the patio.

"Reese, some of the students from my aerobics class invited Timmy and me to the Wet-'n-Wild Water Park in Las Vegas tomorrow. Those of us with kids are taking them along." Nancy nearly laughed out loud because she was never quite sure to whom she was speaking; Reese the child, or Reese the adult. "I thought maybe you'd like to come along with us. Timmy and me that is."

There. She had made it through and the question and it hadn't killed her, even though she expected his answer would be a definite *no*, or at best an ambiguous *maybe*.

He was not accustomed to being asked out on a date, actually, come to think of it, this was the first time. He was pleasantly surprised and seriously considered the offer until Nancy told him a block of rooms had been reserved at the Tropicana. Then he nearly choked.

When he said, "I'd love to, Nancy—" she had found herself sitting up straighter, smile growing a little wider. The weekend may shape up into something encouraging, or so she thought. "—but I have an important conference call I have to deal with Saturday afternoon. A business thing," deflated her with a rueful frown, but only for a moment. She switched to plan B.

"Okay. Dakota can bring you down after you're finished with your call. Or he can bring you down Sunday morning. We'll still be there." She knew she was struggling. "I'll bring you back Sunday afternoon."

Reese stumbled away from the table, nearly tripping over the chair as he made his way to the patio bar. He needed something with a little more punch in his glass than iced tea. He stepped behind the bar with a halo of sweat forming around the base of his neck.

"To be honest with you, Nancy, if all goes well Saturday I'll be meeting with the corporate attorneys on Sunday afternoon. We'll have some important details in need of ironing out."

Reese poured his tea down the drain and reached for a new glass and the bottle of Jack Daniel's.

So much for optimism she told herself. It was time to give Mr. Reese Daniels a taste of some good old-fashioned Nancy Jean Fansler-Robbins's biting sarcasm. "Right, Reese. Attorneys always work on weekends. Everybody knows that."

"Mine do," he said curtly, and then softened his tone. "I'm sorry, Nancy, it's business. It's imperative I make my move when the timing is right."

Nancy's head bobbed from side to side in mock appreciation of his dilemma. "Oh, I see. You have to move when the timing is right?"

Reese poured an extra-stiff drink into his glass and looked, apologetically, across the bar.

How she managed to let herself have feelings for a neurotic-eccentric-reclusive-hermit had suddenly escaped her for the moment. An audible sigh hissed from between her teeth.

"Your grandfather made truckloads of money, didn't he Reese? More than most people will ever see in several lifetimes, and a lot more than he could possibly spend had he not drank himself to death."

Reese's eyes squinted behind dark lenses. The only way she could have come upon that tidbit of information would be directly from Dakota's loose lips. The closest Nancy had ever come to discussing his ancestry was when she asked why there were no family pictures displayed anywhere in the house.

"Your grandfather fell down the staircase drunk off his ass, didn't he? Is that your plan too, Reese? Fall down life's steps trying to fill your grandfather's shoes?"

Reese's eyes fell to the glass full of booze in hand. He poured half of it down the drain.

"How you can sit in this fortress," she swept an arm over the estate, "wasting away in a self-created prison is beyond me. Timmy's told me how you sneak off in the middle of the night at the weirdest times...Oh forgive me." Nancy slashed quotation marks into the air. "At the most *eccentric* of times no doubt to meet with corporate attorneys who line up to kiss your ass because you're one of the richest people in the country."

Reese dropped four ice cubes into his glass.

Nancy rested her chin on folded hands with a cynical grin. "Exactly what is it you're into, Reese?"

He slipped his sunglasses to the tip of his nose and welded dark eyes onto his guest. "I told you, Daniels Industries is a complex diversified corporation with assets in a variety of arenas. And how I make my money is none of your business."

Even before his words made their way across the patio Reese was sorry for what he had said. They'd come out much harsher than he intended. When he opened his mouth to apologize he found himself cutoff by Nancy's raised palms.

She stood from the table, the hurt in her voice evident. "Fair enough. I wont ask you again about your business. But let me tell you something Mister Reese Daniels. There's a lot more to life than money, but I guess since you've always had your ass wiped with hundred dollar bills you wouldn't know about that would you?

"For your information I had a husband who thought that making money was more important than everything else in life, including his family. He fudged his driver's log so he could stay behind the wheel of that stupid truck of his up to twenty hours a day. There were times I wondered if he didn't love that truck more than he did Timmy and me." An angry snort slipped out. "I guess he died in the arms of his lover. He fell asleep behind the wheel one night and left me with a half-assed insurance policy, five thousand dollars in the bank, and a five year old filled with endless questions about when daddy was coming home. All I got out of it was a photo album filled with memories, all neatly packed away under six feet of dirt. So, you can just about imagine how much money means to me," she said, picking up her cup and chugging down two gulps of lukewarm coffee. She slammed it to the table hard enough that coffee geysered over the side of the mug and splashed onto the table.

Reese stepped from behind the bar with a towel in one hand, a spray bottle of disinfectant in the other.

"My God, Reese!" she screamed. "Must you always be such a clean freak? What is it with you anyway? You shower half a dozen times a day, sterilize your hands every time you touch something…or someone, only use a dish or glass once. A couple of germs won't kill you you know."

She snatched the towel from his hand, flung it to the ground, stomped it under her feet, picked it up, mopped coffee from the table, and for good measure wiped her mouth before flinging it against his chest.

"See? Germs! Filthy disease carrying little microbes and I'm not dead."

He shook his head, walked behind the bar, deposited the towel in the hamper, worked thick sterilizing goop over his hands, and returned to the table.

Nancy folded her arms across her chest and shook her head. "Reese, have you ever done anything dirty in your entire life? Something that was totally bad?"

A long buried memory resurrected itself and shuddered to a stop at the top of his spine. "I ate stone-ground bread once," he said, dryly.

Timmy roared out from behind the barn and raced toward the house. He skidded his ATV to a stop amid a cloud of dust. Dakota glided next to him with a little more decorum.

"Watch this, Dakota," Timmy said.

He quickly peeled out of his helmet, boots, socks, and shirt, threw open the gate, and launched himself to the center of the pool, rolled into a tight ball of mischievousness. A tidal wave of laughter and water swept over his mother and Reese.

Nancy brushed drenched locks from her eyes while Reese, on the other hand, capitalized on the distraction. He tossed his sunglasses to the table and leaped into the pool, his cannonball wave slapping Timmy in the face. They took turns horsing around and dunking each other in the deep end of the pool.

Nancy sat down cradling her bowed head in her hands. "A thirty-two year old adolescent," she mumbled.

Chapter 14

After the exchange on the deck, and after Timmy and Reese finished horsing about in the pool, Nancy was ready to head for home. She needed time away from the ranch and, more importantly, away from Reese. She needed to mull over how she was falling in love with such a screwball. Reese, however, managed to instigate Timmy into begging for "...just one more night, please Mom..." Nancy adamantly refused his plea, but finally acquiesced to letting him stay a few more hours on the condition Dakota brought him home before it got dark.

After Nancy left, Timmy and Reese changed, fueled the four wheelers, invited Dakota along for the ride, and then took off for an afternoon jaunt on the quad runners.

Seated atop an internal combustion engine was the kind of horsepower Reese appreciated, not riding on the U-shaped Trixie. With a snap of his wrist Reese coaxed his candy-apple blue quad runner into a tight sideways slide, sending a rooster tail of sand into the air.

Dakota fanned the cloud of dust away from his face. "Reese, that's not a proper display of sound riding practices in front of young Timothy."

"Jeez-al-wheeze, Dakota," Reese groused, shutting down his quad's engine. "You're going to turn him into a Tinker Bell."

Dakota lifted his helmet from his head, set it on the luggage rack, and leaned forward to rest his thick forearms on the handlebars. "Hardly not," he said. "Steel wrapped in velvet is every bit as strong."

Timmy's eyes darted back and forth from behind his mirrored face shield. He rolled his hand on the throttle and juiced his birthday present to life. He cranked the handlebars hard to the right mimicking Reese, and halfway through the slide the back wheel bounced over a rock. Instead of riding it through, Timmy panicked. He let off the throttle, clamped down on the front brake, which tipped the machine onto its right front wheel. He found himself bucked over the handlebars like a drunken fraternity pledge on a mechanical bull.

Reese had already skidded to a stop on his knees and was gently rolling Timmy over by the time Dakota dropped down next to him. Timmy blinked his eyes and jumped from the ground, peeled out of his helmet and offered Reese a high-five.

"Did you see that shit, Reese?" Timmy traced his flight through the air with his hand. "I must have gone ten feet in the air." Three feet was more like it, but young boys have a latent talent for embellishing. "Man was that way cool or what?"

Dakota grabbed him by the shoulders and turned him around looking for unnatural bends in his young limbs. "Timothy, are you all right?"

"Yeah, I'm fine." He pulled away from Dakota and brushed the sand from his clothes. "It was no big deal."

"I've heard that people pay good money at an amusement park for that kind of a ride," Reese said.

Dakota was beyond angry; he was incensed. He viciously turned and confronted Reese. "Nice move, showoff. He could have been seriously injured trying to impress you by imitating your reckless antics. Do him a favor will you Reese? Grow up!"

Dakota's angry glare remained fixed on Reese long enough that the latter turned his eyes away. He turned to Timmy, and said, "You're coming with me."

"Dakota, I didn't get hurt. Honest. I can ride back on my own."

His protest was in vain.

Dakota straddled his machine, slammed his helmet into place, and ordered Timmy to climb aboard. "Get on, NOW!"

Timmy looked to Reese for help but all he got was a head nod to obey.

He took a seat behind Dakota and wrapped his hands around the big man's waist. "What about my quad?"

Dakota fired another glare at Reese. "Let Mr. Showoff smarty britches figure out how he's going to get it home." Dakota fired up his machine, snapped down the face shield, and sprayed Reese with dirt and rocks as he sped off.

By the time Dakota returned to the ranch from dropping Timmy off at home Reese had the old Ford work truck backed up to the barn doors. He was in the process of dropping the tailgate when Dakota walked to the barn and helped him set the ramps in place.

"I owe you an apology, Mr. Daniels," Dakota said. "Indeed, I should not have spoken to you in such a brusque manner. Especially in front of Timothy."

Reese gave a resigning shrug that said he had taken no offense.

"Outside of you, Reese, Timothy is all I have to care for," he continued, thrusting out his big hand. "I overreacted and I'm very sorry."

Reese shook Dakota's hand, vaulted over the side rail and into the bed of the truck. He loosened the tie down straps, and said, "You were right, Dakota. Tim thinks I walk on water. I really should be more careful how I act when he's around." He rolled Timmy's quad to the edge of the tailgate. "Sometimes I forget he's just a kid and that I'm not."

"Nevertheless, I was out of line and apologize."

Reese stood on the tailgate looking down at Dakota with an amused grin on his face. "Dakota, stop apologizing for being the one with good sense and help me roll this thing into the barn, would you?"

Timmy stood in front of the small mirror over the bathroom sink clad in a pair of black boxers covered with silver dollar sized yellow smiley faces, wet shoulder length hair parted in the middle and pulled back behind his ears, toothbrush jammed into his mouth.

"Did you and Dakota and Reese have a good time this afternoon?" his mother asked from the adjacent laundry room.

Foam sprayed from his mouth like a rabid dog as he answered. "Yeah, right up until Dakota tweaked a gear on Reese."

"Over what?"

Timmy spit into the sink. "Reese was clowning around spinning circles on his quad. When I tried it I flipped over."

Nancy's head poked around the doorjamb. "You didn't get hurt did you?"

"No."

"Are you sure?"

He gave her reflection a disgusted eye roll. "Jeez, Mom. You're as bad a Dakota. No I didn't get hurt, and no it was no big deal.

"Anyhow, Dakota went off on Reese. That's the first time I heard him raise his voice. Man was he ever pissed. He told Reese I was trying to impress him so he wouldn't let me ride my quad home. I had to ride on the back of his hanging on like a little girl. After he calmed down we rode out to that canyon I told you about."

Nancy grinned a skeptical smile and returned to folding clothes.

"The same canyon where the eagles hang out with Billy the Kid's ghost?"

She had seen the pictures Timmy emailed to Dakota as soon as he got home. Some of them were actually quite good, but she saw no apparition of the famous outlaw in any of the photos.

Timmy parked the toothbrush in the corner of his mouth and rested his hands on the lip of the sink. "Not supposed to Mom! He really did hide out there. Dakota told me he researched it on the Internet. And now that I have my own computer I can look up shit like that too."

Nancy appeared in the doorway. "Look up what?"

"Stuff." He hooked his teeth over his bottom lip. "I said stuff, didn't I?"

" 'Stuff' doesn't end in I-T. You had better straighten up that mouth of yours before it gets you into hot water, buster."

"Sorry."

Timmy finished rinsing his mouth, dropped his toothbrush into the holder in medicine cabinet, and closed the door with a bang. He inspected his teeth in the mirror. As much as he hated his overbite, he also knew his mother could never afford braces on the money she made. Maybe he would mention braces to Reese and Dakota, offer to work off the cost at the ranch, knowing full well they wouldn't make him. He joined his mother in the laundry room.

"Well maybe Billy the Kid did hang out there," Nancy said. "And maybe he didn't. Just don't fall for every story people tell you."

Timmy reached into the dryer, pulled out a handful of towels, and began folding them in half. "Why would Dakota lie about something like that?"

"I didn't say he was lying. I'm just saying he may be…embellishing." She dropped the last pair of socks rolled into a ball into the wicker basket and handed it to Timmy. "These are yours. Put them in your room while I finish folding the towels."

He carried the basket into the living room, paused, braced it on the arm of the futon, and said, "What does 'embellishing' mean?"

"Stretching the truth so the story sounds more believable." She nodded her head toward the basket. "Hurry up and put those away I need the basket."

Timmy walked toward his small bedroom at the back of the trailer. "How is embellishing different from lying?" he yelled over his shoulder.

"Basically, there is no difference."

He gave a dismissing shake of his head and carried the neatly folded clothes to his room. After a quick head-peek down the hall to see if his mother was watching, satisfied she was not, he crammed tee shirts, boxers, and socks into the drawer until he was able to force it closed.

He tossed the basket down near her feet in the laundry room, and said, "Can we make some popcorn?"

"You just brushed your teeth."

He ran his tongue over his teeth. "So? I can brush 'em again."

"I swear you're a bottomless pit."

Timmy went into the living room and fell back onto the futon, pulling a loom-woven Paiute Indian blanket (a gift from Reese and Dakota shortly after he started visiting the ranch) down over his legs. Nancy joined him, found the TV's remote wedged between the cushion and the armrest, pressed the power button, and sat down.

"What time does the movie start?" she said.

He checked his Timex against the VCR's clock with a mischievous grin. "In ten minutes, plenty of time to make popcorn," he said.

Nancy let out a heavy, exasperated sigh. Before he knew what happened she tossed the remote into his lap as a distraction and raced for the kitchen.

"Cheater!" he cackled kicking free of the blanket and charging after her.

While the two bags of microwave popcorn hiss and popped they chatted about tomorrow's trip to Las Vegas, Timmy's first. Nancy took the health conscious approach giving her bowl of popcorn a light dusting of salt with no butter. Timmy, however, doused his bowl with several pads of melted butter and garlic salt.

"After the movie's over it's bedtime. I want to get a early start in the morning," she said.

They carried their bowls of popcorn into the living room, curled up on opposite ends of the futon, and shared the Indian blanket to cover their legs. Timmy shoveled a fistful of greasy kernels into his mouth to the opening credits of the original uncut version of "Night of the Living Dead".

Chapter 15

"I see your rich boyfriend couldn't make it, huh?" Cora Battles said, her tone nearly as cynical as the expression on her wrinkled face.

Nancy forced a pleasant smile. "He had business to attend to," she said.

No one other than Cora Battles had ever said Reese was her *boyfriend*, and while he was certainly a boy in ways more than not, yesterday's conversation by the pool made it clear he was highly unlikely to become her boyfriend.

Why the elderly and highly opinionated Cora Battles invited herself along to the family outing at the water park was beyond anyone's understanding. Thomas Penter, one of Nancy's advanced aerobic students, hit the nail on the head when he painted a verbal picture of Cora Battles streaking down a water slide, clad in a skimpy bathing suit and wearing a body in severe need of ironing. Penter, who possessed an acidic sense of humor made a strong case for the irreparable psychological trauma the sight of Cora Battles skimming down a waterslide may cause any child in attendance.

"I see," Cora said with a provocateur's sneer. She spun on her heels and tottered toward the elevator.

Timmy made a face behind her back. *Old lady Battles must have some elephant-sized balls to bust on Reese like that,* he fumed. He hooked protruding teeth over his bottom lip and shot Battles the middle finger. Apparently mothers have wider peripheral vision than the average person. Nancy's nostrils flared as she gave Timmy's hand a sharp slap.

"You don't give Miss Battles the finger." She turned and shot Battles the double whammy. "People like her deserve both of them."

"All right, Mom!" he grinned, deciding there was still hope for his mother.

Nancy grabbed hold of his hand and turned for the registration counter. "Let's get signed in."

Thirteen years old and on the cusp of manhood, he was too old to be led around like a child. Timmy pulled his hand away and hoisted the strap of Nancy's overnight bag to his shoulder, picked up his gym bag, and followed her to the front desk.

He stood beside her with an amused grin as he read the engraved nametag pinned to the Head Concierge's monogrammed blazer. With a name like *Ramon* he had to be a head of something, Timmy mused. The concierge held his attention but for a second. A skimpily clad casino hostess wearing little more than two strategically placed Band-Aids and a loincloth sashayed past, the cork-lined tray propped on her shoulder filled with free cocktails intended to keep the gamblers' wallets open. His eyes bugged out and his mouth fell open.

"Whoa, check that out!" he slavered, nearly drooling down the front of his shirt.

Nancy's expression was a combination of shock and embarrassment; she covered his eyes with her hand. "Move it, buster."

He pried a peephole between her fingers and mouthed an exaggerated, silent *WOW*, while visually undressing and eye raping the hostess. He decided right then and there that Las Vegas was without a doubt the coolest place he had ever visited, in spite of Reese's absence. They rode the elevator to the thirteenth floor (only in Las Vegas was the universal unlucky number assigned to a guest floor) and wandered through the labyrinth of hallways until they located their room.

Timmy tossed the luggage onto one of the double beds, and then raced across the room for a look out through the floor to ceiling windows. Below teamed busy Las Vegas Boulevard, "The Strip", an awesome sight to a boy living in a trailer in a tiny desert town. He stood with his hands and nose pressed against the glass, enraptured by the "Manhattan Express" roller coaster roaring around the upper floors of the New York,

New York Casino. The coaster streaked to the backside of the building and his attention dropped back down to the nonstop flow of ant-size pedestrians meandering along the sidewalk. He couldn't wait to take his place in the swarm of tourists pressing along the boulevard, ducking in and out of the innumerable casinos. Quickly bored with being a spectator, his attention turned to the television set recessed in a dark cherry wood credenza against the wall. He found a complimentary copy of *Las Vegas Entertainment Magazine* and flopped down on the bed. He thumbed through the magazine's glossy pages overflowing with discount coupons to restaurants, theatre shows, and advertisements with just enough risqué pictures of flesh to arouse the imagination of any adolescent, pausing on each page and imagining his way into the R-rated performance.

Nancy stepped from the bathroom through a swirling cloud of steam. She was wrapped in a yellow terry cloth robe and had her hair bundled atop her head in a towel. Timmy tossed the magazine aside and bounced off the bed.

"You ready to go?"

She dropped to a corner of the bed unwrapped and fluffed her hair. "Hold your pants on, Timmy. We just got here."

"We didn't come all the way to Las Vegas to sit in a stupid hotel room did we?"

Nancy looked at him through strands of wet hair. "Las Vegas won't go anywhere if we don't rush out there this very instant."

If he couldn't join them he could at least watch them. He walked back to the window with "shit" squeaking out under his breath.

Nancy threw back her locks with a snap of the head, setting hard eyes on Timmy. "What was that?"

He turned from the window with a cherub's smile. "What? I said shoot."

"Sure you did, Timmy. Do me a small favor, would you." She squeezed her thumb and forefinger together. "Don't embarrass me in front of my clients with that foul mouth of yours."

"Me?"

"Nooo," she mocked. "You'd never do anything like that, would you?"

She worked the towel over her head, rewrapped her hair, spun around on the bed, and plumped two pillows together. "It was a long drive. Let me grab a half hour nap and then we'll get something to eat."

Timmy sank back against the window incredulously. "Right now?"

"Yes, right now." She dropped her head to the pillow.

"I'm going to go take a look around," he said, exasperated.

He stopped in front of the dressing table next to the bathroom and slid a ten from the envelope tucked inside his mother's purse. As if she could see around corners she warned him not to take more than twenty. He looked at the bill in hand, and then took her up on her offer. He liberated a twenty-dollar bill and tucked both into his pocket.

Nancy's eyelids drifted closed as he opened the door. "Don't forget your keycard. Stay out of the casino. And don't be gone, too, long."

Timmy rode the elevator to the first floor, stopping at the casino entrance long enough to read the sign: "You must be 21 years of age to enter the gaming area." before he shrugged his shoulders and walked inside.

Fifteen minutes into a "Wheel of Fortune" video slot game Timmy had doubled his money. Overhead one of the security cameras that watched every move on the casino floor zeroed in on the west slots. Children playing slot machines inside a casino has a tendency to bring about enormous fines from the Nevada Gaming Commission. In the time it took security personnel monitoring the cameras deep inside the administrative offices, until two officers—one uniformed, the other a plainclothesman—intervened took less than two minutes. The black nametag pinned to the pocket of his gold blazer identified the plainclothes officer as Assistant Security Director, Thomas Ferry.

Officer Ferry stepped in close behind Timmy, folded his arms across his chest, and said, "May I ask what you think you're doing?"

Timmy glanced at the reflection of the officers in the machine's glass; the muscle-bound uniformed cop was nothing short of mammoth.

Timmy knew he should have quit while he was ahead, but had to try *just one more time* for the big jackpot. "What does it look like I'm doing?" he said caustically as possible to cover his angst of getting caught red-handed.

When Officer Ferry's hand shot forward, Timmy winced. He had seen those "Travel Channel" specials on Las Vegas, how security did not put up with any malarkey. Ferry pressed the cash out button, and said, "You have to be twenty-one to play the games, son."

The commotion of quarters clanging into the metal tray at the base of the machine (purposely designed to draw attention of nearby gamblers, thus encouraging them to pour more money into their machine seeing how their *neighbor* had just hit big) drew the attention of a couple of middle-age tourists wearing matching Hawaiian shirts. Ferry gave them his practiced, squint-eyed smile, the smile that said: Mind your own business. After they got up and moved to a different row off machines, Ferry returned his attention to the business at hand.

"Are you a guest at our facility, young man?"

Timmy pulled his proof from his shirt pocket and held it up in front of the officer's face. "Room 1327. And it is a very nice view, thank you," he said sardonically.

Ferry examined both sides of the card to ensure it was not counterfeit. He passed it over his shoulder for a second opinion. Officer Don Mathers gave the card a cursory glance; it was the longhaired, mouthy towhead that held more of his interest.

"As I stated young man, you must be twenty-one years old to play the slot machines." He took the card that Mathers handed back over his shoulder, and said, "With whom are staying?"

"My mother and some of her clients, that's with *whom*." Timmy snatched the card from Ferry hoping the "her clients" tag impressed the cop enough to use as bail for getting nabbed at the machine.

Officer Ferry, with great difficulty, maintained his professional demeanor just in case the sassy little urchin's mother truly was an important guest. "I see. And may I ask where your mother is at the moment?"

"Taking a nap, that's where." He tucked the key card into his shirt pocket.

Ferry nodded to Mathers, who in turn reached between the machines for a plastic coin bucket and began scooping Timmy's earnings out of the tray, depositing them in the bucket.

"Hey, those are mine!" Timmy protested loud enough to draw the momentary attention of several passing tourists. They received the *Ferry smile* and continued on their way.

His smile faded. He seized the young gambler's arm and marched him on his tiptoes to a house phone mounted next to the cashier's cage. "Your mother can cash your winnings in for you; just once." He punched in the room number and waited for an answer. "What's your mother's name?"

"Mom," Timmy said with a mocking bucktoothed grin that amused neither officer.

Nancy floated in that limbo between sleep and awake, drawing the handset to her ear. "Hello," she said, groggily

"Mrs. Robbins?"

"Yes."

"This is Thomas Ferry, casino security. Do you have a son named Timmy?"

She sat up on the bed and shook off the remnants of her short nap. She glanced at the clock on the night table wondering, exactly how much trouble could he possibly get into in twenty-three minutes? Then she reminded herself of whom she was speaking. She swung her legs over the side of the bed and arched her back.

"Yes. What's he done?"

"Nothing major, Mrs. Robbins. He was in the gaming area playing a slot machine." Nancy rolled her eyes to the ceiling. "I don't think he realized the law requires our guests to be twenty-one years of age before they can play the games." Ferry segued, diplomatically. "We have a video arcade set aside especially for our younger guests. With your permission I'll direct him to that area more appropriate for his age."

Nancy yanked the towel from her head and slammed it to the bed. She ran agitated fingers through her damp hair. "I have a better idea officer," she snapped. "Why don't you direct his butt back to our room? And tell him I said the rest of his body better be attached to it. Pronto!"

Timmy slinked into the room with his head slung nearly as low as his gray cargo shorts, a bucketful of quarters cradled to his chest.

Nancy slid to the edge of the bed, folded her arms across her chest, crossed her legs at the knee, and impatiently tapped the air with her foot.

"Where could you possibly have left your brain to think you were going to get away with that one?"

When he opened his mouth in self-defense she sprang from the bed and slammed her hands to her hips. "Not one word, buster! Not one sneaky, stinking, foul-mouthed, lying, word."

Well aren't we a bit testy when we don't get our nap?

His mother stomped her foot hard enough a shockwave crossed the room and probably rattled the fixtures one floor below. "I'm telling you something right this instant, buster. If you can't behave yourself we'll pack up and head back home so you can get well acquainted with your room for the next, shall we say, three weeks.

"What's it going to be?"

Not only did she look angry enough to carry out the threat, she sounded it too. "Sorry," he said, timidly, knowing enough not to push his luck.

She tipped her head toward the plastic cup he was nervously shifting back and forth in his hands. "What's in the bucket?"

He raised his eyes with a cautious grin. "I won us twenty bucks."

"With my money?" She stormed across the room and snatched the bucket out of his hands. "That makes it mine, because there's no *us* in this conversation!"

Timmy's brows creased. "Hey, that ain't fair! I'm the one who earned it."

"File a complaint with security," she spat acerbically. "I'm sure they'll be happy to see you again." She walked across the room and tossed the cup down on the bed. "Go take a shower while I change. We'll hit the buffet for dinner."

Timmy unpacked a set of fresh clothes from his gym bag and padded to the bathroom. He turned on the shower, mooned his mother through the door, stepped into the tub, and yanked the heavy plastic shower curtain closed. "That blows," he grumbled. "I get busted by a *fairy* and loose my money all in one sweep." He smiled into the stream issuing from the showerhead, and said, "At least I still have the ten."

Nancy counted the bucket's contents spilled contents across the comforter, forty-three dollars and seventy-five cents. She turned and smiled at the bathroom door. After changing and combing her hair she picked up Timmy's shorts where, out of habit, she checked the pockets. Deep inside the front pocket she found the tightly folded ten-dollar bill.

Chapter 16

Timmy sat on the floor at the center of Reese's tiyuguan with his legs split as wide as quivering muscles unaccustomed to the strain would allow. He bounced forward in a futile attempt to bring his nose closer to his knee.

Timmy's sifu (Chinese for teacher) sat across from his protégé, stretched through a full split with his chin easily resting on his kneecap. Out of the corner of his eye Reese watched Timmy's struggle. He sat up straight, pulled his feet together in front of him, and barked, "Bù tántiào! Which means, don't bounce! You're going to tear a muscle bouncing like that."

Timmy brought his hand to the back of his head and pushed down, grunting against the strain. "Why can't I get any lower?"

"It could have something to do with a lack of practice," Reese said, dryly.

Timmy pulled his feet together mimicking Reese's position. "How long did it take you to learn all the shit you know?"

Reese folded his torso forward until the tip of his nose rested on the insides of his ankles. "Tim, the art of Wushu is sort of like..." He searched for the right comparable. "...the game of chess. You never master the arts, just like you never master the chessboard. The more you practice the better, more proficient you become. But in answer to your question, I usually workout a couple of hours a day; and I'm still learning."

He returned to a seated position, locked eyes with Timmy, and said, "I was a little bit younger than you when I began my studies with a Wushu Master from China."

Timmy's eyes widened. "You've been to China?" He scratched the side of his head. "I thought you didn't like leaving the ranch?"

Reese ignored the latter question. "I said I studied with a master *from* China, not *in* China. His name was Fashi Tian Xian Huo. Fashi means *Master*; a title the Chinese give a Taoist priest as a sign of respect. Mr. Huo was brought to the ranch when I was very young, brought here to teach me martial arts. We would work out together a lot. Sometimes up to eight hours a day, five or six days a week."

What Reese chose not to share with Timmy was how he had been forced to beg his grandfather to let him learn martial arts. How he had used passionate devotion to the arts as a means of escaping the loneliness of having no friends or playmates. Early on Reese learned to use meditation (as he still did) like a hallucinogenic drug, a means of escaping his bizarre lifestyle and fleeing deep within himself.

Timmy pulled his feet together and sat erect. "Do you think you could kick Bruce Lee's ass," he said.

"Yep."

Timmy's face bubbled with excitement. "Really?"

"Really."

"There's no doubt in your mind you could take him?"

"Absolutely none whatsoever," Reese said confidently.

Timmy gave him a skeptical glance. "What makes you so sure you could kick Bruce's butt?"

"Ha!" Reese guffawed. "Because he's dead."

"Ah, come on Reese. I'm being serious. Do you really think you could have taken him in a fight?"

Reese lifted his ankles to the insides of his thighs and contemplated his young apprentice for a moment. "Tim, Wushu teaches you how not to fight. There's no honor in fighting. Physical confrontation should always be a last resort because, no one ever really wins a fight."

Timmy spoke with a genuine yearning. "I wish I knew what you know."

A listless smile crossed his teacher's face. Years ago he had said the same thing to his teacher, and now repeated Master Huo's words, first in Chinese and then in English: "Be not afraid of growing slowly, Tim. Be only afraid of standing still."

Timmy's head cocked to the side. "Where do you come up with all these sayings?"

"Not until I met Fashi Huo did I learn about my Chinese heritage. Because he spoke no English I had to learn Chinese, with the help of an interpreter of course."

"Is that why you listen to that Chinese crap on the Internet? So you can practice the language?"

"Something like that," Reese said, adding, with a southwestern drawl, "Not many people speak Chinese in these here parts."

Timmy's young mind switched gears without warning. "Do you like my mom?"

The abruptness of the question caught Reese off guard. He leaned back and propped himself on his elbows. "What brought that up?"

"I don't know," Timmy said, shrugging and letting his eyes drift to the floor. "That's all she talked about while we were in Las Vegas last weekend. Reese this…Reese that…Reese should have been here for this…She must have said a thousand million times how she wished that you would've came along with us. She's worse than the girls at my school."

Reese chuckled at the comparison. "Yeah, I kind of do like Nancy," he said. "She's fun to be around."

Timmy's snarled lip exposed his teeth. "Not if you have to live with her she isn't," he said.

Without using his hands for support, Reese tucked his foot underneath and stood. Timmy almost made it to half-mast before he lost his balance and dropped his hands to the ground. He pushed off the floor and took a place three steps behind and to the left of Reese.

Reese closed his stance by bringing his ankles together. He let his arms dangle loosely at his sides, closed his eyes, remaining tranquilly motionless for a several minutes. After his chi was sufficiently calmed, he stepped to his left with an exaggerated, slow motion step, sensing Timmy mirroring his movements from behind, as they oozed with the viscosity of syrup through the unhurried pace of Yang's Tai Chi Chuan. At the conclusion of "Close Tai Chi" Reese spun about abruptly and barked: "Ma jiashi!"

Ma jiashì was one of the few Chinese phrases Timmy knew by heart. He sank into the dreaded "Horse Stance"—feet spread shoulder width, torso lowered to a half-squat, fists drawn tight against hipbones, palms facing the ceiling. He locked into position and stared straight ahead as Reese walked around him correcting hand and foot position as well as posture. Somewhere near the two-minute mark Timmy's legs began to do what Reese called "the Elvis shake". He stepped in front of Timmy and gave him permission to relax. "Songsan."

Timmy wiggled and kicked the tension from cramped legs, and shook his hands at his sides until the blood was flowing again.

"It looks like you've been practicing a little," Reese said. "That was almost two minutes, sport."

Timmy beamed a big tooth grin at the compliment. "When are you going to teach me how to break boards and bricks and shit?"

Reese pushed Timmy's shoulder knocking him off balance. "I think you had better stick to hot butter and Jell-O for the time being, grasshopper. You have yet learned to stand."

His protégé jumped in front of him and lined up for a round of Push Hands. They seesawed back and forth in rhythmic motion, the backs of their hands in light contact, each seeking the advantage of balance over the other.

"Bala gong; bu tui gong," Reese snapped.

Timmy's brows furrowed together. "What?"

"I said, 'push hand; not, shove hand.' Relax. Loosen up. You're trying to use too much force."

They continued the drill for several minutes before Reese snaked his arm forward, surreptitiously, until his hand made light contact with Timmy's chest. Using a rotating snap of the hip generating internal power that radiated through his torso and out through his arm, he launched Timmy backwards two feet.

"Crap!" Timmy rubbed his chest and jumped back in front of Reese.

"Enough for today, grasshopper." Reese draped an arm around Tim's neck and led him toward the door. The notion entered his mind like a blow to the gut. Reese pulled his arm away; initiating physical contact was very, very unlike him.

Timmy stepped from the studio first and turned as Reese bowed to Master Huo's portrait. He reentered the studio, bowed, and then switched off the light and closed the door.

Chapter 17

The two figures dressed in desert-camouflage military garb barely spoke during the long trip north out of Las Vegas. The passenger, for the umpteenth time, checked the Casio GPS wristwatch strapped to his left wrist.

"Click two miles off on the odometer," he said. "The shoulder will widen, pull off there."

The driver reached between the steering wheel spokes and reset the cargo truck's trip meter wondering how, on a moonless night where the murky desert landscape all looked the same, his counterpart knew there would be a pull off up ahead.

Unbeknownst to him the passenger visited the site earlier in the week and buried a narrow, inconspicuous wood stake in the sand, leaving the top four inches exposed, a "Fire Tack" pressed into the board. During daylight the marker was invisible to the naked eye, but at night it glowed like a blurry white beacon when headlights hit it and unless you were looking, you wouldn't notice it. As predicted, exactly at the two-mile mark the road edge widened and the driver guided the big white unmarked truck to the side of the road and brought it to shuddering stop.

They crawled from the cab, stretched their stiff bodies, and walked to the rear of the truck where the driver unlocked and rolled up the cargo door. He climbed inside and clicked on a low-wattage battery-operated light attached to the interior wall, the dim red glow providing enough light to see by, but not enough to draw the attention of a moth.

"What excuse are we using if the highway patrol or someone from the sheriff's office happens by?" he said.

"The local boys rarely make it this far into the desert during the day. I doubt we have much to worry about them showing up this late at night," Agent Stevens said.

Stevens climbed into the truck and helped Agent Harry Silifax release the tie-down straps, and then jumped from the truck, sliding two lightweight aluminum ramps into place and making sure they locked tight against the truck's heavy steel bumper. Receiving a go-a-head nod from the ground, Silifax pushed a matte-black dune buggy down the ramps into his partner's outstretched arms. Stevens guided it to a stop and then gave the dune buggy a once over while Silifax secured the ramps, double-checking to make sure all the doors were locked.

"Let's rock and roll," Stevens said. He climbed into the passenger seat and checked his GPS wristwatch.

Silifax jumped into the driver's seat, strapped himself into the safety harness, and turned the key. Because it was equipped with a stealth muffler system the buggy's engine purred, rather than roared, to life.

Agent Stevens had spent a week preparing for this late night mission. He had reviewed dozens of aerial military photographs, memorizing the topography of an area simply known as Nevada Grid #36. Using the GPS's backlight to read the dial he guided Silifax with "east-south-southeast" corrections until they had covered better than two and a half miles of barren terrain that included washed out ruts, flash flood runoffs, and perilous cliffs dropping off into a black abyss. They stopped at the crest of a small hill three-quarters of a mile north of their target. Stevens reached overhead and fumbled with a black canvas military bag secured to the roll bar with Velcro strips.

"Kill the engine," he said, pulling a pair of high-tech night binoculars from the bag. He slung the carrying strap over his shoulder, crawled from the buggy, and cautiously moved forward with Silifax in tow, stopping at the lip of a crag overlooking the valley below.

Silifax squatted down to his haunches next to Stevens. "Can I ask what it is you expect to see this time of night, Mack?"

"Who knows?" Stevens said.

The vista below reminded Stevens of the dozens of black velvet paint-by-number artwork kits his grandmother gave him every Christmas, even after he had graduated the FBI's National Academy. Over the years he painted dogs, cats, mallards, flowers, snow capped mountains, pine forests, and more glowing pictures of Jesus than he cared to remember. Bathed by halogen quartz security lighting, Daniels's ranch glowed like a white oasis on black velvet.

To the north of the main house stood the barn; to the west was the servant's quarters (or so indicated the hacienda's blueprints on file with the Lincoln County Building Inspector's Office); to the south a jagged gravel driveway snaking through the foothills and ultimately to State Route 375; to the east, open desert and minimal lighting. Stevens had to admit, Daniels's spread looked even more impressive in person than it did in the satellite photos he had studied.

As if someone might hear him in the middle of this dark isolated place, Stevens dropped his voice to a whisper and swept his hand to the east. "We'll follow this ridge that direction. That should bring us around on the front side of a knoll between the house and the barn. The shadows should hide us pretty well."

Before Silifax could offer a protest, should he have wanted to, Stevens was on the move.

Reese awakened to a high-pitch chirping, and for a moment thought he was dreaming. Sleep quickly abated when he recognized the piercing chirp as that of the perimeter alarm. In the amount of time it took Dakota to make the sleepy climb from his first floor quarters to the second floor security room—a room about the size of a walk-in closet housing the alarm panel and video screens—Reese, much to Kitty's relief had switched off the alarm. Standing inside the door clad in a pair of baggy cotton Kung Fu pants, he stared disbelievingly at one of the monitors.

Dakota stifled a yawn. "Mule deer?"

Reese's eyes squinted at the two iridescent green figures captured on the thermal imaging camera. "Looks like full grown bucks," he said. "Both of 'em around six foot tall and on two legs." He glanced over his shoulder to Dakota. "More the homo sapient variety, I'd say."

Dakota craned his neck over Reese's shoulder and sure enough, there were two figures sliding down the hillcrest north of the barn.

Reese bolted from the closet toward the stairs and bounded down the sweeping mahogany staircase covering three steps with each leap. He yelled over his shoulder, "You stay here with Tim."

He stopped at front door and fumbled to get the lock open.

Dakota ran to the head of the stairs. "Reese, please remain inside. I'll immediately summon the sheriff's office."

Reese yanked open the door and half turned to the figure at the top of the stairs. "All the way from Pioche, Dakota? You've got to be kidding me. They'll never get here in time. Stay inside with Tim!"

He disappeared outside, pulling the door closed behind him.

"Reese!" Dakota's robe fluttered behind him like a full sail as he dashed down the staircase, but by the time he opened the door Reese had already disappeared into the night.

"Kitty, go with Reese," Dakota said, panic-stricken.

Kitty bounded off the porch in time to catch a glimpse of his master's bare feet rounding the east side of the house. It took the coyote a few leaps before he passed Reese ready to confront the unseen danger his master sensed.

"Kitty, huilai! Gen!"

Kitty immediately obeyed the *Come! Heel!* command and returned to Reese's side, hugging tightly against his thigh as they sprinted into the desert.

Reese arched northwest toward a sloping sand dune he judged would bring him out slightly ahead of, and above the intruders. Depending on how fast they were moving he would intercept them near the barn.

They make it to the knoll paralleling the barn moments ahead of the prowlers.

"Pa," Reese huffed, out of breath. When Kitty hesitated, he growled the down command again. Kitty dropped to the ground on high alert, inching forward on his haunches. His chest was heaving as Reese squatted next to Kitty, laid a hand on the coyote's back, and using Zen-like concentration, brought his breathing under control. Kitty's acute night vision spotted the interlopers slithering along the northeast side of the barn moments before Reese sensed the pair's movements in the shadows.

Stevens and Silifax sneaked along the side of the barn until they were directly below where Reese and Kitty sat, motionless, crouching eight feet overhead, muscles twitching. Reese watched Stevens raise his hand and bring his partner to a shuffling stop, slide the night vision goggle strap from his shoulder, remove the protective lens caps, and hand them to Silifax. Stevens flicked the power switch to the "on" position and brought the unit to his eye. The familiar green field of vision seen when looking through a night scope did not appear. He rechecked the switch and brought the unit to his eye a second time, still nothing. Two sharp slaps and a restrained curse, and the instrument still would not cooperate.

"I don't suppose you bothered checking the batteries, did you, Mack? That thing hasn't been signed out in over six months," Silifax said, his voice sounding a little too amused for Stevens's liking.

Stevens had gone through a checklist before leaving Las Vegas. He had checked the dune buggy's battery, checked the vehicle's tire pressure, coolant levels, and fuel gauge. But no, he had not thought to check the night vision goggle's battery pack.

Silifax, having grown up in rural Montana, knew well how to prepare for the hunt. In Montana one always checked and double-checked his equipment before venturing into the field. His tone changed from amused to condescending. "You can take the suit out of the city, but you can't take the city out of the suit," he tittered.

Stevens kept his eyes on the house a few hundred yards away. He stuck his hand out behind him, and said, "Shut up, Harry, and hand me the lens caps."

Silifax handed him the lens covers with another heckle. "Here you go great white hunter."

It was while Stevens fumbled with the lens caps that Reese seized the opportunity for a surprise attack. He sprang from the knoll with his arms outstretched and slammed into both figures, knocking Silifax to the ground and Stevens off balance. The night goggle sailed into the darkness.

Stevens recovered first and drew his government-issued, semi-automatic pistol from the tactical holster strapped to his right thigh. But quicker than the gun could be brought to eye level, a spinning back fist impacted his wrist like a jackhammer. Stevens's gun found a place in the dark with the night vision goggle. A thrusting sidekick caught the agent square in the gut, lifted him an inch or two off the ground, and doubled him over at the waist. Reese dropped to a crouch and pivoted on one leg, the other sweeping Stevens's feet out from under him. The agent landed on his back with a hollow thud.

By this time Silifax recovered from his spill and drew his service weapon. He lined the laser sight on their attacker's center mass. Reese's eyes dropped to the glowing red dot on the middle of his chest. Even with cat-like reflexes, Reese knew he was not fast enough to stop the inevitable result of the increased pressure on Silifax's trigger finger.

Kitty was, and sixty-five pounds of fanged fury crashed into Silifax's shoulder. The weapon discharged, but with a face-full of claws and fangs the bullet missed its mark.

The battle was suddenly bathed in 30,000 candle-watts of handheld spotlight. "Might I suggest you drop your gun, young fellow?" Dakota said from behind the curtain of light, "Before I am forced to drop you."

His polite instruction was punctuated by the distinct sound of a shotgun slide ramming forward to charge the weapon. That sound alone has a tendency to relax the sphincter muscle of even the most courageous. Silifax was no exception.

The backup agent nervously swept his weapon between the available targets—a snarling coyote crouched on the peripheral and ready to spring; the attacker who was quickly fading into a curtain of darkness while calling the dog in Chinese; and a notable British accent calling the shots from somewhere beyond the light.

"FBI, you drop it, mister!" Silifax sure hoped his voice sounded more confident than he felt at the moment.

In the deafening silence, the shotgun's safety clicking off sounded like a crypt slamming shut.

Stevens stepped into the mix holding out from his chest the identification badge dangling from his neck on a chain. "We're FBI agents. I suggest you put down the gun," he said, almost casually.

Dakota kept the light focused on Silifax. "Him first."

Fearing his partner may get trigger-happy, Stevens stepped in front of Silifax and said, "Harry, holster your weapon."

Silifax glanced at the senior agent incredulously, and then immediately refocused on their adversaries. "You've got to be kidding Mack!"

"Harry," Stevens spoke to him as if coaxing a kitten out from under the bed. "Holster you weapon. We don't want anyone to get hurt here."

Grudgingly Silifax returned his sidearm to his holster but kept his hand close by, just in case.

Stevens brought his hand up and shielded his eyes. "There, it's away. Now how about lowering the light, partner."

Reese overflowed with rage. "How about explaining why you're sneaking up on my house in the middle of the night, *partner*."

Stevens squinted between splayed fingers. "To be perfectly honest with you I think we're in the wrong place."

"Indeed you have that correct, sonny," Dakota retorted.

Silifax, more survival conscious than Stevens, noticed the voices had separated, that they were no longer side-by-side, which meant that even if he could draw and fire before they reacted, the chances of bringing down both targets was minimal, a risk he was not willing to take.

Stevens had made the connection. It had to be Dakota Bricker holding the light.

Bricker's military file said he had grown up in England, hence the telltale brogue. Stevens attempted to cover the blunder of getting caught on Daniels's land with a cover story that was as unbelievable as the situation he found himself in.

"We were looking for a marijuana grow and guess we got lost, ended up on the wrong property." He tittered nervously. "It's pretty dark out here."

A skeptical snort escaped Dakota. "No one grows pot in the middle of a desert, Mr. FBI. You need some work on your fairytale."

In an attempt to end the Mexican standoff, Stevens tried the authoritative approach. "Look, mister. I told you, we're Federal Agents." He lifted his badge away from his chest a second time. "Now put down that gun and lower the light."

"I've a better idea," Dakota said, brusquely. "Since it seems only the two of you are impressed with the fact your *allegedly* federal agents, why don't you haul your Yankee rumps back up the hill, back to wherever it is you came from, and we'll call it a night."

Stevens stepped forward pointing his finger beyond the light. "I'm giving you a direct order. Put the gun down and lower the light."

For his efforts he saw the barrel of a shotgun poke into the light, followed by an ethereal growl.

"Under the current circumstances, my good man," Dakota jeered, "it appears you are not in much of a position to give orders. So allow me, instead. For the final time; hightail it the other direction and do it now!"

Stevens was dumbfounded. This was the first time in his career that he had encountered someone not immediately intimidated to capitulation with the invocation of *FBI*. He had no choice but to retreat and regroup. In the spotlight's peripheral glow he found the night vision goggle and his weapon, the latter of which he gingerly slipped it into his holster with two fingers. The agents from the most revered law enforcement agency in the world made a tactical advance to the rear.

Dakota remained vigilant with both the spotlight and shotgun until the agents crested the ridge and were out of sight. Once the coast was clear he extinguished the spotlight.

Reese dropped to his knees and ran his hands over Kitty's coat, checking the coyote for evidence the stray round may have found a lucky mark. He hugged Kitty's neck. "I owe you one you dumb mutt. You could have been killed."

"And, likewise, so could have you," Dakota said tersely.

Reese stood and shook Dakota's hand. "Thanks. I think I got in over my head that time."

"Do tell," Dakota scoffed. "Maybe the next time you'll listen to me, Reese. This was a job for the sheriff's office. You needlessly endangered yourself, and Kitty."

He slung the shotgun over his shoulder and turned for the house, grateful neither Reese nor Kitty were injured during the encounter with the FBI.

Silifax lined up the dune buggy's tires with the ramps and drove it into the truck's cargo hold. After tightening the tie down straps and slamming the hatch closed, he climbed into the cab. "We'll come back in the daylight with arrest warrants," he said. "Then we'll see who the real hot shots are."

A frustrated sigh came from the passenger seat.

"Great idea, Harry," Stevens said, condescendingly. "Why don't we get up real early in the morning and, right after breakfast, run down to the U.S. Attorney's office and tell her how we trespassed on a man's property without a warrant; got attacked by the Tasmanian Devil and his lobo wolf; fired a shot at an unarmed civilian protecting his property against armed intruders; and when she asks us to positively identify our assailant, we'll tell her we can't because we were blinded by a gun-toting English lighthouse." Stevens turned in his seat and glared at Silifax. "That's a wonderful idea you have there, Harry."

Silifax closed his door and stared out through the windshield with his fingers poised on the ignition key. "That first guy materialized out of nowhere, didn't he, Mack? Like a shadow, he just sprang up out of nowhere."

Stevens slammed his door hard enough it rocked the truck. "Shut up and drive, Harry."

Chapter 18

Agent Stevens stabbed his finger down on the red flashing light on line three, wincing in pain as a bolt shot up his wrist. He drew the phone to his ear. "Good afternoon, Agent Stevens, how may I help you?"

"How goes it, Stevens?"

After an unusually long, and hectic Monday he was in no mood for Lincoln County's version of Sheriff Taylor, or any of his bumbling deputy Fifes. He turned his chair toward the window. "Fine, Austin. And how goes it with you?" he replied at his sardonic best.

Austin grinned at Stevens's obviously dour mood and moved on to the point of his call. "Hear tell a couple of your boys had a run in with Reese Daniels over the weekend."

Stevens sat up in his chair. "Is that so?"

"Yep. Said he caught a couple of your fellows slinking around his barn in the middle of the night; thought maybe you was rustlers or something."

The tone of Stevens's response told Austin his snicker had carried the desired effect. "If you recall, Austin, we're conducting an investigation into a dozen or so unsolved homicides the local police can't seem to solve."

Sheriff Austin rocked back and forth in his creaky chair, cradling the phone in the crook of his shoulder. "Mind if I ask who the agents was?"

"I'd love to tell you, Sheriff, but that's confidential Bureau information. Sorry. Why? Did Daniels file a complaint with your office?"

Stevens pulled the phone away from his ear when Austin bellowed, "Hell's bells no! To be honest with you, Stevens—and this is just between you and me—from the sound of it I think Reese had more fun handling it all by himself." Sheriff Austin brought his dusty boots to the top of his desk with a satisfied smile. "Just so happens I stopped by his place earlier this morning and it came up in conversation. He mentioned how he had a little ruckus with the FBI over the weekend, might have ruffed one of you boys up a bit."

Sheriff Austin slipped into his Detective Columbo, stupid-as-a-fox routine. "Didn't I tell you he was a karate nut? I think I did. I seen him break boards and bricks with his bare hands. Sure hope your boy wasn't hurt too bad, Stevens." Stevens remained quiet, so Austin continued with his taunts. "You know, Stevens, you should have called and let me know you boys was plannin' on goin' out there. I could have saved you a lot of grief."

Stevens gingerly adjusted the Ace Bandage wrapped around his wrist. "How's that, Sheriff?"

"Well, for openers I could have told you that Daniels's little kingdom in the desert has a better security system than Fort Knox. Seems the old paranoid Captain had surveillance cameras mounted everywheres. There's a bunch of pressure plates buried in the sand all around the house and barn, not to mention infrared sensors and thermal imagers hidden out in the desert, state of the art stuff. You can't get within half a mile of the house that Daniels or Bricker don't already know you're out there…somewheres."

Stevens, bored with the chastising, said, "Well thanks for the information, Sheriff. If the Bureau needs your services, I'll be sure to give you a call."

"Stevens, the next time any of your boys decides to head out there, try doing what I do to get inside."

"What's that, Austin?"

"Ring the doorbell." The sheriff's annoying chortle trickled through the line. "You may have to wait on the porch for a few minutes but it sure beats the alternative. Trying to sneak up on Daniels can be a little tricky. Kind of like plucking hairs out of a wild boar's nose, if you know what I mean."

"Good bye, Sheriff."

Austin's feet hit the wood plank floor in his office with a thud. "Stevens, just one more thing before you hang up."

"I'm listening, Sheriff, but not for long."

"Soak your hand in a bucket of ice, keep it wrapped, the swelling should go down in a day or two, three at tops."

"Thanks for the medical advice, Austin. I'll give it a try."

It was not until after he hung up the phone that Stevens realized he had as much as admitted to being one of the agents that invaded Daniels's ranch.

Chapter 19

Enough time spent scouting Internet Relay Chat rooms, sitting in the wings watching and waiting, and any dedicated vigilante is able to gather enough information about his target to make a positive identification. Shadow Man had proven the theory correct time and time again. Over the years he had discovered there is one constant in human nature; people like to talk, mainly about themselves. After a few short months researching the Internet, he was ready to move against his next target. Shadow Man had inadvertently stumbled into the IRC room where Don Mathers and his predator friends frequently discussed their sexual preferences with children, as well as disclosing personal details of their lives, all under the Internet's umbrella of anonymity. After a short time he connected the screen name to the person, validated it with a clandestine visit to Mathers's apartment, and then formulated a plan to eradicate him. While the Internet allows a person sitting at the keyboard to become any persona they choose, it also permits those with the patience and dedication to gather enough information to reveal the identities of those they seek.

The staff at the front desk of the Desert Acres Assisted Care facility always gave Don Mathers a long, second look when he arrived wearing his Tropicana Security guard uniform. Each time the routine was the same: Mathers marched down the hallway like a spit-shined, squared-away Marine, the nurses ogled. He flashed a bashful, introverted smile and waved while they tittered like love-struck sixth graders. And considering

Mathers's penchant for children, he may have expressed more interest had they been nearer to that age.

He made a left turn into the B-wing hallway and swaggered to a hesitant stop in front of room number twelve. He poked his head around the doorjamb with the guilty expression of a child caught with his hand in the cookie jar. The old lady sat in a wheelchair parked in front of the window. She was staring catatonically at a panoramic view of the parking lot and lawn maintenance shed. Bolted high in a corner of the room near the ceiling, a nineteen-inch Zenith television set played out the black and white action of the old western, "Only the Valiant", staring Gregory Peck. While medicinally clean, the room still had that distinctive old people smell about it, the sinister presence of the Grim Reaper, which had prompted Mathers's visit, still hung in the air like a thick fog. One of the two single beds had been stripped bare; ninety-four year old Beatrice Starr crossed over to the Promised Land last night in her sleep. The old lady reflected in the glass was happy she had, death being her only affordable means to a private room.

She spoke without turning from the window. "Donny, come give your Mama some sugar," she said in a squeaky, raspy voice.

Mathers jammed nervous, sweaty hands into the pockets of his uniform pants and made his way across the room. He leaned down and moved his pursed lips toward his mother's cheek. Ruth Mathers snapped out an arthritic lobster claw hand, clamped it onto the back his neck and, with surprising strength for a wheelchair bound old lady, twisted his face toward hers, kissing him full on the mouth and plunging her tongue deep inside.

Mathers could not wrench his hands out of his pockets fast enough. He shoved his mother's wheelchair away and stepped back wiping his mouth with the back of his hand, nearly retching. The wheelchair caromed off the wall with a metallic clang.

Ruth Mathers turned unblinking lifeless eyes—irises the color of sun-bleached sand, eyes that had frightened him his whole life—to her son, and said, "That's no way to treat a crippled old lady." She cut loose with a sinister laugh.

Mathers moved to the opposite side of the room and forced his hands back into his pockets.

When Bobby Sheer opened the apartment door, boy was he surprised to see, standing in the hallway wearing a policeman's uniform, his summer camp counselor. The scorn he addressed Mathers with was unmistakable. "I didn't know you were a cop," he spat. "What are you doing here? I didn't do nothing wrong."

"I'm not a cop." Mathers pointed to the shoulder patch on his sleeve. "Casino security at the Tropicana. I had to make a quick stop at Walgreens on my way home so I thought I'd drop by and say hello."

The fact that Mr. Mathers was a rent-a-cop and not a real cop assuaged some of Bobby's hatred for those in uniform.

"I heard that some of the older kids gave you younger dudes a rough time last weekend," Mathers said. "I didn't know about any of that crap until Pastor Davis told me about it." Mathers forced a sympathetic smile. "I wanted to stop by and apologize for what happened."

The previous weekend Mathers took a group of boys (underprivileged kids sponsored by the Mountain Valley Lutheran Bible School) on a canoeing and hiking expedition to the Kershaw-Ryan State Park near Caliente on the east side of Lincoln County. The older boys, led by senior group leader Johnny Edwards, whooped and hollered like a primal tribe while they forced the younger ones to disrobe and jump into Meadow Valley Creek. When Bobby refused, Edwards and several of his cohorts ganged up on him, ripped off his clothes, dragged him kicking and cursing to the creek, and threw him in. The following Monday morning Pastor Davis fielded a complaint from an irate parent and, in turn, confronted Mathers over the incident. Mathers claimed he knew nothing of the hazing, but, in truth, had captured the entire episode on digital video from his hiding place in the bluffs overlooking the creek. The testosterone-filled skirmish reminded him of one of his favorite films, "Lord of the Flies", a coming of age movie where naked and half-naked boys frolic on a deserted island after a plane crash. Uninhibited by social restraint, they established a pecking order through intimidation and brutality, and

Mathers was well accomplished on how to use both to get what he wanted.

Bobby scuffed the threadbare carpet with the toe of his dirty tennis shoe. "It was no big deal, Mr. Mathers. They're a bunch of idiots."

"Pastor Davis and I had a long chat about the whole episode. We decided if Edwards can't act like a group leader, he's out."

Bobby looked up from the floor. "Really?"

Mathers nodded with a rueful smile. "Really," he said, and then turned for the stairs.

Bobby leaned his skinny frame into the hall. "Want to come in for a minute?"

Mathers glanced at his wristwatch as if he had someplace else to be. "Maybe for just a minute."

Bobby nudged a well-used Fisher Price scooter aside and flung the door open wider. "Don't mind the mess," he said. "I'm supposed to straighten up before my mom gets home, but that probably won't be for a while. She took my little sister shopping for school clothes. Megan starts first grade this year."

Mathers stepped over piles of dirty laundry, navigated around scattered toys, and followed Bobby the length of a fingerprint-smudged hallway. In a small bedroom halfway down the hall he saw a pink and blue Barbie blanket rumpled on the corner of a bare mattress resting at the foot of a single bed. Obviously, Bobby's mother and sister share a room.

The living room's condition was no better. Clothes, newspapers, and empty two liter soda bottles littered the floor. A worn coffee table courageously made its last stand in front of a secondhand couch leveled with two thick books. Considering they had not passed a second bedroom, Mathers assumed the couch also doubled as Bobby's bed. The tiny kitchen matched the rest of the apartment. Dirty pots, pans, and dishes flowed from the sink and spilled across a peeling faded Formica countertop. A stack of unopened mail sat on a rickety table at the center of the room waiting for attention. Mathers paused in the doorway, wondering if all people living in government-subsidized housing were filthy slobs, and quickly decided they probably were.

Bobby clanged loudly through the sink until he found an aluminum pot with the handle missing. He rinsed it under cold water, scraped away whatever was fused to the side with his fingernail, set it on the stove, and struck an old fashion wooden match. "Want a cup of coffee? All we got is instant," he said.

After working the midnight shift at the casino, and the horrendous visit at the nursing home, a coffee would hit the spot, but not if it came a' la carte with typhoid. "No thanks, Bobby. I can't stay that long," he said.

Bobby shrugged and tossed the match into the sink where it sizzled out, a smoky finger curling toward the ceiling. He made his way to the table, pushed the stack of mail aside, and said, "Have a seat, Mr. Mathers."

The soles of Mathers's spit shined shoes stuck to the linoleum floor as he moved to the table. The chair Bobby offered was covered with potato chip debris. Mathers brushed the crumbs to the floor, musing on how long it would take the cockroaches to find the feast.

"You start middle school this year don't you?" Mathers said, giving the chair a second look before sitting down.

"Yeah. I should have been there last year but I got held back in the fourth grade."

"I thought I saw on your emergency card that you were twelve," Mathers lied with a thoughtful scratch of his head. He knew Bobby's age.

"Thirteen last week," Bobby said at having proudly crossed the benchmark to the teen years.

Bobby opened the refrigerator, threw back three loud gulps of orange juice, and then noticed Mathers staring at him. He wiped his mouth on his shirtsleeve, returned the carton to the refrigerator, and slammed the door closed with a bang.

Mathers leaned forward intending to rest his hands on the table but thought better of it, and instead, folded them in his lap. "So, Bobby, you got any friends you hang with? I mean besides the kids at camp."

"No, not really. I think that's why Mom signed me up for the campout. She figured I'd meet some kids my age, I guess."

"Where'd you live before you moved here?"

"New York." Bobby's eyes and voice dropped toward the floor. "We moved clear out here to get away from my old man. He's a cop in

Yonkers. He beat the crap out of us whenever he got drunk, which was just about every day. None of his cop buddies would arrest him, so Mom decided she'd had enough and we split. I guess she figured Nevada was far enough away from New York. She got a job at one of the casinos and now we're stuck here."

"What's wrong with Nevada? I've lived here all my life," Mathers said. "I kind of like it here."

"It's too hot," Bobby said. "Especially when you're used to having snowball fights no later than Halloween."

"That's probably true," Mathers chuckled. "I've only seen snow once when I visited my grandma in Maine back when I was a kid. I don't care if I ever see snow again." He wrapped his arms around his shoulders and shivered. "Too cold for me."

"Your folks still live around here?"

"My dad died when I was real young." Another untruth. "My mother's in a nursing home and probably won't last more than a few months. She has Alzheimer's."

Mathers's father wasn't dead. He left twenty years ago when he realized his wife was as crazy as a bat, destined to get crazier, and he wasn't about to stick around for that ride. Ruth Mathers was healthy as a horse, had all her faculties, and, in all probability, would outlive her son—literally. Mathers doubted that Momma actually needed the wheelchair either. He had the sneaky suspicion she was every bit as mobile as he was. One afternoon when he stopped by Desert Acres for a surprise visit, he found her room locked. He bent down and peeked under the door, sure he'd seen a shadow cross on the polished floor. By the time the nurse's aid arrived with a key and unlocked the room, Momma was slouched over the side of the wheelchair, sound asleep.

Seeing how Bobby was alone in the apartment, and that he had established a rapport with him, Mathers made his move. A predator is a predator, whether an animal on the hunt for survival, or a predator hunting to satisfy a perverse self-need, they both possess the uncanny ability of seeking out the weak and cutting them from the herd. Predator

Mathers's choice of prey was one with low self-esteem, yearning for acceptance, and Bobby Sheer's pathetic, poverty-stricken life was a made-to-order shambles ripe for the harvest. Flattery on such kids had worked every time in the past and Mathers saw no reason to change tactics.

"You know something, Bobby," he said. "You did a pretty fair job at handling the canoe last weekend. I'll bet with a little practice you'd been real darn good."

Bobby broke into a large, self-conscious smile. "You really think so?"

"Think so?" Mathers dismissed the self-criticism with a wave of his hand. "I'm sure of it. All you have to do is remember to let the paddle do the work. If you use it like a rudder..." Mathers turned sideways in his chair and gave Bobby a quick demonstration on the art of steering a canoe. "It's that easy," he said with a snap of his fingers.

Bobby leaped onto the counter and copied Mr. Mathers's technique. "Hey, that's not too hard to do when you think of it that way."

"All it takes is a little practice and I'll bet you'd have it down pat."

Mathers snapped his fingers again, as if an idea just came to him. "You know something, Bobby..." He let his voice trail off to heighten Bobby's interest. "With the Edwards kid out, and you being thirteen and all...I could toss in a good word with Pastor Davis if you want me to. We're going to need a new teen leader to help out with the younger kids, and like I said, with a little practice you could be really good at teaching them how to use the canoes."

"Yeah?" Bobby slid to the edge of the counter where his zeal lasted but a moment. "But there ain't many places to practice steering a canoe around here. I mean, like, we're in the middle of the desert."

Mathers laughed with false gusto. "Yeah, I suppose you're right. But Grand Beaver Creek isn't more than a twenty minutes from here."

Bobby was cautious not to let his hopes soar; they'd been dashed too many times before. "So?"

"*So?* So I can borrow a canoe from the church and, if you're into it, teach you how to steer like a pro. Once you've proven to me that you can handle a canoe, I'll tell Pastor Davis we've got us a new teen leader."

Mathers arched his thick shoulders and flexed massive arms. "That's if it's okay with your mom, of course."

Bobby's heart skipped a beat as he grabbed the bait like a bass fresh out of hibernation. The idea of being a group leader, someone the other kids looked up to, came to when they needed help, or advice…well, that appealed to Bobby in a big way. Not to mention he would learn to steer a canoe better than anyone else in the whole camp, except maybe Mr. Mathers.

"Mom don't care what I do just as long as I don't get into no trouble."

"How much trouble can we get into camping?" Mathers lowered his voice. "Unless of course we get attacked by a wild bobcat."

"There ain't no bobcats around here," Bobby said, apprehensively, "are there?"

"I've never seen one, but I heard a couple of duck hunters saw one last spring up in the game refuge near Beaver Lake. And don't forget, Grand Beaver Creek runs out of the north side of the lake."

The tale of a wild bobcat was filled with enough hot air to fan the flames of a young boy's imagination, and Bobby's mind was made up. He would take Mr. Mathers up on the offer, become a teen group leader so the other kids respected him, and maybe, just maybe with a little luck, see a wild bobcat. All he had to do was convince his mother, and that shouldn't be too hard to do considering he would be with his camp counselor, therefore, be safe.

If only Bobby knew what he was getting himself into.

"Well I ain't going to say nothing about wild animals because she might not let me go," he said.

Mathers winked understandingly. "We'll keep that a secret between you and me." He glanced at his watch and stood. "Wow, it's getting late. I've got to get a move on. I wanted to stop by the gym," he gave his arms a posing flex, "and get a lift in before I head home for a little shuteye."

Bobby walked Mathers back through the disaster area and stopped with his hand on the doorknob. "Thanks for coming by, Mr. Mathers."

Mathers dropped his powerful hands onto Bobby's shoulders and kneaded the muscles. His mind was made up, too. After a quick workout he would go home and re-watch the video of Bobby being carried to the creek and thrown in. "Look, Bobby, if we're going to be canoe and camping partners you might as well call me by my name. Don, okay?"

Mathers shot his hand forward. "Well, my man, I've got to get going. Canoe partners."

"Canoe partners." Bobby shook hands while repeating the pledge. "Thanks for stopping by Mr. Mathers—Don. I'll check with Mom when she gets home. I'm pretty sure she won't care."

Bobby pulled the door open and found his mother standing in the hallway balancing a Goodwill bag of Megan's *new school clothes* on her knee and fumbling with a set of keys.

Donna Sheer immediately saw Mathers's uniform, and then looked at Bobby and said, "What did you do?"

Mathers reached a muscular arm into the hallway, relieved her of the bag, and handed it inside. "Give your mother a hand, Bobby," he said looking down at the little girl, curly golden locks framing crystal blue eyes, peeking out from behind her mother's legs. "Aren't you about the cutest little thing."

Megan disappeared behind her mother.

Bobby huffed the bag to his chest and made the introductions. "Mom, this is Mr. Mathers. He's the church counselor I told you about. Don, this is my mom, Donna. And the pain in the butt is my little sister Megan."

Megan's faced darted out from behind her mother long enough to stick her tongue out at Bobby, and the disappeared again.

Mathers shook Donna's hand. "Nice to meet you, Mrs. Sheer."

"Pleased to meet you, Mr. Mathers." Donna reached behind and dragged Megan into the apartment. "For a minute I thought Bobby was in some kind of trouble."

Mathers tossed Bobby's hair ("dirty blonde" was apparently tailor-made for Bobby) and then discreetly wiped his hand on his pant leg. "Not Bobby. He's a good kid." He turned to Bobby and said, "Got to go, my man."

He set the bag on the floor, exchanged a slick handshake, bumped fists, and said goodbye before closing the door.

"What was he doing here?" Donna said on her way toward the living room.

Bobby picked up the bag and followed. "He just stopped by to say hello."

Donna stopped abruptly at the end of the hall, folded her arms across her chest, and said, "Robert Andrew Sheer! I thought you were supposed to straighten up before we got home."

"Yeah, Andrew." Megan stuck her tongue out again.

Donna shook her head and walked across the living room where she dropped heavily onto the lame couch, the books supporting the end gave way. The couch thumped to the floor and Megan covered her mouth with her tiny hands, capturing a girlish titter. She snatched the bag from Bobby, dumped the hand-me-down contents onto the living room floor, and held up each outfit.

Donna propped her feet onto the coffee table, wiggled her toes, and leaned back to close her weary eyes. He would wait until later to mention the camping trip, Bobby plopped down on the floor next to Megan.

Chapter 20

Agent Stevens was glad to be back home. Well not exactly *home*, because home was the tiny borough of Griffith Creek, Tennessee, where he had grown up in a two-story red brick Victorian, along with three siblings and white lace curtains tied back from the windows with cotton sashes; the aroma of southern hospitality in the way of fresh apple pies and fried chicken permeating the air in every room in the house.

He stepped off the plane at the North Las Vegas Air Terminal, grateful to be out of smog-ridden Los Angeles, the only place he found more fetid than Las Vegas.

For the past week the Bureau had played its part in a multi-jurisdictional task force comprised of the nation's most elite law enforcement agents from the FBI, U.S. Marshal's Office-Fugitive Task Force, ATF, and LAPD's S.W.A.T. team. They had spent long days crashing through crack houses in the bowels of Los Angeles' Compton district chasing federal fugitives, not MacKenzie Stevens's idea of law enforcement. But when the Bureau says go, you go.

He drew in a deep breath of arid desert air. Yes, it was good to be back in Las Vegas.

He tossed his luggage into the trunk and slammed closed the lid of his unmarked car, walked to the driver's side, unlocked the door, and climbed in behind the wheel. His immediate plan, right after adjusting the car's air conditioning vents, was to stop by the office and check his voicemail and the "while you were out" messages on his desk. After that it was straight home for a treat of medium-well onion-grilled steak and a bowlful of creamy instant mashed potatoes, dripping with butter. He planned to finish off the evening with a glass or two of velvety red Pinot Noir and relax in the hot tub. But as luck would have it, he found himself bogged down in traffic at the intersection of Sahara Avenue and Las Vegas Boulevard, the north entrance to the Strip.

Stevens would not have complained if someone had kicked him in the seat of the pants for not cutting across Rancho Drive, picking up Industrial Boulevard, and cutting across the casino-laden Strip to his office on East Charleston. Nearly four years at his Las Vegas assignment and he was still amazed at the volume of cars, buses, limousines, and taxis cramming nightly onto the Strip. With heavy eyelids and a growling belly he cast a lethargic glance to the line of cars waiting in the lane next to him. And, as if looking at a mirage, he blinked his eyes and shook his head. When he did a retake his chin nearly bounced off the steering wheel.

Seated behind the steering wheel of a shiny black Lincoln Navigator waiting for the right turn arrow sat the elusive Shadow Man. Stevens easily recognized him from their late night encounter in the desert.

The agent instinctively leaned forward and groped under the dashboard for the hidden microphone, the multiplex T-1 radio transmitter concealed in a false compartment beneath the spare tire well in the trunk allowed him direct communication with any police agency in Nevada, Arizona, Utah, and California, not to mention all the Federal agencies. He keyed the microphone prepared to alert Las Vegas Metro P.D. that they had an unlicensed driver entering the north end of the Strip. Daniels's presence on the Strip could mean but one thing: Shadow Man was stalking his next victim.

Stevens brought the microphone to his mouth and the idea struck, like a piano dropped from a third floor balcony. If he could figure out who Shadow Man's intended victim was, set up a stakeout so he was present when the killer came calling, his chances of catching Daniels red handed was a wager John Dowe would sink an entire paycheck on. He released the transmit button and returned the microphone to its hiding place.

Identifying the next Shadow Man victim and stopping the killer before he carried out his plan had the potential of killing two birds with one stone. He would *finally* have Daniels in custody, as well as his pedophile target. The double whammy brought a smile to Stevens's face, because, while life offers few guarantees, if his plan worked, he would almost bet that his transfer would be fast-tracked, and Memphis' moderate summers were a lot more appealing to him than Nevada's oppressive scorchers.

Agent Stevens nervously drummed the top of the steering wheel and waited for Daniels to make his move. Just in case that clod Austin was right about Bricker and Daniels working as a team, the agent's highly trained eyes searched the line of cars in front of and behind Daniels for the English butler. Although he had not seen Bricker the night they invaded Daniels's property, he was confident he would recognize Bricker from the photo Nevada DMV emailed him.

Stevens glanced between the dashboard clock and the wristwatch strapped to his wrist. Friday night at seven-thirty; surely there would be no one other than the switchboard receptionist at the field office, and time did not permit him calling in agents to help with the surveillance. He, and he alone, would have to handle the tail of Shadow Man.

The traffic signal changed and Daniels's vehicle lurched forward with the rest of the impatient motorists pining for the Strip. The agent broke lanes without a turn signal and cut off a black stretch limousine, earning him a long horn blast and a single finger salute. Daniels was already half a block ahead when Stevens charged through the red light, tires squealing, and found himself pulled to the curb by a L.V.P.D. motorcycle officer's pulsating blue light. He leaped from the car and ran back to the officer with his badge and identification wallet held out, necktie and eyes flicking over his shoulder at the escaping Lincoln. After a curt explanation that he was on assignment, Stevens ran back to his car, jumped inside and slammed the gearshift to drive, his tires chirping as he pulled away.

He caught up with Daniels in the curb lane near the Westward Ho Casino where he hung back several cars in line at the red light, and in the unlikely event Daniels recognized him from their impromptu meeting, Stevens folded down the sun visor. He found chasing a serial killer a whole bunch more stimulating than chasing warrant dodgers. He watched Daniels twist his head back and forth looking at ubiquitous neon signs blazing night into day, at taxicab drivers charging across multiple lanes using a combination of accelerator, horn, and hand gestures, tourists' faces pressed against windows in combined terror and awe.

Daniels continued south along the Strip and, to Stevens's utter amazement, stopped smack dab in traffic blocking two lanes like he owned the boulevard. He watched the swashbuckling outdoor "Pirate's Cove" performance in front of the Treasure Island Casino until an impatient horn edged him forward.

With a conceited smile, Stevens stuck to Daniels like a shadow to its host. They passed the Mirage, Flamingo, Barbary Coast, and Caesar's Palace, where, once again, Daniels interrupted the Strip's frenzied pace and paused in front of the Bellagio to watch the casino's famous Dancing Fountains. Half way between the Monte Carlo and MGM Grand casinos, Daniels sidled the Lincoln across four lanes of traffic and came to a stop at the head of the LEFT TURN ONLY lane. A dozen cars back, Stevens mirrored his objective's movements.

The green arrow appeared and Daniels turned onto Tropicana Avenue, quickly making the right turn into the Tropicana Hotel and Casino. Stevens edged his car up the sloping driveway in time to see Daniels come to a stop in the "Valet Parking Only" lane. He eased the unmarked car to the curb and slid down until his eyes were at dashboard level.

Daniels stepped from the SUV and—dressed as inconspicuous as any other tourist in dark glasses, a baggy white long sleeve shirt, black jeans and athletic shoes, navy blue Nike baseball cap pulled down to eye level—stretched his arms overhead. The agent watched Daniels tip the valet attendant, pocket his parking stub, and then walk toward the building on a cautiously alert stride. He waited until Daniels was out of sight before leaping from his car and making a mad dash for the doors, fearing he may loose Daniels to the crowd inside the casino. Stevens's hand was reaching for the door handle when the parking attendant intercepted him, thumbed over his shoulder, and said, "Sir, you can't leave an unattended vehicle parked there."

Stevens's eyes remained fixed on Daniels as he walked into the crowded lobby. He flashed his shield over his shoulder, and out of the side of his mouth, said, "FBI, official business." The wallet snapped closed, brusquely, and he hurried inside after his quarry.

Where the lobby's glistening marble floors met the bright-red carpeted pathways leading into the casino's gambling area, Reese stood frozen, lost, drawing in deep *dantian* breaths. The close proximity to the jostling crowd, most on their way to the slot machines, did little to console his agoraphobia: the abnormal fear, or avoidance of public places. From behind the safety of wraparound sunglasses, Reese's eyes bounced nervously from side to side taking in the bustling crowd and commotion on the casino floor. He spotted a vacant counter top near the "Tourist Information Booth" and moved warily in that direction. Once he felt safe from physical contact with the throng, he casually leaned his back against the counter and spent several minutes bringing his troubled *chi* under control. Finally, he ventured into the casino and used inconspicuous body adjustments to thread through the crowd with minimal contact.

Employing the techniques learned in the National Academy's "Suspect Surveillance" class, Stevens maintained a comfortably observant distance while pursuing the killer through the casino.

On his trek through the gaming area Daniels stopped occasionally and watched patrons slide currency into the noisy machines. He stood back from the Blackjack tables while mountains of currency passed to the dealer's side of the table, smiling weakly as the well-endowed cocktail hostess, her tray loaded with empty glasses, worked her way around the tables taking drink orders, emptying ashtrays, and being ogled by pie-eyed gamblers.

As she moved away from the tables Reese stepped in front of her. "Excuse me, Miss. May I have a double Jack and water, please?"

She sashayed around him without breaking stride, oblivious to whom she was speaking she said in a gruff voice, "You have to be seated at a table or one of the machines before I can serve you."

Reese's shoulders sagged with disappointment. He looked around for another hostess, and seeing none, bellied up to a bar other than one of the several at his home.

Two young black men in their early twenties sporting dreadlocks, loud Hawaiian shirts, and white cotton slacks worked the congested horseshoe-shaped bar. They tossed liquor bottles between them like a well-rehearsed juggler's act, and with adept precision, poured drinks to the enthusiastic applause of a three-deep mob pressed against the bar. One stopped in front of Reese and shouted above the din, "What ya' drinkin', mon'?"

"Double Jack and water, please," he replied timidly enough to bring the bartender's cupped hand to his ear.

"Say again, mon'."

Reese repeated his order.

"It be comin' right up."

After two years at the "Beachcomber Lounge" he had no need to search the shelves stacked in front an opaque mirror etched with a tropical sunset. Except for the juggling act, he could have done his job blindfolded. He pulled a bottle of Jack Daniel's from the second shelf, tossed it into the air and caught it behind his back, and at the same time snatched a glass from atop a crystal pyramid stacked near the cash register. A scoop of ice, two streams of the bronze liquid, a splash of water from the multi-flow beverage nozzle under the counter, drop in a swizzle straw, set a paper napkin on the bar, and the drink was finished; elapsed time, ten seconds.

"Six-fifty', mon'." He set the drink on top of the napkin.

Reese dropped a ten-dollar bill onto the bar and picked up his drink, but before he had a chance to sample it the bartender laid his change and receipt on the bar.

Reese waved it back to the young man.

"Thank you, sir," he said with a broad smile, scooped up the tip, deposited it in a jar next to the cash register, and then moved down the line to further entertain the crowd.

Reese carried his drink away from the bar to a row of vacant slot machines. He set his glass on a quarter machine, pulled out a foil wrapped anti-bacterial towlette from his back pocket, sanitized his hands, and tossed the towlette and wrapper into the wastebasket. He wandered deeper into the casino leisurely sipping his drink and occasionally stopping to watch gamblers at the slot machines or blackjack tables. After several minutes surveying the craps table, he shook a confused head and moved on. Nearly a half hour was used up studying the Pai Gow tables, seemingly the favored game of the Tropicana's Oriental patrons. He sat through two Kino games and wandering to the Texas Hold 'Em poker room at the back of the casino.

Stevens shadowed Shadow Man's every move, making sure he did not end up in Daniels's direct line of vision.

While the target wandered around the Texas Hold 'Em poker room, Stevens removed his necktie and tucked it into the pocket of his suit coat, undid the top two buttons of his shirt, and mussed his hair. Under the current circumstances it was the best he could do to change his appearance. His badge gave him the liberty of turning the Security Desk into a coatroom kiosk.

Reese emerged from the "Poker Room" and set his empty glass on a nearby combination trashcan/ashtray before heading toward the Tropicana's Island Buffet. He milled about aimlessly near the elevators looking at the framed watercolors hanging on the wall, waiting for a family of five lined up at the entrance to make their way inside.

He hung back until Daniels paid his admission and was deep inside the diner before Stevens paid his way inside, immediately concealing himself behind the salad bar's protective glass hood.

He watched as Daniels meandered about the eatery like an undercover health inspector. He stood in front of the kitchen's swinging doors, peering inside each time they opened until askance glances from the hostesses encouraged him along. The agent was sure he saw a smile on the killer's face when a busboy and waitress launched a two-prong attack on a recently vacated table; the busboy cleared dishes while the waitress misted the table with disinfectant and wiped it clean.

Stevens loaded his plate with onion-grilled filet mignon and mashed potatoes, baptized it with brown gravy, and found a table giving him a covert view of the exit. But, much to his chagrin, Daniels left the restaurant before he had a chance to take his first bite of dinner. He looked at his plate with a rueful sigh, and waited until Daniels's silhouette passed the frosted-glass exit windows before taking up the chase.

His quarry walked the length of the glass-enclosed Island Tower Walkway, and disappeared into the crowded Tropics Lounge.

Stevens's eyes adjusted slowly to the bar's hazy interior. Initially he thought the room was filled with smoke, but quickly realized the swirling smog was the work of a fog machine meant to give the illusion of a mist rolling in off the ocean. Brilliant red, blue, and yellow spotlights bathed a small bamboo thatch stage, contrasting sharply with the room's gloomy interior. Two barefoot olive-skin Polynesian princesses—wearing traditional Hawaiian grass skirts and revealing vibrant pink halter-tops—stood at the center of the stage. A dozen brilliantly colored parrots, macaws, and cockatoos sat on perches, as well as on the girls' shoulders, while entertaining the audience with their linguistic skills and tumbling antics.

Stevens had no difficulty spotting his objective; he stood out like a second thumb at an empty corner of the bar, sipping a reddish-orange drink with a tiny parasol attached to the side of the glass, a crumpled foil wrapper on the bar in front of him. Daniels stayed for most of the fifteen-minute "Exotic Birds of Paradise" performance, but quickly picked up his drink and departed as the crowd sprang to their feet, applauding fervently.

Once they were back inside the casino, Stevens gave serious consideration to following Daniels into the men's room but decided the quarters could prove a little too cramped for his anonymity. Instead, he hid behind a rambunctious throng crowed around a craps table. He watched Daniels emerge, glance around hesitantly, gather his bearings, and again go on the prowl. Shadow Man's shadow melted from the crowd and followed.

Daniels responded to a squealing player seated at a nearby slot machine with an abrupt about face and almost bumped into his stalker. Stevens's hands snapped in front of his face as he turned away and faked a sneeze; thanking his good fortune the prey's attention had been focused on the progressive slot machine with three red-white-and blue 7s across the pay line. He watched Daniels edge away from the gathering crowd as the slots host validated the win, cleared the machine, and counted aloud with the crowd as she deposited fifteen crisp one hundred dollar bills in the guest's quivering palm. Reese found himself drawn into the excitement, almost to the point of joining in. But the good sense to avoid crowds returned by the time the tenth bill landed in the outstretched hand. He turned away and walked through a set of thick, double glass doors.

Stevens stayed inside the casino and watched from a vantage point behind floor-to-ceiling windows carved with flamingos and palm trees. A puzzled brow wrinkled when Daniels strolled across the wooden footbridge connecting the casino to the "Island Wedding Chapel's" gazebo. He vanished inside.

Reese stepped into the gazebo with a quick neurotic look around. Satisfied he was alone, let his weary, lithe frame sink to one of the bamboo benches. He set his glass on the window ledge and brought his chin to rest atop his folded arms. Like a defeated puppy he sat staring listlessly across the empty Lagoon Swimming Pool's sparkling blue-green water.

Although Stevens changed locations several times he was unable to see what Daniels was looking at, if anything. He did, however, watch intently as a Tropicana security guard approached the gazebo.

Officer Mathers stepped into the gazebo and said, "Excuse me, Sir. You're in an area that's closed for the evening." Mathers found he was being ignored by the little Chinaman who *plobably no-speaka'-the-Engrish*, and he stepped closer, jabbing Reese's shoulder with his finger. "Hey buddy. I said you're going to have to move along. This area is closed."

Reese slowly craned his neck around until his ominous eyes landed on Mathers. For a moment, he thought about latching hold of the guard's finger and snapping it like a pencil. That should teach him to keep his hands to himself. But, there would be time in the not too distant future to deal with the towering oaf's unwarranted touching. Wordlessly, Reese rose and walked back into the casino with Mathers close on his heels.

Daniels retraced his steps back toward the lobby.

Stevens realized his quarry was leaving, so he quickly reclaimed his apparel from the security desk and waited inside the lobby until Daniels exchanged his parking pass and empty glass for his black SUV. He again tipped the valet, and then climbed behind the wheel of the Lincoln.

Daniels was pulling out from beneath the overhead canopy when the agent burst through the doors. Keeping his eyes fixed on the SUV he sprinted to his car anxious to see where Daniels would venture next. He skidded to a stop near the curb and slapped his hands against his thighs.

"What do you mean you had it towed?" he bellowed to the attendant. "I told you I was on official business!"

The Valet shrugged and pointed to the "NO UNATTENDED PARKING" sign. The sign had not expedited the removal of Stevens's car nearly as much as the fifty-dollar bill tucked into the attendant's palm by the grumbling patron in the black Lincoln. While he complained about how some people think they're above the law, he also promised another fifty if the car was gone before he returned.

Reese drove north out of Las Vegas on I-15 with his eyes focused on the rearview mirror as much as the road ahead. He exited and reentered the freeway three times before he was satisfied enough to relax in his seat. With a white-knuckle grip on the steering wheel, he pondered why the FBI had followed him the length of the Strip and through the Tropicana.

Chapter 21

The essence of qigong [Chi' Kung] is the healing of mind and body through meditation, deep breathing, and movement. Well-disciplined Wushu masters, like fashi Tian Xian Huo, are quite capable of achieving hours of meditative tranquility, unlike most Westerners, whose ambitious thoughts are silenced but for moments. The recent intrusions into Reese's solitary lifestyle were creating too many demands, too many distractions. He found himself thinking and acting like a harried Westerner more than the Eastern mystic practitioner he was, and he did not like it, not one bit!

A clap of thunder rumbled him back to the here-and-now side of consciousness. He opened his eyes from where he sat on the hardwood floor at the center of his tiyuguan. The candle on the altar had melted down to a one-Lux puddle of wax. A second reverberating crack rattled the house and spoke volumes to the rapidity of the approaching storm. He rose from the floor in a fluid motion, walked to the altar, blew out what was left of the candle, and then made his way to the door, pausing with a reverent bow.

Kitty skidded to a frenzied stop in the hallway, nearly crashing into Reese's legs as he backed from the room. The coyote did an about face, clawed for traction on gleaming Brazilian hardwood, and raced ahead of Reese toward the family room. He was prancing in front of the doors as if his bladder was about burst when Reese crossed the room and slid the door open. Kitty bounded out onto the pool deck.

Reese looked northwest to ominous black clouds sweeping down over the ridge and boiling to the desert floor like an overflowing caldron, fueled by hell's fire. He had watched many storms cross the landscape during his years at the ranch, but only once recalled one so menacing. For a moment he stood motionless in the doorway, his thoughts drifting back to when he was a youngster.

The storm blew up out of nowhere as he raced to the barn, sand biting his skin like a swarm of stinging bees. Once he was inside the barn, he killed the quad's engine, peeled out of his helmet, and decided to wait out the storm with the horses. The wind's velocity reached a point that he actually thought the barn was about to collapse. Suddenly, Dakota filled the doorway shouting unintelligible words. He found his arm clutched in Dakota's powerful hand, held so tight he had bruises the following day, and, amid swirling sand and flying patio furniture and fence rails, was dragged to the house and shoved inside. It had taken all Dakota's strength to force the doors closed.

The Captain stood on the other side of the room swishing his drink around in his glass. "What's the matter, Brick, afraid of a little wind?" he guffawed on his way to the French doors. That maniacal laugh of his lasted but a second; the wind launched a patio table through the doors and knocked the drunken fool flat on his butt.

Reese shook the ancient memory from his head and stepped out of the house, the chilled air riding the leading edge of the storm hit him full in the face and rocked him back against the house, stealing away his breath for a second. Sensing impending doom, Kitty raced around the pool, leaped over the wrought iron gate, and disappeared into the wall of sand sucked from the desert floor.

Reese fought his way to the barn amid blowing debris. It took all his strength to pry the barn door open, the force of the wind tearing the handle from his hand and sending the door crashing against the side of the barn. He dove through the opening as the door slammed closed with enough force to amputate a limb.

Upon seeing Reese roll out of a summersault, and spring to his feet with cat-like grace, Dakota gave a sigh of relief. They sandwiched Timmy between them, each holding an arm in a tight grip, and pushed out into the storm. With the wind at their backs they were practically carried to the house.

Once he was sure everyone was safely inside, Dakota left Timmy in Reese's care and ran from the family room, taking the stairs to the upper level three at a time. He made a left at the top of the staircase and sprinted down the hallway where he yanked open the security room door, clapped his hand against a red plunger switch next to the control panel, and fell back against the wall breathing a sigh of relief to the sound of heavy galvanized steel hurricane shutters (installed on all doors and windows after the late R.B. Daniels caught the patio table on the chin) electronically sealing the house from the elements. He paused to catch his breath before returning to the family room.

Reese clicked a light on just as the power went out, three seconds later the emergency generator kicked in. "Are you okay, Tim?" he said.

Timmy was terrified and on the verge of tears. "What in the hell is it, a tornado?"

Dakota supplied the answer from the doorway. "It's a microburst."

Timmy's bottom lip was quivering when he asked what a microburst was.

"An extremely strong, concentrated downdraft," Reese said. "Every once in a while a wind shear crashes down out of the mountains and races across the desert floor. They're short lived, but because there's nothing in their path, they scream across the desert with tremendous force."

"Are you sure you're, okay?" he asked again.

Timmy swiped a tear from the corner of his eye and nodded his head.

A solid, sickening thud crashed against the outside of the house.

Timmy looked around the room. "Where's Kitty?"

Reese and Dakota looked toward the sealed, steel door. All they could hope was that Kitty's natural survival instincts had not been domesticated out of him.

Chapter 22

Dakota was looking out through the family room doors (formally dressed in a black velvet butler's vest, white long sleeve shirt, black bowtie, slacks and patent leather shoes) when a blue and white Bell 427 helicopter descended out of the cobalt sky, the Daniels Industries' logo disappeared from sight as the blades thumped the desert into a miniature sandstorm. The aircraft touched down between the house and barn as lightly as if landing on a bed of eggshells. After the dust settled, Dakota opened the doors and walked around the pool, and stopped with his hand on the wrought iron gate. The blades whined to a stop, and three suit-clad figures jumped down from the aircraft, the last passenger to the ground carried a black leather attaché case. Dakota held open the gate for the guests, and then silently escorted them into the house. The pilot waited until his cargo was inside before dusting the desert floor with a liftoff whirlwind.

Dakota ushered the gentlemen on a crisp pace through the family room and down the long hallway ending in front of a set of double oak doors across from Reese's workout studio. He grasped the media room's antique brass doorknobs and pushed, waving the entourage inside. Dakota moved across the room, stood stiffly next a table covered by a red tablecloth with black linen napkins, folded in pyramid fashion, standing up in little peaks. With panache, he removed the lids from two British sterling hors d'oeuvres trays, and said, "Gentlemen, for your pleasure I have prepared Salmon Mousseline on toasted rye, and jumbo shrimp wrapped in garlic-roasted kelp. Mr. Daniels will join you in a few moments."

He made his way across the room and backed through the doors, closing them with a soft click. Dakota returned to the kitchen and went about putting the finishing touches on dinner: crisp garden salad, French onion soup, and roasted quail with duchess potatoes. He stood in front of the double oven donning oven mitts, whistling while he checked on the quail.

Reese materialized in the doorway like an apparition.

Dakota turned to his employer with an approving smile. It was rare Reese wore anything more formal around the ranch than shorts, a tee shirt, and sandals. He stood on the kitchen's threshold dressed in a tailored, white Italian-silk suit and pastel Perry Ellis Crosswick shirt, the top buttonhole and cuffs fashionably sporting black opal studs. On his feet he wore formal white dress shoes with black soles. The ensemble made him appear taller and stockier than he actually was. His choice of formal attire spoke volumes of how important this afternoon's meeting with two of the corporate attorneys, and the third person Dakota did not recognize, was to Reese.

Dakota worked the oven mitts off his hands, set them on the island countertop, rested his elbows on top of the mitts, and dropped chin to his palms. "You look very nice, Reese," he said.

It had been more than a decade since Reese took over control of the reigns that guided Daniels Industries. Always anal about his appearance when it came time for those rare face-to-face meetings with the highfalutin attorneys because he lacked a formal college education—although he had studied more mail-order tomes on business principles and philosophy than most corporate executives—Reese hid his insecurity by dressing the part of a highly successful CEO, and that was exactly what he was.

Reese took two nervous steps into the kitchen, and said, "Do I look *nice*, or do I look *professional?*"

Dakota chose the centerline. "You look professionally nice," he said.

Reese rolled his eyes and then locked them on Dakota. "Have I ever told you what Master Huo told me whenever I refused to make a decision about something?"

Dakota gave his best boy-am-I-going-to-be-bored-with-this-conversation look as Reese imparted tidbits of Chinese wisdom learned from his martial arts teacher.

"He used to say, yongbu xingzou zhengzhong daolu, nin shibi shoudao ya liangbian." That roughly translates into; don't walk in middle of road, get run over from both directions."

"Well thank you Kwai Chang Caine," Dakota said with a reserved applause better suited for a golf match. "Thank you so much for that most wonderful moment of philosophical Chinese reflection." He snatched the mittens from the counter and turned toward the oven to hide his smirk. "You look as professionally nice as any well-starched albino penguin, meeting with corporate attorneys he'd rather not be bothered with, should look. Now excuse me, sir. Dinner is about to burn."

Reese shifted his weight from foot to foot while Dakota transferred two Pyrex casserole dishes from the oven to the hot plate on the counter, and then closed the oven door.

"Dakota," Reese heard his voice falter, "I'd appreciate if you'd sit in on this afternoon's meeting."

Dakota did a slow about-face, his thick eyebrows furrowing. Early on Reese frequently asked his input regarding Daniels Industries' affairs, but over the years his contribution had been sought less and less until he was completely removed from the loop, business-wise speaking.

He gracefully declined the offer. "Thank you for the invitation, Reese, but I must keep an eye on dinner."

"Which eye would that be, Dakota? The chickens—"

"Quail."

"—birds look like they're finished to me. Besides, this won't take long."

Dakota leaned back against the counter and folded mittened hands across his chest. "Reese, it has been quite some time since you've involved me in your business affairs. Why this sudden change?"

"Because today I feel like involving you," Reese said with a playful twinkle in his eye. He added in his best Tarzan voice, "Me employer. You employee. Follow." He turned on his heels and strutted from the kitchen before Dakota could offer resistance.

Dakota gave his head a shake, hung the mitts on the hook next to the stove, and then joined Reese, who paced the hallway in front of the media room doors like a caged animal.

"Shall we?" Reese pushed the doors open.

Dakota tugged at the bottom of his vest, straightened his bow tie, and followed Reese into the private theatre.

Reese moved forward on bouncing steps and greeted his guests, all of whom were crowded around the hors d'oeuvre table and heavily indulging on Bricker's snacks. As if they had rehearsed the move, they all set their plates down in unison and tidied the corners of their mouths with a black linen napkin.

Reese dipped his head to the eldest guest. "Nelson."

Nelson Grover, senior partner of Grover, Rusk, Diamond, and Associates stepped forward to shake Reese's hand.

"Nelson," Reese tuned toward his butler. "You know Dakota."

Grover smiled and waved across the room. "Nice to see you again, Dakota." Grover nodded his head toward the display on the table. "I must say I believe those are the most delicious appetizers I've ever tasted. Garlic-roasted kelp, amazing, simply amazing."

Dakota humbly accepted the compliment. "Thank you, Sir."

Grover turned toward the approaching figures. "Dakota, this is Thaddeus Diamond. Thad, meet Dakota Bricker, he's been with the Daniels family longer than we have," he added with a chuckle.

Dakota stepped forward and gave a half bow as he clasped the outstretched hand. "Mr. Diamond."

"My honor, Mr. Bricker. And please, Thad. Everyone calls me Thad," Diamond said, his voice not betraying the fact that he was sucking up to the butler in hope of favorably impressing the host. "Nelson speaks of you often," Diamond continued, "and rather highly I might add."

Dakota offered Diamond a reserved smile and cordial nod while Grover introduced the last guest.

"Reese, Dakota, allow me to introduce Bill Masters. He's the newest addition to our firm, and a damn good numbers cruncher. He comes to us straight from the Nevada Gaming Commission. Hired him myself right after Reese called and told me…"

"Anyone care for a drink?" Reese blurted. He motioned Dakota to the bar with a nod, ignoring the butler's quizzical gape.

More in line with his duties, Dakota stepped behind the bar and prepared each guest's beverage of choice: a Scotch and soda for Grover, Diamond was a Seven&Seven, Masters a bottle of Corona. While the trio moved to the front of the room, Reese stepped behind the bar and discreetly sanitized his hands.

"Impressive media center you have here, Mr. Daniels," Masters said, carrying his briefcase down four tiers.

The media room was a horseshoe-shaped, four-tier amphitheatre. It had cushy gray carpeting and matching plush velvet theatre seats, six to a row. Added to the main house to accommodate corporate video presentations, and the late Captain's paranoia about leaving the ranch, the Sony rear projection television got more use out of Timmy than for its original purpose. He would often curl into a ball in the front row with a bowl of popcorn cradled in his lap, remote control in hand, and watch larger than life figures of Steven Seagal, Bruce Lee, and Jackie Chan dispatch legions of villains without so much as a scratch.

Reese stepped from behind the bar, accepted the whiskey and water Dakota handed off to him, and acknowledged Masters's compliment while taking a seat in the third row. "Thank you, Bill."

Dakota served the guests, and then claimed the aisle seat next to Reese. Grover and Diamond settled down in the second row, while Masters took his place at the front of the room. "Is it okay to set my drink here?" He waved his bottle over an expensive looking teak, octagon-shaped quartz-top table.

Reese raised his glass and nodded permission.

The accountant gingerly set his Corona and briefcase on the table, unpacked a laptop computer, and held up the connecting cord. "Mr. Daniels, sir, is your system USB compatible?"

"There's a receptacle recessed into the floor at your feet, Bill," Reese said, grinning at the notion the accountant insisted upon calling him 'Sir', even though he was twenty years senior.

While Master was busy setting up his computer Dakota leaned in closer to Reese and whispered, "What's going on?"

"A presentation of some sort, I suspect." Reese stared ahead at the blank screen.

Dakota cocked his head to the side and studied Reese's profile for a moment—something was definitely afoot—before he leaned back in his seat and quipped under his breath, "You don't say."

Master was plugged into the multimedia system and ready to begin his presentation. While they waited for Masters's PowerPoint presentation to load, Reese leaned to his left and whispered to Dakota the purpose of the meeting.

"Dakota, a few months back when our *visitors* showed up here in the middle of the night I told you I was working on taking Daniels Industries in a different direction." In his peripheral vision he saw Dakota's head bobbing.

"I apologize for being so evasive with you, but I wasn't ready to divulge my intentions. Now I'm ready. The *new direction* I was speaking of is that, as of last week, Daniels Industries made an offer to purchase the Tropicana Casino and Resort on the Las Vegas Strip."

Dakota snapped around in his seat and hissed under his breath. "What in the world would possess you to buy a casino?"

"Dakota, think about it," Reese whispered with a wary smile. "Name me one other place on earth, besides a casino, where the house makes up the rules…rules that border on cheating, and people flock there from around the world to spend money like it's made of toilet paper."

At the conclusion of Masters's presentation, Grover rocked his chubby frame out of the chair and waddled to the light switch. He turned up the lights, but not so bright as to obscure the spreadsheet display on the screen. Masters, nervous as the day he interviewed with Grover, Diamond, Rusk and Associates, six weeks ago, turned and addressed Reese.

"So as you can see, Mr. Daniels, Sir, with an aggressive marketing plan directed at the locals, those who live in and around metropolitan Las Vegas, Daniels Industries could realize as much as a fifteen percent increase in the Tropic's current casino revenues, which, incidentally, translates into somewhere between three-point-three, and four-point-one million dollars quarterly.

"I know you're probably thinking that's not a huge amount of money in the grand scheme of things, but it's only a start."

Reese leaned back in his chair, his drink cradled between his hands, and spent several minutes pondering the figures on the screen. He abruptly rose from his seat, and said, "Feel free to correct me if I'm wrong, Bill. But what you're telling me is that with as little as a five percent increase in the buffet line you feel confident our dinner guests, most probably, would be inclined to stay at the Tropicana and play our games? Increasing gaming profits, I believe you said, by as much as fifteen percent."

"Yes, Sir, Mr. Daniels. And keep in mind," Masters nodded toward the screen, "those figures aren't etched in stone. After going over the Tropic's books several times, I'm confident my projections lean toward the conservative side."

All eyes fixed on Reese when he stepped over Dakota's outstretched legs, walked to the bar, and poured a fresh drink (in a fresh glass of course). He sanitized his hands, returned to his seat, rested his chin on the rim of his glass, and mulled over the figures for several more tedious minutes. His voice echoed out of his glass when he finally elected to speak.

"Well then, gentlemen, as I see it the only obstacle to initiating our plan is finding the right person to take over control the buffet line and banquet rooms. Am I correct?" The question being rhetorical, Reese continued without waiting for a response. "According to your figures, Bill, if we draw as little as three percent of the business away from the casinos that cater to the locals—the Stardust, Palace Station, Riviera, so on and so forth—the Tropic's take should increase exponentially."

Grover turned around in his seat and rested his empty Scotch and water on the back of his chair. "Reese, we'll advertise nationally. Worldwide if need be. We will find that *someone* who's in line with our way of thinking. Once we plug Cinderella into the ballroom," Grover's skipped his fingers across the backrest of his seat. "The Tropicana will dance all the way to the bank on glass slippers."

The time had come for Reese to execute step one; one of several methodically planned changes to take place over the next few weeks. He sat down in his seat, sipped his drink, scanned the gigantic screen, and remained silent long enough that not only did Masters begin to question his figures, so did Grover and Diamond.

Grover nervously cleared his throat, and said, "Reese, if you're having second thoughts, it's not to late to back out. I built several CYA contingencies into the contract. They allow us thirty days to withdraw the offer."

Reese's dark brown eyes ignited. "Gentlemen, please allow me to introduce you to Cinderella." He turned in his seat. "The Tropicana's new head chef and buffet manager is going to be Michael Dakota Bricker."

Bricker, rather than Reese, or the numbers on the screen, became the center of their attention.

"I trust Dakota with my life, so what's a few hundred million dollars?"

The corporate stooges waited until Reese's face melted into a broad grin before Diamond and Masters joined Grover's disproportionate laughter.

Speechless, Dakota struggled to his feet, walked to the bar, and mixed himself a much stiffer gin and tonic.

"Reese..." Dakota quickly looked at the staring faces. "Excuse me, Mr. Daniels, I have far too many responsibilities here at the ranch to consider such a generous offer. After all, if my time is engaged managing a restaurant, who will do the cooking? And let us not overlook the domestic issues of laundry and cleaning."

Reese sat with his back to Dakota, rolling his glass between his hands. "I have an idea for all those *issues* Dakota."

"What of the voluminous maintenance projects? Who will care for those?" A nervous chortle escaped his throat. "It seems something is always going on the fritz around here."

"If I pinch my pennies, Dakota, maybe clip coupons out of the newspaper, I'm pretty sure I'll have enough left over to hire a maintenance man."

Grover and his minions laughed at the absurdity of Reese Daniels pinching pennies to hire a janitor. Dakota, on the other hand, shook a disconcerted head and continued to stammer for excuses.

"The horses also need to be considered. Who will care for the horses?" He glared at the back of Reese's head. "I will not stand by while Gus and Mollie and poor Trixie are sold off."

A sigh escape as Reese turned, buried both knees into his seat, and said, " 'A horse! a horse! my Kingdom for a horse!'

"My goodness, Dakota. Gus and Mollie and Trixie aren't going anywhere. Next problem?"

"Kitty!" Dakota blurted. "What about Kitty? Have you given thought of him, Reese? As you well know not just anyone can deal with Kitty."

After the hurricane shutters were retracted following the microburst phenomenon, Kitty stood in front of the sliding doors wagging his tail, none the worst for wear, except for a small gash across the bridge of his nose. He lay on his side in the family room, tail thumping the floor, while Timmy played Florence Nightingale with a bottle of peroxide and cotton balls.

"Kitty's taken care of," Reese said.

Grover, who had been to the ranch enough times, dating back to the late R.B. Daniels's days, was growing bored with the exchange. He nodded Diamond to the hors d'oeuvre table. Masters, on the other hand, had only met the wealthy host and his man "Friday" a little over an hour ago. He remained at the front of the room intrigued with the exchange.

Growing short on excuses, Dakota became ridiculously defensive. "You won't put Kitty down just to fatten your substantial bank accounts, Reese. I will not stand idly by for such an atrocity!"

Angrily, Reese launched from his seat, stopped in the aisle, closed his eyes for a moment to check his anger, and then said, "Michael, stop being obtuse. I'd never put Kitty down, not for money, or any other reason, and you know that."

Annoyed at the way Grover and Diamond were stuffing themselves at the hors d'oeuvres table, Reese said, "Nelson, you know your way around. Why don't you show Thad and Bill the swimming pool? Take them out to the barn and show them the horses."

Grover took the hint, set his plate on the table, and motioned for Diamond and Masters to follow him from the room. Reese waited until the door closed before storming across the room and slamming his glass down on the bar.

"What in the hell is wrong with you, Dakota? I thought this offer would be a pleasant surprise, my way of repaying you for taking care of me all these years. For putting your life on hold for this stupid ranch." He sank to a padded leather barstool and massaged his forehead. "Haven't you always dreamt of being a chef, owning your own restaurant?" His eyes drifted to Dakota's. "Don't you get it? Buying the Tropicana can make that dream a reality."

Reese shook his head wearily, stood, and walked to the front of the room. Maybe if he gave Dakota time to ponder the proposal, gave himself time to digest his unexpected rejection it would all make sense. He stared at the figures on the screen.

"It's not about money, Dakota. Goodness, neither of us needs to worry about money. The wacko, demented Captain saw to that. I'm sure he rolls in his grave at the mistake of not cutting me out of the will, but the fact still remains that we're both pretty damn wealthy.

"My buying a casino is about doing something different, something exciting for a change. Dakota, I'm no longer afraid to leave the ranch now and again. For months I've found myself looking forward to Nancy and Tim's visits, particularly when they stay overnight, and even more so when they stay over for the weekend. When they're around I find myself looking forward. I'm able to see the future instead of living in the past." Reese turned to his housekeeper with sad eyes. "I'm tired of living life with my eyes closed, Dakota.

"It all still scares me to death, but my life has changed over the past year and a half in ways I never thought it would, or could.

"Dakota, you hit the nail square on the head the night the FBI showed up here. I had been sneaking away, or at least thought I was sneaky." He flashed a shallow smile. "I had to go to Las Vegas to see it for myself. I had to see what it was like down there before I marched Daniels Industries into an unknown arena. I had to know, firsthand, what I was getting *all of us* into.

"Trust me, bouncing and jostling around all those people inside the Tropicana was terrifying. It's still unnerving, and I'm buying the place!"

"But you want to know what the weirdest thing for me to get a handle on is? No matter how apprehensive I was—am—around all those strangers, I find that I tingle with excitement at the thought of breaking out of this self-created prison the Captain taught me is a normal way of life. It excites the heck out me."

He walked to the top riser and buried his knees in the aisle seat of the back row, rested his forearms on the backrest, and studied Dakota's bowed profile.

"Dakota, look at me," he said, softly.

Bricker raised his eyes to Reese.

"Look at what I've become. I'm a pathetic, thirty-two year old social reject. My goodness, I'm the very person I hate the most. The Captain chose his hermit's lifestyle, and then forced me to live that way until I didn't know any other way existed. I don't want to live that way anymore. I'd rather join him than continue like I have been.

"I'm not so sure buying a casino is the right thing to do, but to me, it's far less important that I take Daniels Industries someplace new than it is I take Reese Daniels someplace new."

He walked to the bar and leaned his forearms against the chair rail. He looked directly into Dakota's eyes. "I don't give a rat's behind if the Tropicana makes a pennies' profit. If it doesn't," he shrugged, "so what. It becomes another tax shelter column in Masters's ledger book. Who cares?

"What do I care about is that it gives me a reason to step outside of this sterile bubble I've been living in. And that, my friend, is a good thing."

Reese migrated to the hors d'oeuvres table and sampled the kelp-wrapped shrimp. He popped the last morsel into his mouth as he reached the spot where Dakota stood, set his plate on the bar, licked his fingers, and thumbed over his shoulder.

"Now that's what I'm talking about. Those are way beyond delicious. Nobody can match you in the kitchen, Dakota. Nobody! Your managing the casino's bistro is important to me. It's not that I couldn't find someone else to do it, but I'll never find someone I trust as much as I trust you.

"I want to take the people I care about with me on this ride." Reese gently laid a hand on top of the thick arms folded on the bar. "In case you haven't noticed, Dakota, Reese Daniels, *'the kid millionaire'* the tabloids wrote about years ago, ain't so normal. He wants to cruise down a brand new road he never dreamt he'd have the courage to travel a year ago. Please Dakota, let me give instead of taking all the time. Let me repay you for everything you've done for me."

Reese toyed with the glass he had slammed to the bar for a moment, and then turned for the door. When he reached the edge of the media room's plush carpet he turned, shoved his hands into his pockets, and said, "Let me repay you for my freedom. And I think you know what I mean."

Dakota heard the fading sound of Reese's heels clicking down the hall.

His touching discourse stirred emotions within Dakota he thought he had buried with Emy. No matter how fast he blinked, a tear found its way down his cheek and splashed onto the ceramic tile bar top. In the years since baby Reese uttered his first words, never had he spoken so openly, so passionately as to cause Dakota's eyes to mist. The big housekeeper's frame sagged against the bar for support, his fingertips massaging his temples. He pulled a paper napkin from beneath the bar and wiped his eyes, looked over the bar at the open doors, and spoke to the empty room. "Let me think it over, Reese."

Chapter 23

Shadow Man sat slumped on a park bench looking more like a homeless vagrant than a murder, and that was the plan.

After months of tedious Internet searching, along with some careful planning and downright good covert stalking, he was seated across from Don Mathers's apartment waiting to strike—for the last time.

His final target, before retiring from his calling, would step from the apartment in the next few minutes and, if past practice proved consistent, would emerge wearing a skimpy onionskin jogging short and no shirt. The crowd of predominately elderly park goers' heads would turn, as they always did, to gawk at the chiseled Adonis' physique as he jogged through the park.

The thought that pedophile Don Mathers would strut past him without noticing (*see*, but not *perceive*) the person about to kill him brought an amused smile to the killer's face.

He lowered the newspaper slightly when Mathers stepped from the building, and with surreptitious eyes he watched the target saunter across the intersection, flexing his immense muscles.

Unlike the first few pieces of filth he had eliminated, Shadow Man no longer displayed any outward sign of nervousness. Killing experience bred confidence, along with a sense of invincibility.

Mathers strolled into the park and sat down on a withered patch of grass in the sparse shade of a palm tree, less than ten yards from the killer. He stretched his legs and looked around to see if he was being admired. The only person in sight was a bum on the park bench (wearing a black short sleeve shirt, charcoal sweats, and black athletic shoes), his face buried behind a newspaper that in all likelihood he'd rescued from a trash barrel. Mathers watched the bum listlessly toss handfuls of cracked corn to a bevy of pigeons milling about at his feet. Without an audience, Mathers stood and wandered deeper into the park.

After a furtive glance in all directions, and satisfied he was no more the object of anyone's attention than the pigeons at his feet, Shadow Man lowered the newspaper, stood, and stretched his arms overhead that sent a dozen of the more skittish pigeons fluttering a short distance away. He crammed the newspaper into a green wire trash container, vaulted over the bench, and silently disappeared into the undergrowth like a hunter in the forest, a soldier in the jungle, or a vigilante on a mission.

Unbeknownst to Mathers, his route and schedule had been monitored for several weeks. Every Monday, Wednesday, and Friday, like clockwork, he left his apartment between ten and ten thirty and zigzagged a lazy gait between geriatric walkers, kids on skateboards, and stroller pushing mothers.

The park, located in the placid southeast corner of Las Vegas, away from the hustle and bustle of the gambling Mecca, was twenty-five acres of triangle-shaped park bordered on the east by St. Claire Avenue, on the west by Clear Mountain Boulevard, and on the south by Spring Water Drive with its mid-range priced condominiums and well-kept apartments. An asphalt jogging trail meandered languidly through the park, splitting into a V in front of a shaded gazebo landscaped with eight foot tall tuffs of ornamental zebra grass, ground hugging green and white hostas, and bright red and yellow tulips.

The left fork followed a gentle sloping hill that leveled off near a concrete pond with white water lilies poking above the surface. The SnoCone kiosk next to the pond sold frozen treats and compressed pellets people tossed to the orange and black Japanese koi gliding between the lilies. The trail to the right, however, was a horse of a different color. It paralleled a bulldozed path created for BMX and mountain bike enthusiasts. The trail was hidden from view behind a row of thick manicured hedges and looped around the park's perimeter until connecting with a wooden footbridge spanning a runoff ditch that channeled rainwater to the city's aqueduct system. Taking into account Las Vegas averages four inches of rainfall annually, the gulch was powdery dry sand most of the time.

Unfortunate for the cause Mathers never displayed a discernable pattern as to the path he would take. On two previous attempts to cleanse the gene pool of Mathers's DNA, Shadow Man watched with disappointment as the pedophile took the left fork. There were too many witnesses loitering about near the pond for an assassin to ply his trade. If, on the other hand, Mathers chose the trail to the right, Shadow Man could execute his plan. The wooden footbridge at the base of a steep incline that led up to St. Clair Avenue would be the perfect spot to strike.

Shadow Man easily covered the moguls and valleys that kids on expensive trick and mountain bikes leaped over with glee, purposely holding back on the target's right rear flank. He kept Mathers in sight while remaining undetected by his prey. When they reached the split in front of the gazebo and Mathers made a right turn, Shadow Man's pulse quickened with a surge of adrenaline. From three meters behind, he matched Mathers step-for-step; something the jogger should have heard had his footfalls not sounded like those of a charging elephant. Fifty yards from the footbridge the killer picked up his pace and closed the gap to barely one meter. The trail arched to the left before it made a sharp right that would connect it with the bridge, and ultimately to St. Clair Avenue. The bicycle path, however, was the shortest distance between two points and the shadowy figure behind the hedges reached the bridge several seconds before the target.

Mathers's right foot was on the downward step to the first plank when a charley horse like he had never felt before slammed his right thigh into a painful spasm. Shadow Man stood on the edge of the planking looking on in total disbelief. The well-placed kick should have snapped Mathers's femur and sent him crashing to the ground, but instead of dropping like a stone, he limped onto the bridge unaware he had been struck. Mathers grabbed the railing for support and hobbled to a stop like a car with a flat tire.

Mathers stood on the bridge, bent over at the waist massaging his quadriceps. The second blow struck his neck like an angry fist from God and sent stars dancing before his eyes. The follow-up punch broke the third and fourth vertebrae without the desired effect. Fractures high in the cervical region have a tendency to sever the spine near the base of the skull bringing about instant paralysis, and death.

Instead of collapsing to the ground, Mathers flew into a rage. He spun to confront his attacker. He grabbed Shadow Man by throat in a vise-like grip, and jerked him up off the ground.

Suspended three inches above the bridge with his throat in Mathers's powerful grip, Shadow Man knew he would loose consciousness, quickly, unless he reacted, and reacted fast. A front snap-kick to the groin released Mathers's grip and doubled him over. Shadow Man gasped in a quick breath, and then kneed Mathers in the forehead hard enough to split a coconut. Mathers's staggered backwards, blood spurting from a three-inch long gash above his right eye, and again clutched the rail for support. It was obvious to the killer he had severely underestimated his target. He drove a pile driver fist into Mathers's chest, felt the sternum splinter, but remarkably, the target was still standing. And even more remarkable, he blindly flailed those massive arms, hands clenched into cannonball fists. A lucky blow found its mark and Shadow Man careened to the opposite side of the bridge with enough force that his ribcage broke one of the two-by-four treated-lumber posts. Mathers seized advantage of the lull in action and blindly scurried toward St. Clair Avenue. He clawed his way up the steep dirt embankment like a wounded animal.

A hand clamped onto his ankle and, like a dog playing tug-o-war with a rope toy, jerked, and tugged him back toward the shadowy coppice. Mathers knew if he allowed himself to be dragged back into the cover of the thick brush he might never see the light of day again. More out of survival instinct than conscious thought, he kicked back with his good leg, landing a solid blow, followed by a deflating "umph."

Again free of his attacker, Mathers struggled up the embankment, and no matter how much pain he felt, he had to make it to the sidewalk, it was a matter of life and death. With one last mighty heave he burst into the bright sunlight, staggered to his feet with blood streaming into his eyes and blurring his vision, and dragged his injured leg behind him to the edge of the sidewalk, where he stumbled off the curb directly into the path of a passing shuttle bus. He stuck to the grill for a moment like a bug on a windshield, and then slipped beneath the wheels with a blood-curdling scream sure to haunt the driver into years of therapy. The horrified Pakistani immigrant driver paced the sidewalk squeezing his turbaned head between his hands, wailing: "Oh my god! Oh my god!"

Several of the less squeamish tourists disembarked for a better look at the crumpled, bloody mess pinned between the chassis and the pavement. One even pulled out a camera and snapped a few digital pictures for posterity.

Shadow Man pressed his hand against damaged ribs and eased back into the shadows; the approaching sirens signaled him it was time to take his leave. He slid over the shattered railing and retreated down the concealed bicycle trail.

The following day Donald G. Mathers's obituary declared his death a tragic accident. It would be weeks before his landlady mustered up the courage to enter his apartment, and gather together his personal effects. Not until after her *discovery* behind a partially open plumbing access door, and her subsequent notification of the police, did Agent MacKenzie Stevens finally understand why Daniels visited the Tropicana Casino.

Donna Sheer stood behind Bobby's chair with misty eyes, her hands resting on his shoulders. He sat hunched over the morning edition of the *Las Vegas Sun*'s account of Don Mathers's accident.

After their escape from a tyrannical, abusive, alcoholic husband and father, she was happy a gentleman of Mr. Mathers's caliber had stepped into Bobby's life serving as a positive male role model. Now through a disastrous twist of fate that life had been prematurely snuffed out, her heart ached for how Bobby must feel. Not only had he lost his camp counselor and canoe partner, he had lost a truly good friend, too. *Bobby must be devastated*, she told herself.

Bobby read the article with macabre interest. After he finished the obituary for the second time, he pushed away from the table, walked into the living room, flopped down on the braced up couch/bed, and buried his face under a pillow. Donna shooed Megan back into the kitchen to leave Bobby alone with his grief.

Bobby kept his broad smile hidden underneath the pillow until he heard Megan and his mother's voices in the kitchen. Thanks to a tour bus his secret was safe, he wouldn't have to make up excuses for never going camping—or anywhere for that matter—with Mathers.

Late last Sunday afternoon Mathers dropped Bobby off at home. After a long shower, Bobby slept most of the afternoon and evening. Donna attributed his fatigue to a fun-filled exhaustive weekend canoeing and camping. The truth was that Bobby was hung over.

During the camping trip Mathers *graciously* shared a jug of sweet homemade wine with Bobby. They stayed up late, sitting around a campfire and passing the jug back and forth, while Mathers regaled him with grandiose stories about the mystery bobcat. Never having drunk alcohol before, Bobby didn't realize wine was sipped and not gulped like grape soda pop. He was inebriated in no time, but that didn't stop Mathers from goading him into taking another gulp. Even after Bobby dashed off into the bushes to throw up, Mathers was able to taunt him into taking "just one more small swig, my man". It was after midnight when Bobby finally staggered to the tent and promptly passed out.

Mathers sat near the fire, pulled out a glowing ember, and lit his cigar. He lay on his back watching the stars until he heard Bobby's deep rhythmic snoring, then he made his move.

Inside the tent, Mathers stripped the unconscious Bobby out of his clothes and laid him on top of the sleeping bag, settling down next to him with his head propped on his hand. In the battery-operated lantern's dim light he watched Bobby's chest rise and fall, the sight of naked Bobby, sound asleep, drew Mathers back to his youth.

Growing up in the Mathers household, the standard operating procedure had been sharing baths with his mother. The older he grew, the more intense the demented matriarch's haranguing about the dangers of "evil girls" and how they looked to "get good boys in trouble" became. Mathers stirred the images with a shake of his head, and the just as *Momma* did for him on his fourteenth birthday; Mathers reached across the tent and deflowered Bobby.

Bobby awoke during the attack and tried his best to escape, but Mathers was too strong. He held him tight against his chest while he explored Bobby's "no visitors region", whispering into his ear that what he was doing was okay, that it meant he loved him. Bobby wept and begged Mathers to stop, but his pleas were ignored as his counselor tossed him off to a quivering orgasm. Bobby actually threw up all over the inside of the tent when Mathers said, "We can do this every time we come camping, Bobby."

Bobby rolled off the couch and headed for the bathroom, he had an urgent need to shower Mathers's filthy hands from his body again. He was glad Mathers was dead. His only regret was that Mathers had not died a slow, painful death of AIDS, lung cancer, and a brain tumor. Only two people knew what had taken place on that ill-fated trip, and with one of them dead, the other, for the rest of his life, would bury the humiliating experience deep in the recesses of the mind especially reserved for such traumatically disturbing events.

Chapter 24

Agent Stevens swiped his magnetized parking card through the reader, waited for the traffic arm to rise, and then drove into the "employees only" parking lot of the Lloyd George Federal Building on S. Las Vegas Boulevard. After he located an empty parking space close to the building and parked his car, he climbed out, slipped into his suit coat, and, with briefcase in hand, hurried toward the air-conditioned building.

The elevator jolted to a stop on the second floor and he stepped out, turned left, his heels clicking against the tile floor, until he came to a stop in front of the last door on the right, office of the United States Attorney. He closed the door behind him and announced his arrival at the receptionist's window before taking a seat in a molded plastic chair against the wall. Stevens leaned over and wedged his briefcase between his chair and his feet, and picked up a *U.S. News & World Report* that he flipped open to the cover article, a feature on the history of "Air Force One".

It only took a few minutes, not enough time to learn much from the article, before U.S. Attorney Kerrie Bridger greeted him from the doorway. She propped the door open with her foot, and wearing a friendly smile, said, "Come on in, Mack."

Stevens tossed the magazine back down onto the table, picked up his briefcase, and followed Kerrie to her office.

Shortly after he had transferred to the Bureau's Las Vegas office, Stevens and Bridger shared a brief romance, but so as not to interfere with their respective careers decided, *mutually*, to end the relationship.

Attorney Bridger returned to her desk and moved manila folders around until she found a pen, scribbled a note on a legal pad, and inserted it into one of the file folders piled on her desk. Stevens, on the other hand, walked directly to a conference table opposite her desk where he set his attaché case, draped his jacket over the back of a chair, and thumbed open the tumblers.

"How are Max and Erma?" He pulled out a thick folder held together with two rubber bands and set it onto the table.

Bridger trapped a chuckle behind her hand. "They're fine," she said. "They eat, poop, swim, and wait until late in the afternoon to sun themselves on their rock."

"That's what turtles do best," he said, with an affable smile.

Kerrie crossed the room and leaned on the back of a chair. "The Bureau make any headway on the counterfeit fifties passed at the Rio?"

"We've narrowed it down to one of the bartenders, or a cocktail waitress, or possibly both. Washington wanted it turned over to the boys in Treasury; it's more up their alley than it is the Bureau's. I heard someone around the office say something about the Rio's surveillance cameras getting it all on video."

Stevens closed the lid on his case, pushed it aside, and waited until Kerrie claimed her seat before he, too, sat down.

She glanced at the stout folder on the table. "What do you have for me, Mack?"

"What I have," he flashed a wary smile, "and what you'll agree to are probably two different things, but I'm about to give it my best shot."

Stevens's professional experience with Attorney Bridger showed her to be a stickler for detail, holding fast and true to the philosophy the longer the paper trail the better. And that was precisely why he had padded the file with superfluous pages to make it thicker than necessary.

On the conference table between them, being shared for the first time with someone outside of the Bureau, sat "Operation Candy Cane". Incorporated into the file was a multicolored hand-drawn timeline and aerial photos, along with archived Lincoln County Medical Examiner's reports. The fifteen page typed synopsis (Sheriff Austin's theory come to life in Stevens's hand) included the agent's official documentation of Daniels's clandestine visit to the Tropicana Casino a few days before the latest Shadow Man victim—one Donald G. Mathers—was ingeniously murdered to look like a traffic accident.

Stevens hoped a presentation of the facts would get him the search warrant he so desperately wanted. If that came to fruition, and only Bridger could make it happen, he would organize a dozen agents to swoop down on Daniels's property and seize computers, floppy disks, files, or anything else that a fishing expedition of Daniels's property may yield that could even remotely link him to Shadow Man. He hoped the Behavioral Science geeks in Washington were right about how many serial killers keep trophies; newspaper accounts of their work, photos of the crime scene, or, dare he hope, personal effects taken from the victims.

Stevens used up the better part of an hour imparting the pure facts of the case, at least as he saw them.

Kerrie listened patiently until he was finished, leaned back in her chair and tucked several loose strands of shoulder-length jet-black black hair behind her ears. She began smoothing her eyebrows with her fingertips, which annoyed the heck out of Stevens. That peculiar little quirk alone spoke volumes of her impression of the presentation. Several minutes of brow grooming elapsed before she leaned forward, and darned if she didn't repeat his exact words when Austin first brought Reese Daniels to his attention, "Mack, you're taking huge leaps in logic, considering the majority of your dubious foundation comes from an unlawful excursion onto Mr. Daniels's property."

Stevens winced. Maybe he should have held back on that part of the story. Oh well, as they say, "the cat's out of the bag".

"Actually," Kerrie broke into his thoughts. "You should probably consider yourself fortunate Daniels didn't file a complaint with my office. Or worse yet, seek redress through the local courts." She arched her flattened brows. "In light of the fact the statute of limitations window hasn't expired, that option remains open to him.

"I'm not sure if I were you, Mack, I would provoke him by executing a search warrant; particularly when you're not standing on very solid ground."

Stevens grew taller in his seat at the rebuff. "Not on solid ground? Come on, Kerrie." He stabbed his finger on the satellite images resting on top of the file. "The guy slinks around like some sort of somnambulistic phantom; helicopters in and out of Las Vegas on an increasingly frequent basis; and keeps a wolf—"

"Coyote," she interjected with a patronizing grin.

"—whatever, as a pet.

"He cruises up and down the Strip like he owns the place. My god, Kerrie, he doesn't even have a valid driver's license. Don't you find it a little peculiar that whenever Daniels decides to leave his fortress in the desert, a trail of bodies appears?" Stevens rose from his chair and hiked up his trousers. "A lot more than coincidence, if you ask me."

Attorney Bridger grinned at the ridiculous line of his reasoning. He was obviously taking the case personally, and she wondered why.

"No driver's license is a state issue, Mack, not federal," she said, almost condescendingly. "I will grant you that keeping a coyote as a pet is a little bizarre, considering they're about as welcome as a root canal without Novocain, but to the best of my knowledge, not illegal. And in case you haven't noticed, a lot of corporate helicopters fly in and out of Las Vegas on a daily basis.

"As for *Shadow Man* being a sleepwalking phantom, I beg your pardon, but I'll have to disagree. From what little I know about the case, I'd say your mystery man, whoever he is, seems well in charge of his faculties. As a matter of fact, it appears he's both systematic, and methodical in his selection of victims, as well as his execution of plan."

Stevens walked to the window, and pressed his knuckles to his eyes hard enough to trigger a kaleidoscope of light behind his eyelids. "Trust me, Kerrie, I'm aware of all that." He turned intense eyes from the window and crossed the room, punching his finger to his palm as he ticked off the essential points.

"Daniels is a martial arts expert; ergo *ability*!

"He's a recluse. *Secrecy*!

"He's filthy rich enough to move about totally undetected. *Opportunity*!

"And he's a half-breed Chinese, most probably abused by his grandfather. *Motive*!

"Kerrie, it all adds up." He reclaimed his seat.

"Not the way I do the math it doesn't." She fidgeted in her seat as she adjusted her green and black tartan skirt. "Have you tried a tail?" she asked, diplomatically.

"Yeah, I tried one the afternoon he was busy stalking Mathers. You know," he added, sarcastically, "the last guy he killed."

She ignored the cynicism. "And?"

" 'And', I got the agency's car towed for my efforts."

Attorney Bridger was unable to trap her laughter. She quickly recovered, rested her elbows on the table, planted her chin in her palms, smoothed her eyebrows, and stared across the table for a long time before she spoke. "Mack," she glanced at her watch. "For forty-five minutes you've regaled me with coincidental innuendo and speculation, nothing tangible. Care to hear my opinion?"

No, he did not want her opinion but knew he was going to get it anyway. He hated when she lectured him like one of her pre-law students. Dejected, he crossed his arms over his chest and flopped back in his seat with a groan.

"Based on what you've told me I think you're too close to the forest." She laid a benevolent hand on top of the file. "I can't justify asking Judge Greenleaf for a warrant.

"Good lord, Mack, rumor has it when she leaves the bench next year she's already been tapped for a top slot at the A.C.L.U. There's no way she'll sign a warrant on such weak supposition."

Weak supposition? How dare you! Stevens fumed. He slowly rose from his chair and leaned forward, rested balled up fists on the table, his tie brushed across the top of the "Operation Candy Cane" folder.

"Come on, Kerrie, we're so close. I've got a psychotic, cold-blooded killer right in my hands." He crushed his fist closed. "My goodness, days before the last victim's death Daniels just happens to show up at the casino where the guy works? I personally saw him talking to his victim out by the pool. Doesn't that count for something?"

Stevens locked onto her bright green eyes and found the twinkle a little too snooty. Conversely, Kerrie's eyes took in her former partner. She recognized he was on the verge of detonating into one of his angry conniption fits because he was not getting his way.

"Mack, how many other people were in the same exact casino, at the same exact time? Are you telling me they're all suspects, too?"

Stevens's nostrils flared as he gathered the file together. He knew he was wasting his time talking to her. "I should have let Harry shoot the slant-eyed SOB."

Attorney Bridger's mien darkened. "Beautiful, Mack, just beautiful. Exactly what the Bureau needs is another Ruby Ridge."

"MacKenzie Stevens, I suggest you and your agents tread lightly, before you find yourself on the opposite side of the badge."

Stevens tossed the file into his briefcase and slammed the lid with a sharp report. "What is it that you need, Counselor? Maybe you'd like me to bring you the next victim? Would that change your position?"

U.S. Attorney Kerrie Bridger bolted out of her chair and snapped to attention, pointed a harsh finger at the center of Stevens's chest, and said, "Agent Stevens, don't you dare play your little intimidation, bullshit games with me. I work with facts, not speculation, false assumptions, and weak implications. If you can manage to come up with something concrete..." She couldn't pass up giving him a jab. "A little thing we in the legal profession like to call *evidence*, I'll go to Greenleaf. But I'm not taking a farfetched, hackneyed story to the most liberal federal judge between the Atlantic and the Pacific to ask for a warrant I know she won't grant."

His marriage to his job was no doubt why he was divorced, Kerrie mused; and precisely why she suggested they move on, separately, with their lives.

Stevens snapped the clasps on his briefcase closed, wrenched it from the table, and turned for the door. He spoke over his shoulder, his voice dripping with indignation.

"Fine, Kerrie. Fine. I'll bring you a body. You think if we dump a body on Greenleaf's bench that might make the two of you a little more conservative?" He ripped open the door ahead of Kerrie's stern warning.

"Make sure it lands on her bench legally, MacKenzie. Because if it doesn't…you, and your agents, might find yourself in need of a good attorney."

He turned to her from the doorway. "You happen to know one?" He slammed the door with a malevolent sneer.

Stevens's briefcase bounced off the passenger door and landed on the floor. He climbed into the driver's seat, pounded the heel of his hand against the top of the steering wheel, and looked up to Bridger's second story window. It was no wonder he had dumped her; that woman was totally unreasonable.

Chapter 25

To lessen his wind resistance, Timmy had his tear-streaked face buried in Mollie's flowing mane, his boots working ribs overtime for more speed. He blazed over the hill north of the barn ahead of a cloud of dust, spotted Reese raking the limestone path that connected the pool deck to the barn, and with a tug of Mollie's reins, turned her thundering hooves in that direction. Unable to rein her to a stop he bounded from the saddle as the horse shot past Reese. Loose-fitting cowboy boots were not made for running. Timmy stumbled and fell face first in the dirt at Reese's feet.

Reese dropped to his knees and grabbed a hold of Timmy's arms. "What's wrong? Are you all right?"

It was not until Timmy choked out "It's Dakota!" did Reese realize Bricker's absence.

"Where's Dakota, Tim?"

Because Timmy was sobbing so hard, Reese had to give him a gruff shake to make sense of him.

"He fell off of Gus," Timmy said with a shudder. "I think he's dead."

"Where?" Reese screeched.

"Seashell Rock! We were on our way back. I heard a thud and turned around, and Dakota was lying face down in the dirt. I jumped off Mollie and ran back to him and rolled him over…Ah, Reese, he was all blue and shit. I freaked out. I didn't know what to do. I didn't want to leave him out there by himself, honest." Timmy began crying again. "I didn't know what else to do, so I came to get you."

Reese pulled Timmy to his chest and stroked his long blonde hair for a moment. "It's all right, Tim," he said, soothingly. "You did the right thing."

He held Timmy out at arm's length. "I have to get to Dakota, Tim. Take Mollie to the barn and give her some water. We'll unsaddle her when I get back."

Timmy wiped his nose on his shirtsleeve. "Reese, it's bad. I know it. It's real bad."

Reese tipped Timmy's chin up with a gloved thumb. "Tim take Mollie to the barn and give her water. Then go to the house and wait for me. Okay?"

Timmy swabbed his face with his shirttail and nodded.

"Good. Move it, sport."

Reese swatted him on the backside as Timmy jumped up and ran to Mollie, grabbed a tight grip on her reigns, and tugged and pulled and dragged her toward the barn.

Reese sprinted to the battered Ford truck, tossed his gloves to the seat, and dove inside. He turned the key and waited, for what seemed like forever, as the diesel engine's glow plug heated. The yellow light on the dashboard finally blinked out signaling the powerful 6.5 liter engine was ready to fire. He pumped the gas pedal twice, brought the engine to life, slammed the gearshift into first, and stomped the gas pedal to the floor. The rear wheels dug into the loose dirt and buried in a deep rut. He stomped down on the clutch and ground the gearbox into reverse. Sand sprayed in the opposite direction, and the truck buried to its axle.

Reese was not in control of his emotions. He paused, drew in a deep breath, held it for a moment, exhaled forcefully, reached down to the floorboard and worked the shifter forward into its lowest setting, creeper gear. This time around he released the clutch slower, coaxing the truck forward until it clawed out of the rut. Once the wheels were free, Reese mashed the gas pedal to the floor. The truck fishtailed left and right as Timmy jumped onto the passenger running board and hung on through the open window. Reese jammed the clutch and the brake to the floor in unison, abruptly bringing the big 4X4 to a halt.

Timmy scampered through the side window, flopped down on the seat, and with frantic hand gestures, screamed, "Go! Go! Go! Go!"

"Yu buyao youzhao shifen quyu bianlun. Chuqu!" Reese said, agitated at another unexpected delay.

Timmy pulled his seat belt into place and, said, "Yeah, whatever."

"I said; *I don't have time to argue. Get out!*" Reese snarled.

Icy blue eyes snapped around and glared at him from across the cab. "I'm going with you, Reese! So shut the fuck up and drive the goddamn truck." He turned back in his seat and stared straight ahead, afraid to look at Reese.

Reese regarded him for the split second it took for him to jam the truck into first gear, and then roar across the freshly raked path into the desert.

The truck cleared a small mogul behind the barn and went airborne, crashed to the ground, sent Reese's head against the roof and stars waltzing before his eyes. He steered the truck with his left knee, snapped the seatbelt across his lap, and pressed Timmy against the seat with his right as the truck left the ground again. He piloted the truck around rock formations and towering Saguaro cacti, around clumps of parched scrub brush and darting hares, racing across the desert at perilous speeds near seventy miles per hour. A trip that normally took more than an hour on horseback was covered in less than ten minutes.

Timmy pointed through the dirt-streaked windshield to where Gus stood faithful guard over Bricker. "Over there," he shouted above the roar of the engine.

Reese spun the steering wheel hard, rocked the shifter into neutral, stomped on the emergency brake, and leaped from the truck before it skidded to a stop. By the time Timmy reached his side, Reese had already pressed his fingers to Bricker's neck, ripped open his blue flannel shirt, and pressed an ear against the butler's hairy chest. He squeezed his eyes closed and sank back on his heels, biting at his bottom lip. Dakota was gone.

Timmy looked down at Dakota with a yuck-face, and said, "Is he...?"

Reese opened his eyes to Bricker's blank, pasty, skyward gape. Under the blazing sun a chill quivered up his spine and shuddered to a stop between his shoulder blades.

Few people have any desire to touch the dead, and Reese was firmly rooted in that camp. He reached down uneasily and closed Bricker's eyelids with his fingertips, brushed the sand away from the butler's face as if it was bothersome, and returned to his haunches, squeezing his eyes closed and pinching the bridge of his nose.

Timmy stood behind him for several minutes, and then laid a sympathetic hand on his shoulder. "Are you okay, Reese?"

Reese grabbed a tight hold on Timmy's hand, pulled him to the ground, and hugged him close. A single tear trickled out of the corner of his eye, coursed down his cheek, and splashed onto the top of Timmy's head. He cleared his throat, and said, "Let's take Dakota home."

Reese carried Dakota to the truck while Timmy ran ahead and opened the tailgate. They eased Dakota's body into the bed of the truck as gently as if laying a baby down for a nap. Timmy climbed into the saddle and rode Gus home behind the makeshift hearse.

Reese stood in the driveway as the coroner's wagon pull away, arms dangling limply at his sides. Sheriff Austin stepped next to him, and said, "I need to talk to Timmy, Reese."

Reese slid his sunglasses off and folded the stems together. He turned to the sheriff with moist eyes, and said, "Go easy on him, Cody. He's pretty shaken up."

Sheriff Austin reached out and compassionately patted the back of Reese's neck. "Just a few routine questions, and then I'll leave you folks be."

Kitty sensed something was wrong, but didn't know what it was. He paced around the pool tight on Reese's heels, each lap they stopped long enough to peer into the family room where Timmy relayed the details of what happened. When the sheriff stood to leave, Reese hurried into the house and silently walked the lawman to the front door.

Sheriff Austin stopped on the porch steps, turned, and extended his hand. "I'm sorry for your loss, Reese."

Reese chewed the inside of his cheek for a moment, took Austin's hand, and choked out a hoarse "thank you" before returning to the family room.

"The two of you are staying here tonight, aren't you?" he said from the doorway.

Nancy arrived at the same time as the coroner's van, and sat with Timmy during his interview with the sheriff. "If that's what you want," she said, leaning against the billiard table.

"That's what I want."

"Then we'll stay."

He gave a slight nod. "Good," he said.

Reese went upstairs, changed clothes, and then buried himself in his tiyuguan for several hours of meditation to quiet his thoughts.

Chapter 26

"Didn't I tell you this place was way cool," Timmy said, once again overwhelmed with the audiovisual, sensory overload of the Las Vegas Strip.

He walked along the boulevard's sidewalk sandwiched between his mother and Reese as he took in the voluminous sights. Nancy and Timmy squeezed into an open spot against the concrete railing in front of the Bellagio to watch the Dancing Fountain show. Reese, conversely, stood several steps back from the crowd to watch. Nancy shanghaied a passing tourist long enough to snap a picture of the three of them in front of a replica of the Eiffel Tower at the Paris Casino—the first photograph taken of Reese in nearly three decades. Both ignored Timmy's insistent begging for another ride on the roller coaster atop the New York, New York Casino. They spent almost an hour inside the MGM Grand Casino watching a Rock & Roll tribute show featuring impersonators from the Beatles to Diana Ross.

At the intersection of Tropicana Avenue and Las Vegas Boulevard, Reese, Nancy, and Timmy stood at the back of a crowd waiting for the traffic signal to bring the perpetual stampede of cars to a halt. When the light changed they crossed the intersection, strolled down the sidewalk, and walked up the sweeping arched driveway leading to the front doors of the Tropicana Hotel and Casino.

At the back of a line of customers lined up at the registration counter, Timmy's face was aglow. "I can't believe we own this place," he said.

Reese gave a phobic look around. Thankfully no one had heard the pretentious boast. "Daniels Industries owns it," he said, softly.

Timmy's face contorted into a sardonic sneer. "Duh! Hello! And what did you say your name was?" He looked into the gaming area with a salivating gaze. "Now I can play the slot machines, right?"

Reese snorted, and brought a contemplative finger to his chin. "Ah, let me think about that for a minute NO!"

"Well that's bullshit," Timmy grumbled under his breath.

"Keep something in mind, sport. Just because your mom and I are getting married today doesn't mean you can act like a schmuck," Reese said. "You've been getting pretty lippy as of late."

Nancy smiled. Immature as Reese was at times, she was still sure he had the potential to be a good stepfather.

Several weeks ago, only a few days after Dakota's death, and prior to asking her to marry him, Reese invited Nancy along for a sunset ride on the quad-runner. Timmy decided he would tag along until Reese, none to diplomatically, told him he wanted to talk with Nancy, *alone*. Timmy shrugged it off, assuming they had grown up stuff to talk about, probably things concerning Dakota. He dropped to his knees in the kitchen, went nose-to-nose with Kitty, and announced they would microwave a bag of popcorn and "chill" to the media room and a movie.

Nancy wrapped her hands around Reese's waist and held on tight as he pulled the quad-runner out of the barn for a drive around the perimeter of his expansive estate, finally stopping at Seashell Rock as the last rays of sunlight faded over the horizon. They sat inside the stone formation listening to the sounds of a moonless night. Total silence.

Reese marshaled up the courage to slip an arm around Nancy's shoulders and draw her closer; something that took her totally by surprise considering his usual show of affection was an occasional spicy wisecrack.

Because he was afraid to look at Nancy, he stared straight ahead and spoke in a voice so soft, she strained to hear him. "I have something to ask you," he said.

"Ask away," she lilted, nervously.

"Before I *ask*, there's something I need to *tell* you."

She folded her hands between her knees and giggled like a teenager. "Tell away."

Reese turned on the bench and faced her, folded his ankles into his lap and took hold of Nancy's cold trembling hands. He drew in a quivering, hesitant breath, and then walked her down the labyrinth of twisted corridors that made up his life. She sat listening quietly while Reese spoke of the mother he never had the opportunity to know; spoke with detached indifference of a father he would never meet; spoke with admiration of Tian Xian Huo, and how he had introduced him to his Chinese heritage; spoke with deep reverence and respect of the void Dakota had filled in his life; and seethed with rage when he spoke of his grandfather.

Tears of sympathy poured down Nancy's cheeks as he relayed the graphically sordid details of fourteen years of abuse and emotional torture at the hands of the Captain. When he asked her if she had ever heard of Shadow Man, Nancy's blood froze, she pulled her hands free of his. With chest raking sobs, he divulged the account of his grandfather's murder and the birth of Shadow Man, assuming all responsibility for creating the monster and for allowing it to continue for so long. After she recovered from the initial shock, Nancy pulled his head to her shoulder and rocked him like a child as he wept away years of his self-imposed dilemma.

It took some time before he regained his composure enough to timidly *pop the question*. She cupped his tear-streaked face between her hands. "Of course I'll marry you, you eccentric, recluse of neurotic, phobic emotions," she said with a mixture of romance and sarcasm, and then planted a virgin kiss on his quivering lips.

From the back of the slow moving registration line, Timmy said, "Now that we're rich, Mom, we're going to hang out in Las Vegas more often, aren't we?"

"Timothy Michael Robbins…"

Reese squeezed her hand and winked. He turned to Timmy and said, "*We're* not rich, sport, *I* am. And because *I* happen to be rich don't be a wiseass. Got it?"

Timmy rolled his eyes and snarled, "Whatever."

Behind the service counter Ramon, Tropicana's Head Concierge, craned his neck to the back of the line of incoming guests. He rushed around the polished marble counter crimson faced, stumbled over himself with apologies, and quickly ushered the casino's new owner, and guests, to the opulent VIP lounge.

He reached for the telephone on an antique mahogany desk. "Mr. Daniels, why didn't you notify us you were coming in today? We didn't expect you until later in the week. You should have called. I would personally have attended to your needs." He snatched the phone to his ear and summoned a bellhop. "One of the bellboys will take your luggage to your suite, sir."

One of the four suites on the penthouse floor was the only extravagance Reese insisted upon during his first Board of Directors meeting. Presidential Suite A overlooking the Strip was no longer available as a rental. Professionally remodeled, it was now the Daniels's home away from home.

Nancy handed Ramon the keys to the Navigator, steadfastly refusing to let Reese drive (which prompted one of Timmy's favorite taunts "…yeah, Kung Fu, we see who wears the pants around here, don't we?") until he obtained a driver's license; which Reese steadfastly refused to do.

Reese sat next to Nancy on a rich leather maroon settee in the corner of the VIP lounge. Ramon hung up the phone, and then immediately returned it to his ear, his finger hovering over the keypad. "May I order you and your guests a complimentary beverage, Mr. Daniels?"

"Jack and water, please." Reese turned to Nancy. "Would you like anything?"

"No thank you, I'm fine."

Timmy rolled a high-back leather chair from beneath the desk and plopped down. He spun several circles, skidded to a stop, and slammed his tennis shoes down on top of a blotter protecting the desk's surface. He tilted back in the chair and snapped his fingers. "I'll take a beer, *Ramon*. That's if you got one handy."

The sudden pressure on his hand told Reese that Nancy was about to take a huge, and maybe not so figurative, chunk out of Tim's backside. He placed a silencing finger against her lips.

Ever since being told his mother and Reese were going to marry, Timmy's arrogant behavior grew tenfold worse. Reese thought it was the perfect time to make it irrefutably clear that because he was about to become stepson to one of the wealthiest men in the country, that did not give him the right to talk down to anyone. Having been raised by a proper English butler the least Reese could do was to pass along some proper English decorum.

He stood, casually walked across the room, and, probably using more force than necessary, slapped Tim's feet from the desk, pinning his shoulders to the chair. "I'd better never, *ever*, hear you speak to an adult like that again," Reese hissed, his face inches from Timmy's. "Don't think for a second that you're going to get away with acting like a jackass. Not as long as I'm around. Understood?"

Out of a possible ten on the shock-o-meter Tim's face registered a solid thirteen. The grin hidden behind Ramon's hand, on the other hand, brightened the room. The head concierge decided that he liked the Tropicana's new owner, liked him a lot. Not until after Ramon received a timid apology from Timmy did Reese return to his seat.

Nancy checked her smile and took hold of Reese's hand as he sat down. There was no doubt in her mind; Reese Daniels was going to be one heck of a stepfather.

Ramon directed the bellhop to deliver the Daniels's luggage to Presidential Suite A, and then led the way through the casino, through the lush botanical gardens (its air heavily laden with the fragrance of fresh orchids) and across the footbridge to the Island Wedding Chapel's gazebo.

With his ego still smarting from the unexpected reproach in the VIP Lounge, Timmy quietly sat in the back row of pews.

Like most casino chapels in Las Vegas the Tropicana supplied a best man, maid of honor, witness, and a nondenominational clergyman. The reverend had already begun the short service when Reese interrupted the proceedings.

"I can't get married." He stepped from the riser and started for the back of the room, stopping in the aisle next to the last pew. He looked down with apologetic eyes. "Sorry, sport. I can't marry your mother."

Timmy looked up at him dumbfounded, and then to his mother's ashen face at the front of the room. *How can he walk out on her like this?* In the time it took for the idea to formulate—get up and kick the rich bastard

Reese Daniels right square in the jimmy—Reese dragged him from the pew by the arm.

"Not until I have a proper best man," Reese said. "Would you honor me as my best man?"

Timmy smiled and threw his arms around Reese "Hell, yes!" he blurted; loud enough Nancy covered her face with her hand.

Reese laughed, and then bent down, and whispered, "Please. For your mother's sake, watch your mouth."

Timmy curled his finger, drawing Reese closer. "Ok, Dad," he said.

By the time they stepped onto the riser at the front of the room Nancy's color had returned. She shook her head as her two men, boys, moved beside her.

With an innocuous grin, Reese held up his open palms. "What? You thought I was going someplace?"

The Daniels family walked out of the chapel, back through the casino, and onto the private elevator that serviced their penthouse suite.

Tim shot an elbow to Reese's ribs as the elevator glided to a stop on the top floor. "So...what do you two have planned for tonight?" He gave the newlyweds a lewd eyebrow dance.

"For us, dinner at the Luxor and the Blue Man Group show, for you, a babysitter and muzzle."

"Is she cute?" Timmy said with a wide grin.

The ornate doors opened and Reese playfully shoved him into their palatial accommodations. "Just as cute as a fifty year old nun can be," he said, with a deadpan stare.

Nancy burst out laughing. Timmy moped across the room and slumped onto the sofa. "Damn. I am in Vegas and stuck in a stupid hotel room with a nun." He sank into the cushion, tipped his head back, and rolled his eyes. "Can't you do something to help me out here?"

Chapter 27

Dakota Bricker's memorial service was one of the smaller gatherings Reverend Penn, hired by the funeral home, ever officiated. Wearing black preacher's attire and an appropriately somber smile, he addressed the small group of mourners, the collective total not coming close to filling the first pew.

Reese, casually dressed in a navy blue sport jacket and matching slacks, a white long sleeve shirt open at the neck, sat in the front row between his wife and stepson. Nancy chose a conservative black pantsuit and gray pastel blouse, while Timmy observed tradition by festooning himself in a black long sleeve Megadeath tee shirt, black bellbottom cargo pants with chains dangling from the belt loops, and eighteen-hole, calf-high black lace up boots. Nelson Grover sat to their left, Cody Austin to their right, the latter two's attendance more for Reese's benefit than for the guest of honor, whose earthly remains had been reduced to a fine powder and sealed in an ornamental 24-karat gold urn.

Throughout the service Reverend Penn made pleasant observations about a person he had never met, recited several applicable passages from the Old and New Testaments, and at the conclusion of the service, dismissed the assemblage with deep assurance that "Mike" rested with Jesus. Timmy blasted through the chapel doors, ignored the funeral director's outstretched hand, and, like a wide receiver, charged into the parking lot with the gold urn clutched to his chest.

More than six weeks since the memorial service, and Reese's life had changed dramatically. A married man with a readymade family and the new owner of a Las Vegas casino, he sat behind the desk in his upstairs study, deep in thought, rocking gently back and forth in a high back office chair. He resigned to the fact he could not delay the inevitable. He leaned forward, picked up the telephone, and made the call.

The receptionist's cheerful voice answered halfway through the third ring. "Good afternoon, Lincoln County Sheriff's Office, how may I help you?"

"May I speak with Sheriff Austin, please?"

"Who's calling?"

"This is Reese Daniels returning his call."

When Sheriff Austin arrived at the Daniels ranch forty-five minutes later, he did not have to ring the doorbell, nor was he subjected to the customary wait on the porch sweating until someone chose to answer the door. Reese paced the veranda, anxiously watching as Austin crawled from the Bronco.

Once inside, Sheriff Austin popped his head into the family room and said his hellos to Nancy and Timmy, and then followed Reese upstairs to his office.

Before the door could close, Kitty scampered into the room and flopped down near a corner of the desk where he could see his master, as well as keep a watchful eye on their guest.

Reese walked behind the desk and dropped into his chair, folded his hands in his lap and waited. Sheriff Austin set his white Stetson, and the plain manila folder he had carried into the house tucked under his arm, on the floor next to his chair.

Austin squeezed into his seat, and said, "So, how's everyone holding up?"

Reese was in no mood to mince words. He kept his reply succinct. "Fine, Sheriff." He leaned forward and rested his arms on the desk. "I seriously doubt you drove all the way out here," he glanced at the chrome clock on the corner of the desk, "this late in the afternoon just to check up on us."

Austin drummed his fingers on the armrest of his chair for a moment, and then with a thoughtful nod, reached over the side of his chair and picked up the folder under his hat. He tossed it to the desk, the folder sliding across the desktop and coming to rest against Reese's forearms.

Reese glanced down to the folder and then to Austin, but he made no effort to pick it up. "Okay, I give up," he said.

Austin leaned back in the chair, hooked his thumbs inside the front of his gun belt, and sucked air through his teeth. "Open it."

Reese pondered the sheriff's blank expression for a moment but made no attempt to move. "What is it?"

Sheriff Austin unhooked his thumbs and brought crossed arms to rest on his barrel chest, tipped his head toward the desk, and repeated, "Open it, Reese."

Reese picked up the envelope, devoid of any markings, examined both sides, unfastened the metal tab holding the flap closed, and dumped the contents onto his desk. He slid the paperclip off and thumbed through the pages.

Although he didn't understand a majority of the medical jargon the report contained, he understood enough to comprehend why the sheriff's voicemail message insisted they meet this afternoon. At least Sheriff Austin had been considerate enough to sanitize the packet; the autopsy photos were removed. He slid the pages aside, closed his eyes, leaned back in his chair with an audible sigh, and reflected on the day Dakota died.

That morning he thought Dakota looked a little pale. He had also skipped breakfast, something highly unusual for a man who relished bacon and eggs and strong black coffee in the morning. He had watched as Dakota and Timmy mounted the horses; Dakota eased into the saddle clutching his abdomen, rather than bounding onto Gus's back as he normally did. The Coroner's report explained the elastic bandage he'd found wrapped around Dakota's midsection when he ripped opened his shirt to listen for a heartbeat. The checkmark in the "primary cause of death" box stated Dakota bled to death internally from a lacerated liver.

Reese moved his hands from the armrest to his eyes and gave them a thorough massage, but Sheriff Austin was not about to grant him the opportunity to organize his thoughts.

"Bricker died of a ruptured liver, Reese. Any idea how that could have happened?"

Reese eased his hands away from his face and rested them on his desk. "No idea, Sheriff," he said, without expression. "I assumed Dakota died of a heart attack."

The sheriff made no effort to conceal his disgust with Reese's layman diagnosis. He glared across the desk. "Do me a favor would you, Reese?"

"What's that?"

"Shovel the horse pucky someplace else. Dakota died of blunt force trauma to the thorax."

"Maybe he fell off his horse," Reese offered with a shrug.

"Yeah, right," Austin mocked. "And maybe Trixie kicked him to death. The old nag needs put down, Reese. She's dangerous."

"I'll look into that tomorrow."

"Maybe it was you Reese." Austin canted his head, quizzically, to one side. "Was you using Dakota as a punching bag, practicing your Kung Fu Karate crap on him?"

Reese's jaw muscles twitched at the accusation. He sat up a little taller in his seat. "I guess it could be any of the above," he said, stoically.

"I'm guessing that maybe Shadow Man bit off a little more than he could chew," Austin said, candidly.

Reese's eyes narrowed, his head cocked to the side. "What's that supposed to mean, Sheriff?"

"Well…" Austin squirmed into a new position, crossed his legs at the knee, and then continued. "It seems this muscle-bound pedophile security guard that works—used to work—at the Tropicana down in Vegas bought the big one a day or so before Dakota died. Officially, he ran in front of a bus. But the FBI is pressuring Doc Earl to change his final report. There's even talk about a court order to exhume the body."

Upon seeing the color drain from Reese's face, Sheriff Austin sank deeper into his chair with a triumphant smirk.

"I still fail to see what all this has to do with Dakota's death. Or with me," Reese said.

"Like I said, seems Mr. Muscle was a pedophile. Leastways that's what was found out, after the fact. Anyhow, a *little bird* told me the FBI snooped into the death and found evidence of a pretty intense struggle not more than thirty yards from where Hercules became a hood ornament.

"It also appears that someone, or something, broke a pretty hefty handrail on a certain bridge where a certain fight might have took place. Like maybe during the struggle someone got bounced off the railing hard enough to break it. Hard enough to damage a liver."

Reese pushed his chair back and stood, leaned his weight on balled fists, and glared down menacingly at the lawman. "So what's your point Sheriff?"

The sheriff let the tension build with a pause that carried the chrome desk clock's second hand one full revolution. "I thought it was you, Reese," he finally said. "Maybe you and Bricker as a team, but I was sure-fire ready to bet a paycheck that you were Shadow Man. It was Bricker all the time."

A nervous scoff escaped Reese as he dropped into his chair with enough force it rolled away from his desk. "I have no idea what you're talking about, Sheriff. And apparently neither do you."

Reese's diverted glance to the window was all it took to convince the experienced lawman that he was right.

"The FBI dogs are huntin', Reese, and they're sniffin' up your tree," Austin said.

Reese regained his poise, leaned back in his chair, intertwined his fingers behind his head, and smiled, arrogantly. "Let 'em sniff. All they're going to get is a nose full of bullshit."

Sheriff Austin slid closer to the desk, causing Kitty to snap to his feet, warily.

Reese growled in Chinese "Pa." and grudgingly, Kitty dropped back to the floor.

"Reese, let me explain to you how the legal system works. The FBI don't have to prove crap. All they have to do is convince twelve knuckleheads seated on a Federal Grand Jury they're right, and you can bet you'll find your backside indicted.

"Sure, you got the money to hire yourself some topnotch lawyers and do battle with them, but the fact remains, you'll go to jail. Because with all that money of yours…well…that makes you a flight risk, so you can dang well bet the U.S. Attorney will petition the court to deny bond. You can plan on sitting in jail for months while those high-priced attorneys of yours play "Lets Make A Deal" with your life. And that's only the beginning, my friend. It'll get worse, because we all know ho much you like being in the spotlight," Austin said impertinently. "I can guarantee you that every newspaper and TV station from here to Timbuktu will plaster your name and mug shot across the headlines."

Austin saw Reese's defeat. He settled back in his chair, victorious, having brought Reese Daniels to his knees.

Reese struggled to his feet, stepped over Kitty, and walked to the window overlooking the back of the house. He stood with his hands folded on top of his head, staring out the window at nothing for five full minutes, his mind racing through a plethora of scenarios, none promising. On his way back to his seat he paused long enough to bend down and scratch Kitty's muzzle, glanced at Austin, stepped behind his desk and pushed his chair aside, and then dropped to his knees. He slid a caster-mounted bookcase aside and dialed in the combination to a hidden floor safe. When he turned to face the sheriff he held in his hand a small package wrapped in a brown paper lunch sack. He set it on the desk, dropped his backside into his chair, and let several tedious minutes pass before speaking with careful deliberation.

"It seems a bunch of you lawmen-type have been looking for a certain person for quite some time." He slid the package closer to the sheriff's side of the desk.

Sheriff Austin picked up the sack and opened it. Inside he found a Samsung, 40-gigabyte hard drive. His face did not belie his confusion. "What is it I'm supposed to be seeing here, Reese?" He returned the computer hard drive to its wrapper and laid it back on the desk.

Reese slid the package to his side of the desk, and locked his dark alert eyes onto the sheriff's. "The identity of Shadow Man."

The sheriff's back stiffened noticeably, while his jaw slackened.

Reese extended outstretched palms toward the sheriff. "Sit back and I'll explain," he said.

Austin scooted his chair away from the desk, stretched out his legs, and rested his chin on his fingertips. Reese, conversely, hunched forward and rested his elbows on the desk.

"A few days after Dakota's memorial service I looked at his computer. Something you could have no way of knowing, Sheriff, was that Dakota was a stickler for keeping a daily journal. I found shelved in his quarters voluminous handwritten, hardback chronicles of his life dating back to his days in Viet Nam. I guess you could call it a diary of sorts.

"I also kind of supposed he'd keep the most important journal entries hidden on his computer. It took me a little over an hour to figure out his password." Reese paused with a chortle at the simplicity. "DEAR EMY, all in uppercase."

Austin stirred in his seat and dropped his hands to the armrest. "I'm listening," he said.

Reese tapped a rhythm on the bag as he continued. "This disk is all anyone needs to prove the identity of Shadow Man. It's Dakota's diary of a serial killer's work."

Reese leaned back in his chair, dropped his hands to his lap, and explained, in graphic detail, the origin of Shadow Man.

"The evening it all started, Sheriff, I was in my room pleading with the Captain to stop. I'm not really sure, but I think I was about thirteen or fourteen at the time." Reese bounced his shoulders. "Back then, days and months and years all muddled together like grains in a sandstorm.

"Anyhow, Dakota must have been in the upstairs hallway putting towels in the linen closet. He would do that sometimes. Do the laundry late at night. I don't know, maybe that was when Emy did the laundry, late at night. I don't remember her much, she died when I was very young…"

"Reese," Austin interrupted his reverie.

Reese looked up with an embarrassed grin. "I guess I'm wandering off target a little, huh?"

Austin nodded. "You said you were pleading with your grandfather to stop. Stop what Reese?"

"Hurting me."

"Hurting you how, Reese?"

He had seen a lot of sadness in his long career as a lawman, but at that moment, Reese brought to bear upon him the saddest eyes Austin had ever looked upon. He watched Reese draw in a quivering breath, and then forge ahead.

"Dakota burst into my bedroom and found out what was really going on in this house back then." Reese's eyes fell to his lap. "He found me kneeling in front of the Captain's open robe, my hair twisted in a knot between his fingers.

"The Captain glanced over his shoulder completely unconcerned that Dakota was standing there. I still remember his rum-slurred words. 'Just like the old days in Nam, hey, Brick?'"

"It took several years of begging before Dakota finally told me about the countless number of Vietnamese girls and boys my grandfather raped during the war. I guess Dakota's seeing it happening all over again dialed his rage meter past the point of no return.

"Thanks to Agent Orange, Dakota and Emy never had any kids. I guess when he saw the Captain molesting his own flesh and blood, so to speak, because the good Captain made it real clear, from as far back as I can remember, how much he hated me." Reese sunk deeper into his chair. "When it dawned on Dakota what was going on…I guess in his mind it became the unpardonable sin.

"He grabbed the Captain by the throat and yanked him clean up off the ground." Reese's eyes bounced to the sheriff's for a split-second, and fell back to his lap. "You remember the Captain, sheriff. He sure wasn't a little man.

"I don't know if Dakota was that strong, or that mad, but he hurled the Captain into the hallway like he was a rag doll. I'd never seen Dakota so angry. As a matter of fact, up until then, I'd never heard him even raise his voice, or swear. But that day…the look on his face…two black holes like an animal on the hunt.

"I followed them into the hallway and saw what happened next. Jesus—" Reese squeezed his eyes closed as if the old vision would go away, but with closed eyes it only became more vivid. "I was just a little kid."

"The Captain was babbling and slurring commands like he was still in the service. Who knows? Maybe when he got drunk he thought he was. 'Private,' Reese mocked his grandfather's gravely voice, 'you just bought yourself a month in the stockade.'

"If Dakota heard the slobbering drunk's threat he sure didn't show it. He was like a fired bullet. On a trajectory, and there was no calling him back. He blasted his fists into the Captain's chest hard enough to knock the old fool down and take the wind out of his sails. The Captain choked and coughed, groped around until he found the railing and struggled to his feet. Only then did he have the presence of mind to tie his robe closed.

"He was so drunk, Sheriff, even though he was holding onto the banister he kept swaying back and forth…"

Reese looked to Austin with a pained expression, on the edge of tears. "He told Dakota I was nothing more than a 'slant-eyed mongrel.'" Reese shook his head and swallowed the lump building in his throat. "Can you believe he actually called me that?

"He had that same shit-eating grin on his face as he did the day Blaze broke my wrist. He looked right past Dakota like he wasn't even there. Looked at me and said 'You like it, dontcha' boy? Been your pacifier since you was a babe.'

"He had been making me do that to him when I so young I didn't even know what I was doing," Reese said, contemptuously.

"I guess Dakota reverted back to his military days—he was Special Forces you know," Reese said like a child boasting about his father. "I suppose at that point he saw the Captain as the enemy. Dakota's words came out like one of those slow motion movie clips: 'He's your grandson you sick son of a bitch. Your flesh and blood!'"

Reese's eyes grew vacant, as if suddenly someplace else, twenty years in the past.

"Before I knew what was happening, Dakota spun him around, snaked his arm around the Captain's windpipe, and…Sometimes when the house is quiet, late at night, I still hear the bones in the Captain's neck snapping."

Sheriff Austin's face was ashen. He leaned forward, heavily resting his hands on his knees, lowering his eyes to the floor. While Reese's account baffled comprehension, there was no reason not to believe every word was the gospel truth.

"Anyway," Reese continued, "after he went limp Dakota lifted him overhead and pitched him down the staircase with the gentleness of a sack of dirty laundry."

He reached across his desk, rearranged the pens in the holder, and adjusted the clock by centimeters.

"I didn't know what to do," he said with a heavy sigh. "I thought Dakota was going to kill me, too, because of what I'd witnessed. I figured his choo-choo had jumped the track. I'd read stuff about returning Viet Nam vets and, how years later, they suffered from post-traumatic stress disorders, snapping for no apparent reason.

"When Dakota started toward me with those glazed eyes," Reese paused to shake his head, "I stood there absolutely terrified; literally peed myself when he grabbed a hold of me.

"He dropped to his knees and pulled me against his chest, crying like a baby about everything gone wrong in his life; every failure suddenly bubbled to the surface. He kept apologizing like it was him who'd been abusing me, said he had no idea of what was going on or he would have stopped it sooner, if only he'd known.

"He rambled incoherently about failing Emy by not fathering children; failing her because things hadn't worked out for them to be mister and misses restaurant and casino managers. My goodness, Sheriff, he was weeping so hard he had me crying right along with him." Reese blinked away the tear trying to form in the corner of his eye. "I was crying as hard as he was, and at the same time happy, consoling him, patting his back and telling him it was all right, that we'd be okay."

Reese slid his chair away from the desk and clasped his hands behind his back on his way to the window again.

"How screwed up is that?" he said from across the room. "There I was, feeling more sorry for the guy who just murdered my grandfather, right in front of me, than I am for the old buzzard in a heap at the bottom of the staircase."

He turned to Sheriff Austin with a self-deprecating laugh.

"You want to know something, Sheriff? I'd trade this whole stinking ranch and all of my bank accounts to have been a normal kid who led a normal life."

Austin looked to the figure silhouetted in front of the window. "Why didn't you say something to Dakota? Or tell me, or Pops when we came out here. Somebody could have helped you."

Reese returned to his desk with a snide laugh.

"What was I supposed to say back then, Sheriff? Hey Cody, want to shoot a game of eight ball, take the quads for a ride in the desert—where the only things I had to worry about were poisonous snakes and scorpions. Maybe I should have asked if you wanted to hang out by the pool so I could have said; oh, yeah, by the way Cody, my grandfather's raping me and forcing me to give him oral sex." Reese collapsed into his chair. "You have absolutely no idea how humiliating it was being forced to perform on him like some kind of cheap whore whenever he got drunk. I'm not ashamed to say it; I was glad then, and I'm still that he's dead. I hope he rots in hell! Better yet, I hope they're making him do the same thing down there.

"I can't count high enough to tell you how many nights I lay awake, afraid to sleep, waiting for him to throw open my bedroom door and stammer his famous words of foreplay: *You know the drill, chink dog. Get them clothes off and get down on all fours.*"

Reese moved to the front of his desk and sat on the corner closest to his guest. "It was me Sheriff, I'm the guilty one. I came up with the story about the Captain stumbling down the steps. Dakota wanted to call your predecessor and tell him everything. He said there was a good chance they might rule it justifiable homicide because of what the Captain had been doing to me. I talked him out of making the call.

"Dakota was my savior. I couldn't risk them sending him to prison, stick me in a foster home because he'd killed an abusive, child-molesting, drunken piece of shit. Twelve, thirteen, fourteen—whatever age I was at the time—and never off the property? You can't imagine how thoroughly confused and terrified I was back then."

Reese reached behind his back and slid the disk toward the sheriff. "All the evidence you need to prove Dakota Bricker was Shadow Man is on this disk. It's yours, conditionally."

Sheriff Austin reached for the disk. "On what condition, Reese?"

The martial arts expert clamped onto the sheriff's wrist with a surprisingly powerful grip. "The contents can never be made public," Reese said.

"Reese, I have a sworn duty to uphold the law. If what you say is true—and I believe it is—this disk clears up something like eleven unsolved homicides."

"Sixteen," Reese said, increasing the pressure on Austin's wrist.

"Did you miss the part," Austin yanked his hand free, "where I told you the FBI thinks you're Shadow Man?"

The first smile in more than an hour curled the corners of Reese's mouth. "Not right off I didn't, but I kind of figured it out after a while.

"Remember several months back when I told you they showed up here in the middle of the night?"

Austin massaged his wrist. "I remember."

"Well after that *lovely* encounter, one of them followed me up and down the Strip and through the Tropicana. Originally, I thought they were looking at me because I was trying to buy the casino. I had Nelson Grover do a little snooping around. Apparently, his niece is the U.S. Attorney for this district. Although she swore Nelson to secrecy, he's too well paid not to tell me what he found out. She intimated that after the FBI tailed me through the Tropicana, they came to her for a search warrant, she even hinted at what they were up to."

Austin reached out a cautious hand and tapped the disk. "This is evidence. It has to be turned over to the FBI. It has to, Reese!"

Reese smiled with the confidence he could back up his words. "Trust me, Sheriff, the disk won't leave this room until I have your word its contents are confidential."

The sheriff's eyes drifted between the hard drive and Reese's ominous smirk. He huffed out of his chair, Kitty's piercing yellow eyes following his stroll to the window. He thought for a moment about an authoritative dash across the room, take possession of the disk, but dismissed the idea because he doubted he had the physical ability to carry out the plan, and even if he got past Reese, there would be Kitty to contend with.

"Look, Sheriff, won't do any good divulging what's on the disk. Granted, it'll close out a whole bunch of open investigations of dead people who molested children as a hobby. But the bottom line, it accomplishes nothing. Dakota's dead, and, as far as I'm concerned, thank goodness his victims are too."

Austin turned and let anger creep into his voice for the first time. "Don't you think the victim's families deserve some closure, Reese?"

"Screw the victims! And screw their families for giving birth to such perverted offspring! You can almost imagine how much compassion I have for anyone who abuses a child."

Austin pointed an angry finger at the disk. "Reese, there lies the conclusion to a fifteen year mystery!"

The indifferent shrug told Austin his host could not care less.

Austin slapped his hand against his thigh. "Gosh 'dangit, Reese! I'm the one who set the FBI hounds on your trail. I was so sure-fire positive you were Shadow Man...I never dreamt it was Bricker who was the nutcase."

Reese slammed his fist to the desk hard enough it startled both Kitty and the sheriff. "Dakota wasn't a nutcase, Austin," he retorted, vehemently. "Misguided? Maybe. Mixed up? Definitely. But don't you ever call Dakota Bricker a nutcase in my presence again. You got that, Austin?"

Sheriff Austin walked across the room and leaned his thick arms on the back of the chair. "Reese, the FBI is coming after *you*, not Dakota Bricker. What are you fixin' to do if they build a strong enough circumstantial case to indict you?"

Reese picked up the disk and held it out in his open palm. "Guess you'll have to come bail me out."

Austin snatched his Stetson off the floor and stood in front of Reese, nervously fingering the brim of his hat. "Why is it so important for you to keep Dakota out this? Hell's Bells, Reese, he's a galdarned murderer, and a dead one ta' boot."

Reese moved back to his side of the desk, eased into his chair, and set the hard drive in his lap. "Because Dakota was—is—the closest thing I'll ever have to a father, and I can't allow you to ruin his memory. But more importantly, Tim thinks he walked on water, and I'm not about to tell him different; and neither will you, or anyone else."

The conversation grew stagnant under piercing glares, each to the other. Reese broke the face-off.

"I had Nelson do a little more research on some other things." Reese said with a wry grin.

"What things, Reese?" Austin said, suspiciously.

"I know criminal law isn't Grover's strong suit, but, he is an attorney, and according to him there's nothing in the law that says you have to tell the FBI you have the disk, unless, of course, they subpoena your files. Grover said the disk could loosely be considered investigative notes, and investigative notes don't necessarily fall into the realm of public record."

Sheriff Austin was incredulous. "Grover knows what's on the disk!"

"No, not exactly," Reese said. "Based on our conversations he may have surmised, but even if he did, now it falls under attorney client privilege." Reese flashed a conceited smile. "He's not allowed to divulge its contents."

Austin gave his head a despairing shake. "You think you're so smart don't you, that you have all the bases covered, don't you, Reese?"

"I don't think I've missed any."

Austin parked his Stetson on top of his head and turned for the door. "What about home plate, Reese?" he said over his shoulder, crossing the room with long strides.

"Home plate? I don't understand."

Austin turned and paused in the doorway. "My home plate, Reese. How many people you think will vote for me if they ever found out I withheld evidence from the FBI?"

"Maybe you should think about doing what's right, instead of worrying about getting re-elected for a paycheck."

Austin's big frame melted against the doorframe, head shaking ever so slightly, eyes closed. Reese didn't get it. There were far easier ways to collect a paycheck than being a cop. He opened his eyes and, more out of hurt than anger, said, "You know something, *Mr. Daniels*, you remind me of your grandfather. Just like he was, you're an arrogant punk with too much money, and no life. Don't bother to get up. I'll let myself out."

His taunt about a government paycheck was way out of line, and Reese knew it. He agreed with Sheriff Austin; sometimes, most times, he was too arrogant, definitely had more money than he would ever need, but had little else. He grabbed the disk and hurried across the room, Kitty tight on his heels, intercepted the sheriff at the top of the staircase, and said, "Sheriff, wait!"

Austin stopped and turned on the first step. "What?"

"You're right. I have a fistful of overpaid attorneys and accountants, a casino staff who purses their lips every time I walk through the doors, a new wife and stepson I'm trying to get used to, but I have no friends. At least not anymore now that Dakota's gone.

"You're one of the few people I know I can trust, Cody." Reese lifted Austin's hand and set the disk in his palm. "Do with it as you see fit.

"And I'm very, very sorry for what I said. That was uncalled for, I was out of line, and I apologize."

Sheriff Austin looked into Reese's dark eyes for a moment, wagged his head, and then removed his cowboy hat. "You have my word, Reese. I won't say nothing about what's on the disk. Unless…"

"Unless what?"

Austin dropped the disk into his hat with a broad grin. "Unless I need it to bail your sorry butt out of jail."

"Deal."

They sealed their contract with a handshake.

Reese stood in the front doorway squinting into the sun. "By the way, Sheriff. There's one more thing."

Sheriff Austin stepped from the veranda, stopped, and turned to Reese.

Reese nodded toward the sheriff's hat. "When you get the time to look at what's on the disk, you'll find Dakota's version of how the drunken fool murdered my mother. If it wasn't for Dakota, he would have killed me, too."

Reese closed the door.

Chapter 28

Reese sat quietly behind his desk, Kitty curled into a ball next to him, the chrome clock ticking away...a Norman Rockwell painting. A light knock on the doorjamb drew him back from convoluted thoughts. Had he done the right thing by giving Sheriff Austin the disk?

"Can I come in?" Nancy said.

He swiveled his chair around and motioned her into the room. She sat on the rich brown leather sofa against the wall, watching with amusement as his bare foot tapped the air in time with his thoughts. It wasn't long before Timmy appeared in the doorway. Kitty rose and greeted him with a vigorous tail. He bent down and ruffled the coyote's hackles, entered with a hesitant "hey there" and sat in the chair Austin had vacated less than twenty minutes ago.

" 'Hey' back, sport."

Timmy clapped his hands together, intertwined his fingers, rested his hands nervously in his lap, and said, "You know it's...well...like," he stammered. "It's kinda' windy outside. Might be a good day to get Dakota and Emy back together." His eyes darted to his mother, and then to Reese. "That's if you guys don't mind."

Both Nancy and Reese had agreed Timmy would decide when and where to disperse Dakota's ashes.

"Are you sure you're ready?" Reese said, soberly.

Timmy's bottom lip trembled a bit as he spoke. "Yeah, it's time for a reunion."

"I take it from 'Emy' and 'reunion' we're headed for Seashell Rock?" Timmy nodded. "Give your mom and me a few minutes, and then I'll drive us out there."

Timmy tucked his hands under his thighs and fidgeted in his seat. "I was kind of thinking of riding Gus out there, if it's okay with you."

Reese's head bobbed. "You know something, Tim? I think Dakota would very much approve of the idea. Go saddle up Gus, we'll give you a head start and catch up with you." He saw the look on Nancy's face, knowing she thought Gus was too headstrong for Timmy to ride into the desert, especially at dusk. "It'll be all right," Reese said.

She acquiesced with a shrug.

Timmy slid out of the chair and walked with Kitty to the door, where he turned to Reese, and said, "Thanks, Dad."

Since Dakota died, and since the widow Robbins became Mrs. Reese Daniels, they were all still getting used to the new arrangements. Timmy and Kitty were the resilient ones, they took to each other as if they'd been together since birth. As unsociable as Kitty could be at times, he displayed a genuine fondness having a young boy to romp about the ranch with.

Reese waited until Timmy and Kitty left from the room and bounded down the stairs. He dropped his foot to the floor, propped his chin in his hands, and looked at Nancy. "I told Austin everything. I gave him the disk."

"Are you sure you can trust him?" she asked.

"He gave me his word, and Cody's not one to break a promise. Besides, whom else can I trust?" he winked at his wife, "present company excluded, of course."

Nancy smiled coyly. "I thought you planned to give it to Grover, use the attorney-client privilege shield."

"If Grover's willing to divulge confidential information acquired from his niece, how much can I really trust him?"

He gather the photocopied pages of Dakota's autopsy report, slid the pages into the folder, turned his chair around and dropped them into the floor safe, closed the lid with his foot, and spun the dial with his toes. After he slid the bookcase back into place he walked around the desk and wrapped an arm around Nancy's waist, and kissed her lightly on the neck. They walked from the room, hand-in-hand.

While Reese piloted the extended cab pick up truck into the desert, maintaining a quarter-mile buffer between the front bumper and Gus rear flank, Nancy fussed with the radio's buttons searching for a country western station.

Her third trip around the dial, and Reese said, "Car radios don't pick up so well out here."

"I see that." She turned around and looked toward the rear seat area. "Got any CDs?"

"Not really," he said, steering around a clump of cacti. "I'm not that much into music."

Nancy flopped back down in her seat and pressed the *search* button on the radio, again. "Maybe I can find the CNBC business report, in Chinese of course."

An amused smirk crossed his face, he slid his hand from the gearshift to her knee and squeezed. "Cute, Nancy, very cute," he said, in Chinese.

Only her third visit to Seashell Rock, the advancing shadows had the landscape looking all the same to her. "We almost there?"

Reese pointed through the sun-streaked windshield. "Over that ridge."

By the time the truck rolled to a dusty stop, Timmy had Gus's reigns wedged into a crack on the face of Seashell Rock and was sitting inside with the gold urn pinned between the toes of his sneakers. Kitty jumped from the bed of the truck and sniffed around until he found the perfect spot to mark his territory, and then wandered off to the pool in front of Seashell Rock for a drink. Reese and Nancy crawled from the cab, joined Timmy inside the shallow cave, and sat silently for a very long time.

"Anyone want to say a prayer or something?" Reese finally offered.

Timmy turned to him with a heavy frown. "I don't see Dakota getting off on that shit." He snapped his head around to his mother. "Stuff! Sorry. Stuff."

Timmy turned and stared into the setting sun's reflection on the still water.

"The preacher at the funeral home was lame," Timmy said. "He kept calling Dakota, 'Mike'. I felt like walking up there and banging him upside the head with the urn and saying, the guy's name is Dakota, you stupid moron.

"What a bonehead. You'd think he'd at least get his name right."

"Honey, he meant no harm," Nancy said. "It's difficult talking about someone you've never met."

No excuse was going to satisfy Timmy. "Maybe he should have kept his stupid trap shut then."

Nancy laid a hand on his knee. "Reverend Penn was simply reading from the information sheet the funeral director gave him."

Timmy turned to her. "Yeah? Well then maybe the nitwit funeral director should have asked us, huh?"

Reese reached out and pushed Timmy's head. "Let it go, Tim. No harm done. Now would anyone care to say a prayer for Mike?"

Timmy spun around and glared at Reese through narrowed eyes. "Mom, why did you have to pick such a jerk to marry? Couldn't you have found somebody else for us to hang out with, some homeless guy or something."

"The jerk has money," she said. "It's the only way I could afford your braces." She raised her right hand. "I swear, once the braces come off, the jerk's history."

Timmy ran his tongue over the stainless bands realigning his teeth, and turned to Reese. "Get it while it's good, dude. Two years and you're to the curb."

Reese forced out a dejected sigh. "I guess I'd better start searching the Internet for one of those mail-order brides."

"You really are a jerk," Timmy giggled.

He snapped his fingers until the coyote trotted into Sea Shell Rock, laid his head in Timmy's lap, and succumbed to a massage of the insides of his ears.

"I remember the first time I came out here with Dakota." Timmy gave Kitty's head a pat. "And you too Kitty.

"He brought along a godda—gosh darn—plastic bag for the garbage."

Timmy tucked his chin to his chest, lowered his voice two octaves, and, with a not too bad English accent, said, " 'Young Timothy, we should leave nothing behind to soil the landscape of our forefathers but our footprints.'

"Can you believe I had to take a poop out here once and he made me take a shovel and dig a hole? Now I ask you, who carries a shovel and toilet paper with them into the desert just so they can bury a stink pickle?"

"Michael Dakota Bricker, that's who," Reese said, giving them all a good laugh.

"You know something, Mom? I think Dakota was the coolest person I've ever met." He quickly added, "Sorry, Reese. You're cool, too, but in a different kind of way."

Reese tossed Timmy's white locks. "Don't worry about it, sport."

Reese's status as "step-dad" appealed to his ego in a huge way, and he hoped, in the not to distant future, to drop "step" from "dad" and have a child of his own.

"My real dad was cool, too, I guess, but I don't really remember him all that much." Timmy looked back to his mother. "How old was I when Dad died?"

"Almost six."

He turned his fierce blues on Reese. "You'd better not croak off on me."

Nancy reached around Timmy and took Reese's hand.

"No intention of going anywhere for a long time. At least until the braces come off," Reese said with a grin.

"Good! Because if you decide to croak off, I'll never speak to you again." He flashed a sardonic, tinsel-toothed grin, pried their hands apart, and reached down between his feet to pick up the urn. "It's time for a reunion. You two wait here.

"Come on Kitty," he said, bounding to his feet. Timmy and the coyote disappeared around to the backside of Seashell Rock.

"What's he got up his sleeve?" Nancy said.

"Just being Tim, I suppose," Reese said.

Now that they were alone inside Seashell Rock's narrow cave, Reese leaned in, kissed Nancy's lips, and slid his hands under her sleeveless blouse. Great, she was braless.

Timmy's voice interrupted them from above. "Hey! Up here."

Nancy pulled Reese's hands out, smoothed her top, and stepped from beneath the overhang. Timmy stood fifteen feet overhead on the lip of formation.

"Timmy! Get down from there!" Nancy hollered into the wind.

Reese nudged her with his elbow. "He's okay." He cupped his hands around his mouth and shouted, "Be careful up there. If you fall and get hurt your mother's going to kill me."

"A broken arm is all it takes to get rid of you?" To further inflame his mother's angst, Timmy leaned farther over the edge and waved. "It's okay, Mom. Dakota showed me how to get up here."

He moved back away from the ledge, set the urn down on a flat rock, squatted over Dakota's remains, and stared at the sun's ebbing orange rays, speaking with a quavering voice only Kitty heard.

"You know something, Dakota? You're a butthead for dying on me like you did. That wasn't a very nice thing to do." He snorted and smudged away a tear tricking from the corner of his eye. "But I guess I'll forgive you, because I really don't think you meant for things to turn out the way they did."

Kitty pressed his muzzle against Timmy's cheek. He kissed the bridge of the coyote's snout and turned his attention to the urn.

"Thanks for everything, Dakota. Thanks for all that you've done for me; all the neat stuff you showed me.

"You taught me how to look for the desert's dangers, scorpions and rattlesnakes and stuff, and at the same time showed me its beauty; crawling tortoises, darting lizards, and soaring eagles. You always said kids are *God's little angels' sent to earth to bless our lives*. But, most important of all, you talked about how much you missed your 'dear Emaline.'"

He undid the urn's lid and set it aside, pulled out and untied the plastic bag insert, stepped to the rim of Seashell Rock, and lifted Dakota overhead.

From the desert floor below, Reese and Nancy squinted at the silhouette of Timmy and Kitty, highlighted against a brilliant orange ball balanced on the horizon.

Timmy closed his eyes, drew in a deep, shuddering breath, whipped the bag into the air, and shook it violently.

"Go find Emy, Dakota! Now it's your turn to soar with the eagles, fly with the angels!"

The wind carried Timmy's words, and Dakota's ashes, across the landscape, and into eternity.

Timmy sank to his haunches, hugged his shins to his chest, and watched the powdery-gray cloud of Dakota's earthly existence disappear on the breeze. After a few moments of reflection, he folded the plastic bag, tucked it into his back pocket, tightened the lid down on the urn, and started toward the back hump of Seashell Rock. Kitty scampered down the rock ahead of him; he paused for a last look at the beautiful desert Dakota Bricker had introduced to him.

That's when he heard it. It was the wind, but he would swear (and he was pretty good at that) to the grave he'd heard Dakota's ethereal voice on the wind:

"Thank you, young Timothy. Indeed, thank you so very much for being an integral part of my life. Although we only had a short time together, I shall always love you as the son I was never fortunate enough to father.

"And now, my young ward, I have a charge for you. I charge you to take care of Reese and your mother in my absence. But, more importantly I charge you to take care of yourself as you travel through life. And, my dearest Timothy, I charge you to always remember—leave nothing behind except for your best footprints."

"Man, am I really, really going to miss you, Dakota. Miss you like you can't believe," Timmy said, wiping a tear from his eye.

"And, likewise, I shall always miss you," the wind said. *"Now go to your mother and father."*

Timmy smiled into the breeze, tears began streaming down his face, he nodded he understood. He wiped his eyes on his shirttail, and then scampered down the hump of Seashell Rock, jumping the last few feet to the ground he was met by Reese's radiant smile.

"What?" Timmy said, self-consciously wiping the tears from his face again.

Reese nodded toward the top of Seashell Rock. "Nothing, sport; just looked like maybe you heard something up there."

Tim's mouth gaped. "You heard it, too?"

"Heard what?" Reese said with an innocuous grin.

"You did. Didn't you? You heard Dakota talking to me."

Reese smiled as Nancy stepped to the back of the rock and wrapped herself around Reese's arm. "All I hear is the wind picking up," she said.

Reese peeled out of his flannel shirt, slipped it over Nancy's shoulders, draped an arm around Timmy, and escorted his family into the dimpled face of Seashell Rock, where the Daniels family, Kitty included, serenely sat and watched the horizon fade from orange, to purple, to black.

Epilogue

Mr. and Mrs. Daniels were entangled in an amorous embrace when their private elevator glided to an easy stop on the casino's main floor. The doors opened and they stepped from the elevator car, Reese greeting both men, one positioned on each side of the spotless brass doors.

"Good morning boys," he said with a playful smile. "Will you be joining us for breakfast?"

He knew they would.

Neither responded, however, the elder's hateful glower made it crystal clear of what he though of Reese Daniels. The pair marched with military precision behind Daniels, following the hand-in-hand couple through the Tropicana's main floor, and into the Calypsos Café.

As soon as they entered the café, Reese and Nancy were immediately ushered past the waiting crowd to a private cabaña on the outdoor VIP terrace, shaded by towering scabrous palm trees. Their government escorts sat in a booth near the exit and waited impatiently while the couple enjoyed a light breakfast of blueberry crepe suzettes and strong Chinese black tea. Reese and Nancy chatted idly for more than an hour before Reese finally motioned to the waitress, signed his name to the bottom of the check, dropped a twenty-dollar bill on the table, and assisted Nancy from the table.

When they stepped from the veranda, Reese insisted upon stopping at the booth where the FBI agents nursed a third cup of coffee.

"I'd like to pick up breakfast, if you don't mind," he said, graciously reaching for the check.

Stevens's angry hand slammed to the table and crushed the check into a tight, wrinkled ball. "I mind," he said, petulantly. "You know, Daniels, one of these days you're going to trip over that rich dick of yours."

"And you'll be there to catch me? Oh, goody." Reese clapped with child-like glee.

Stevens slid from the booth, rose to his full height, and then added another inch and a half by rising to the balls of his feet. He glared down at the Tropicana's owner, and said, "No, Daniels, I won't be there to catch you. I'll be there to step on your spoiled-rich, scrawny, little neck."

Reese chuckled.

"Agent Stevens, Agent Stevens, Agent Stevens, you are most irritable this morning, more so than usual. I can't help but wonder if your inner hostility rises from a lack of proper rest, nightmares possibly," Reese brought a contemplative finger to the tip of his chin, "or, possibly it's a lack of fiber. Maybe you should try our bran muffins tomorrow. I hear they're delicious. Who knows, a tasty bran muffin may help you overcome that most unpleasant disposition of yours."

Reese took Nancy's hand and stepped around Stevens, who, for nearly six months, had been an irritating fingernail on the chalkboard of Reese Daniels's life. Other than the sanctuary of the ranch where they were beyond the reach of the Federal Bureau of Investigation, the Daniels family was followed and spied upon the proverbial twenty-four-seven.

Stevens was not about to let such arrogance go unchecked. He puffed out his chest like a Banty Rooster defending his harem, and said, "Is that right, Shadow Man?"

Reese froze in mid-step. Stevens's obvious attempt to provoke a response brought him face to face with the agent, a tolerant smile concealing a burning desire to drop the agent like first period Trigonometry. Reese stepped in close enough to purposely invade Stevens's personal space, and then locked dark eyes on the agent.

"Stevens, don't allow something so nonexistent as a shadow destroy you from within," he hissed, in a menacing timbre. "Or from without."

Stevens brought balled fists to rest on his hipbones, conveniently exposing his firearm. "Are you threatening a federal agent, Daniels?"

Reese's eyes darted to the gun for a nanosecond, and then back to Stevens, his countenance remaining as expressive as the figures etched into Mount Rushmore. "Haven't we traveled down this path before, MacKenzie?

"By the way, Stevens," Reese said, with an unexpected snap of the fingers close enough to the agent's face to startle him backwards a half step. "Where'd you park your car? I sure hope it wasn't in the fire lane."

"Don't you worry yourself about my car," Stevens retorted childishly. "If you're smart, Daniels, you'll watch your step. Your butler isn't around anymore to protect your ass."

"Maybe it was yours he protected that night, Stevens."

Reese abruptly turned, took Nancy's hand and led her from the restaurant; he on his way to a Board of Directors' meeting, she to the Blackjack tables to waste time until Daniels Industries corporate helicopter shuttled them back to the ranch later this afternoon.

"Mack, what did he mean when he said 'traveled this path before'?" Agent Tolson asked.

Senior Agent Stevens was not about to tell the rookie, fresh out of the National Academy and newly assigned to the Las Vegas Field Office, of his previous embarrassing encounters with Reese Daniels.

"Shut up, Tolson. Don't ask questions, just do what you're told, go follow the bitch."

"You really shouldn't provoke him, Reese," Nancy said, laboring to keep up with his agitated gait.

"He'll get used to it. Or get over it," Reese replied, curtly. "I've put up with him all over my ass for over six months." He glanced at Nancy. "Now I've grown weary of him. I'll have Grover talk to his niece. If she can't reign in her lap dog, I'll file an injunction in Federal Court to keep Stevens, and the rest of his minions away from us."

Nancy squeezed his hand and tittered. "Darling, if you continue hurting his feelings, he's going to drop us from his Christmas card list."

"Good," Reese said with an amused grin.

In front of the security door to the Tropicana's Administrative Offices, Reese kissed his wife goodbye, and then carded his way inside. Stevens folded his arms across his chest and parked next to the door.

Nancy motioned for Tolson to walk with her, chatting amiably with the agent on her way to the Blackjack pit. He stood back from the table and watched as she signed her name for two thousand dollars worth of chips without so much as batting an eye.

Tailing a rich couple he found rather pleasant—except when Agent Stevens was around—through a casino was not Barry Tolson's idea of a first assignment. His mind was made up. This afternoon when they returned to the office, he intended to file a complaint with the SAC (Special Agent in Charge) about Agent Stevens's hostile and unwarranted behavior this morning.

Printed in the United States
72172LV00002BB/124-147